RACHA0

HEIR OF
MEMORY
AND
SHADOW

KINGDOM LEGACY BOOK TWO

Heir of Memory and Shadow

Kingdom Legacy, Book Two

Editing and proofreading by Tom Loveman

Cover art by Fiona Jayde Media

Also by Rachanee Lumayno

Kingdom Legacy
Heir of Amber and Fire
Heir of Memory and Shadow

Prologue

I BOW OVER THE LOVELY young woman's outstretched hand as I agree to assist her. As we ride together, I see the sunlight halo behind her head, hearing her sweet laughter as she smiles hopefully at me, believing the world is full of possibility.

But, unfortunately, her hope is misplaced.

I watch as her face crumples in tears. Not the restrained, dignified sniffles that I would have expected from someone of her standing. Instead, the tears are great gulping sobs that rack her thin frame, threatening to break her in two.

Just as her heart was breaking.

I had been taught to remain neutral, but it is difficult to see to see the poor young lady react so violently to the news. But what had she honestly expected?

I try to calm her, to comfort her, even though it isn't my place nor my business. I hold her firmly by the shoulders, speaking in a low, soothing voice as if she is an easily spooked animal.

The wild look in her eyes begins to settle. The tears begin to slow.

I breathe easier. It will be all right now.

Then, without warning, her hand shoots out toward me. I instinctively recoil, expecting to feel the sting of a slap. Instead,

1

she grabs the hilt of the dagger sheathed at my belt. In one swift motion, she draws the knife out and plunges it into her heart. Her eyes never leave mine as the light fades from them.

I scream.

Or, at least, I think I do. All I know is, my mouth is gaping open in shock as she falls gracelessly into my outstretched arms. Her blood is everywhere. On my hands, my arms, splashed all over the front of my shirt. Pooling on the floor beneath her crumpled body. Her now sightless eyes are still fixed on me.

Accusing me, forever, that I could have prevented this needless death.

Couldn't I?

I CAME OUT OF THE MAGICALLY-induced memory doubled over, gasping for air, even though I wasn't bound by enchantment or by physical means.

No, I was just bound to the lady Rosemary through my memories of my failed commission.

"Thank you for allowing the Council to see that once more," a deep, gravelly voice above me said. "I know that isn't easy for you to relive, over and over."

The voice recalled me to where I was: in my home country of Orchwell, standing before the kingdom's other governing body, the Council of Seekers, on day ten of what seemed like a never-ending trial.

My trial.

Because my commission had ended so brutally, the Council had called me before them, repeatedly going over the events that led to Rosemary's death. This was the fifth time I had had to relive the memories of what had occurred.

While the memories were painful, they were nothing compared to the possible futures before me. Depending on the Council's ruling, I could be stripped of my Seeker ability, which at best meant I would lose my livelihood and at worst meant I would go insane. Or they could even sentence me to death.

I didn't know which was the better outcome.

My breathing now under control, I looked up to regard the seated members of the Council of Seekers. Pellham Ravenwood, head of the seven-person Council, regarded me from his place at the center of the raised stand where he was flanked on both sides by the other council members. I recognized some of their faces: elderly Madame Kenestra, her white hair piled high on her head as she turned her shrewd brown eyes on me; the former knight Sir Lantley, a lean, athletic man with silver-streaked black hair; and Lord Olivera, the queen's cousin, a bulky, solidly-built man with long blond hair that he often wore tied back from his face. He was at least a good five or ten years younger than his peers on the Council.

Orchwell's ruling king and queen were the ultimate authority in our country, but they tended to delegate many of the day-to-day affairs of governing to the Council of Seekers. It made sense; Orchwell's royal family was, by design, one of the few families of nobility that did not have the Seeker ability running through their veins. Or, if any of the royals did, it was often an extremely weak ability, akin to a minor magical skill. If anyone in the direct line of succession showed a strong aptitude for seeking, they weren't eligible to inherit the throne. There were too many headaches as a Seeker — and in my world, heartaches — to wish upon a future king or queen. Orchwell needed their rulers at home in the kingdom, fully able to focus on their duties.

Which was another reason why the Council of Seekers existed.

Several of those on the Council were members of the royal family who had been ineligible for succession. The rest were former Seekers who had since passed on their duties to other family members, but still wanted to serve the kingdom in some way. Members of the Council weren't paid, but would occasionally receive monetary gifts from the Crown.

Pellham Ravenwood was a rare combination: as the king's fourth younger brother with strong Seeker abilities, he had actually been allowed to pursue his Seeker career since he was never a strong contender for the Orchwell throne. Being a part of both worlds gave him remarkable insight and made him a formidable leader, which helped him earn the position as Head of the Council.

Pellham turned to Lord Olivera. "Well, as you were the one who requested Kaernan go over his commission yet again, are you satisfied with what you saw?"

Lord Olivera tapped his chin thoughtfully. He was wearing an extravagant wide-brimmed red hat with a silver feather; as he nodded, the feather nodded in time with him. "It was thorough, to be sure, but it didn't give us any new information. It would be nice to have another perspective on the situation."

I ground my teeth, pressing my lips into a thin line to stop myself from blurting my thoughts. Of course my story, rehashed multiple times, wouldn't have given the Council new insights. *The only person who could give the Council another perspective is dead.*

While I hadn't expected much sympathy from the Council during my trial, I found I really disliked Lord Olivera. The man seemed to enjoy torturing me, asking the same questions repeatedly, making me relive the commission over and over before the Council, and casting doubt on every move or motive I had during Rosemary's commission. I already had recurring nightmares about it, and had barely slept for the last four months since returning home with the lady's death on my hands.

Besides my nightmares and insomnia, I was constantly on edge from not exercising my Seeker ability. Seekers had to use their gifts regularly or potentially go mad, and I had been denying my gift for several months. And pre-trial, when I had to undergo the Council's intense process of magically sealing witnesses from talking outside of the courtroom, I had barely recovered from it.

So I was definitely not in good physical or mental shape right now. And Lord Olivera's "attention to detail" — as he called it, although I would have termed it otherwise — wasn't helping me. I firmly believed that the Council would have come to a decision about my fate much sooner if he hadn't been present.

"Perhaps we could —"

"Pause the hearing here, and meet again in ten minutes after we get some refreshments." Madame Kenestra smoothly interrupted Lord Olivera. "These old bones can't go for much longer without some sustenance."

"But —"

"I, for one, agree with Madame Kenestra." Sir Lantley also cut off whatever Lord Olivera was going to say. "A short break would do wonders to clear my head."

"If we could just —"

"Sir Lantley, you agree with me? Now that is a first! Pellham, did you hear that? Have the Council secretary note this day, for it truly is a momentous occasion: Sir Lantley agrees with me." The twinkle in Madame Kenestra's eyes as Lord Olivera's face grew mottled red with rage told me she knew exactly what she was doing. I almost felt sorry for Lord Olivera.

Pellham Ravenwood sighed. After spending a few days with the Council, I had a vague idea of what he had to put up with on a daily basis. I ducked my head so the Council members wouldn't see my smirk.

"Who would like to continue the hearing?" he asked the group. Only Lord Olivera's hand shot up. "Who would like to take a short break?" Everyone else, including Pellham, raised a hand. "All right, then, the majority has it. We will take a break and reconvene in, oh, about ten minutes."

Pellham looked at me, then, really taking in my haunted eyes and drooping shoulders.

"And then, we will decide on the fate of Kaernan Asthore."

Chapter One

LET IT BE KNOWN TO all that I, Kaernan Asthore, really, really hated love.

It wasn't because society expected young men of my age and status to find love silly, unnecessary, or inconvenient. It wasn't even because I saw, all around me and all too frequently, people blissfully happy with their soulmates, their one true loves.

No, I hated love because, in my experience, it usually involved death, or worse. If I was involved, it was definitely *or worse*.

The sound of approaching footsteps pulled me from my gloomy thoughts. Their echo against the wooden floor vibrated in my skull, causing my daylong dull headache to spike. I squeezed my eyes shut against the pain as a young woman's lilting laugh floated gently my way.

"There you are." It was the voice of my twin sister, Kaela. I opened my eyes to see her dark brown eyes shining as she smiled down at me. She pushed her long black hair away from her face, so like mine, but softened in her round feminine features.

"I just got home from the Veilan commission — can you believe it took three weeks, but at least we have another happy patron! — and ..." She stopped, really getting a good look at me. "Are you all right?"

I started to shake my head, then winced as the headache pulsed again. Kaela sat down next to me, rubbing circles on my back like our mother used to do when we were little to soothe us. "Rough night again?" she said, indicating the circles under my eyes.

I sucked my breath in between my teeth, forcing the word out. "Yeah. I keep seeing Rosemary's eyes in my dreams. Wild. Hopeless. Accusing. Dead. I'm afraid to sleep anymore. Once night falls ..."

"It's been a month since the trial, Kaernan," my sister said. "Longer still since ... well. I'm surprised you still have the nightmares. The Council said it wasn't your fault. Rosemary was mentally unstable. The rigors of travel and the commission had set her over the edge. You were not responsible for what happened."

The words came out in a rehearsed rush, a well-worn argument Kaela had used repeatedly on me to try to make me feel better. But even though I wanted to wholeheartedly agree with her, a small part of me kept insisting: *You could have done more. You could have stopped it.*

"Aren't you glad they didn't take away your Seeker ability?"

I shrugged. "I don't know how I feel. I'm sure the Council thought they were granting me some small mercy by letting me stay a Seeker. But perhaps the real mercy would have been to take away my gift permanently, and with it the chance that I could ever hurt someone again."

Kaela stopped rubbing my back and instead pulled me to her, hugging me fiercely. "Don't ever say that. Orchwell — no, the whole of the Gifted Lands — needs your ability."

I shrugged again, effectively removing Kaela's arm from around my shoulders. I turned away, trying to pretend I didn't see the hurt look in my twin's eyes.

She pressed her lips together. "Have you talked to Father or Mother about it? Maybe we should fetch the doctor."

"No." I hated how weak I sounded, but the restless nights were definitely taking their toll on me. "I don't want to alarm Mother. And Father thinks I should be over it by now. It's easier to just avoid both of them when I can."

"Ah ... speaking of avoiding them ..."

When Kaela used that tone, it usually meant trouble for me. Warily, I said, "What?"

"I saw Father right when I walked through the door. He sent me to find you. He wants to talk to both of us."

I groaned. "Do we have to? Can't you tell him you couldn't find me?"

"I'm sorry," Kaela said again and sighed heavily, wincing as if she herself were in pain.

It was quite possible she was. As twins, Kaela and I had a sympathetic connection, often sensing each other's feelings and physical presence.

"Come on," Kaela stood, grabbing my hand and turning to go. She stopped short; I hadn't budged from my spot. Turning back, she dropped my hand and sat down next to me on the wooden window ledge.

We sat in silence for a moment, until my thoughts spilled out:

"I can't do this any more, Kay. I know I'm dangerously close to the madness; if I don't use my ability soon my mind will break. But I can't handle the outcome of my commissions. They often end poorly. I wish there was some way I could just be rid of my 'gift' for good."

My shoulders slumped. I turned away from my sister to face the wall, not wanting her to see the tears that threatened to fall. "You're the one with the proper gift, Kaela. I'm just … an aberration."

Kaela threw her arms around me and pulled me close. "That's not true." It was a well-worn argument from my sister, but after all this time — and all my failures — her argument was showing its wear.

Fading sunlight through the window illuminated a golden tassel that adorned the braided rope tying back the heavy red curtains. I reached out, absently flicking the tassel back and forth in my hand. I remembered a time, many years ago, when I played hide-and-seek with Kaela, using these very curtains to shield myself from her view. Not that I was ever successful in hiding from her, thanks to our bond. Life had been so much simpler then. Before Kaela and I had come into our gifts properly.

Kaela gently took the tassel from my hand and tugged me to my feet. This time I let her. "Come on," she said.

I followed, unhappy but unresisting.

KAELA MOVED QUICKLY down the familiar hallways, me on her heels. Our hurried footsteps echoed on the wooden floors, even as the tasteful tapestries and family portraits on the walls blurred past in our haste. Stately and elegant, the Asthore family manor lay near the palace in the kingdom of Orchwell, just on the border of the merchants' district. Our family had a long and storied history of seeking in Orchwell, making us one of the richest and most revered families in the kingdom, second only to the monarchy.

Of course, it helped that even the royalty of Orchwell occasionally sought out the Asthores for their services. Because who didn't want to find their true love?

In the Gifted Lands, Orchwell was known as the Land of Seekers. If you needed to find something, you came to Orchwell, where even the lowliest citizen possessed the ability to locate what you sought. But Orchwellians weren't hunting dogs in human form; depending on a patron's needs, the finder would have to solicit a specific group or family, as certain abilities ran only in certain bloodlines.

One Seeker family was renown for its ability to find dragons. Another famous Seeker clan had built its reputation upon finding other families' lost fortunes. For a fee, of course. But they were very popular, as so many people were convinced they had a spectacular destiny.

The Asthore family was known for its ability to find a person's true love.

We weren't matchmakers, exactly. Most often, a patron just wanted to find their perfect match, and didn't care about their future beloved's background. But occasionally, a patron had specialized requests — such as needing a good love match who also happened to be a good political alliance — and they would bring those specifications to an Asthore Seeker.

The Asthore Seeker found the person's perfect match every time.

Each successive Asthore generation, drawing on the wisdom of their predecessors, was more gifted than the last. My sister and I were still refining our abilities, but we had already showed immense promise. Indeed, Kaela was so talented that she was taking on commissions instead of our father, Lord Asthore, even though it would be at least four or five more years before we were considered fully trained Seekers who could take over the family business in earnest.

But what made Kaela such a formidable talent was the same reason that I hated the family business.

Stopping in front of the plain wooden door that led to Father's study, Kaela knocked. She barely waited for the deep baritone on the other end to say, "Enter," before she pushed the door inward. She sailed into the room confidently, with me reluctantly following behind.

Father stood to greet us. As Kaela moved eagerly into Father's arms, I realized with a start that I was now taller than my father, who had always seemed to loom over me. When had that happened?

Sunlight illuminated the gray that feathered Father's temples. The crow's feet at the corner of his eyes deepened when he smiled and embraced his daughter.

Kaela stepped back so Father could greet me. "Look who I found," she chirped.

Neither Father nor I made a move to close the distance between us.

"Good, you found him," Father said warmly to Kaela. He nodded to me. In a voice just a shade colder, he said, "Son."

I nodded back in an equally chilly manner. "Father."

Kaela flopped down on the leather love seat in front of the fireplace. I followed suit with less abandon than my twin sister. Kaela was acutely aware of the tension between Father and me, but she often was at a loss as to how to handle it. While our mother, Lady Asthore, tried to play the peacemaker between the two men in her life, Kaela chose to ignore the issue, hoping that if she pretended all was well, then it would be.

While I appreciated her optimism, I sometimes wished my sister would take a stronger stance in regards to the family dynamic. Father would listen to Kaela, if she truly wished to exert her influence.

Father sat down at his desk, angling his chair so he faced Kaela and me. "Children, another commission has come our way."

Kaela clapped her hands in delight.

Father smiled indulgently at Kaela, but turned his gaze on me. "This one is for Kaernan."

I couldn't help it; a small groan escaped my lips. Kaela's happiness dimmed a bit as she gave me a sympathetic smile, but Father frowned.

"You're not still upset over what happened with that Rosemary chit, are you?" he asked me.

"I —"

"It honestly couldn't have gone any other way," Father said dismissively. "You did your job. What the client does next is no concern of yours."

"That's a bit callous to say, don't you think, Father?" I said hotly.

"Really, Father, it was a most unfortunate situation —" Kaela said at the same time.

Father slammed his hand down on his desk, hard. The echo of the slap stunned us both into silence.

"When will both of you learn?" he said sharply. "A commission is just that — a commission. We may help people find the one they are fated for, but there is always a choice. People always have a choice. Our family is proof of that. The sooner you understand that, the happier you will be in your careers as Seekers."

Maybe I don't want a career as a Seeker. The thought came unbidden to my mind, startling me with its intensity.

The room suddenly went deathly silent.

I looked around, at my sister's horrified stare, at my father's cold and steely gaze. I realized belatedly that I had actually spoken those words out loud.

"You don't really have a choice," Father said. His tone left no room for argument.

"But you just said —" I began.

"In your private affairs, yes," Father said. "But when it comes to seeking — no. No Seeker has a choice about accepting their fate. You know that."

"But there must be —"

"You will take this commission, and you will fulfill it to the best of your ability." Father's jaw worked back and forth, and his breathing was heavy, like he was trying to keep himself under tight control.

There was a knock on the door, which was still slightly open. A servant's voice sounded timidly through the small crack. "Milord, there is someone here to see you."

Father stood. "And here is your new patron now, Kaernan."

Chapter Two

THE POTENTIAL PATRON waiting in our parlor was a petite, dark-haired woman. She was wearing a simple black dress, but the fabric and cut made it clear she was a woman of means. She had refused to take a seat in one of the plush chairs the room boasted for guests. Instead, she was standing in the middle of the room, hands clasped in front of her as she gazed around shrewdly. When the three of us entered, she turned her shrewd assessment on us, as if *we* were the ones visiting *her* domain, and not the other way around.

Inwardly, my earlier groan of dismay resurfaced. While I disliked taking any commission, working with women always seemed to be worse. I had been hoping for some sort of reprieve after the Rosemary fiasco. But apparently that was not to be.

Could nothing go right in my world?

Beside me, Father bowed to our visitor. "Lady Pahame."

Lady Pahame nodded slightly at Father. "Lord Asthore. Thank you for agreeing to meet with me."

"Of course," Father said. "Although I'm afraid I won't be of any help to you." Lady Pahame frowned, and opened her mouth to speak. Father smoothly cut her off before she could say anything.

"May I introduce my children, Kaernan —" he indicated me, standing uncomfortably just behind him "— and Kaela." He pulled Kaela closer to him, beaming proudly, leaving me to awkwardly shuffle to fill the empty spot on his other side. "Kaernan, Kaela, this is Lady Adallia Pahame. Lady Pahame, my son Kaernan is the one you actually came to see."

Lady Pahame leveled her gaze on me. I tried not to fidget under her silent stare, although it felt like her intelligent dark eyes were sizing me up, judging me ... and finding me lacking. Did she know about the Rosemary commission? She had to, I swear the whole kingdom had been talking about it ....

My palms began to sweat, and I fought to keep my breathing even.

Kaela, ever aware of my feelings, put a comforting hand on my arm to steady me.

"I see," was all Lady Pahame said. "Very well. When do we leave?"

"In two days," Father said. "If that suits you."

"It does," Lady Pahame said.

"Wait," I said. The word tumbled out fast, as if I had just discovered I had a voice. But I had to say *something* — this was all happening too fast for my liking. "What do you mean, in two days? Who are we even seeking?"

"A lost love," Father said. "I would think that was obvious, Kaernan, given your ... unique... abilities."

I bit my tongue so hard I tasted blood. Gritting my teeth — against both my anger and the metallic taste — I said, "Of course, Father. But who, exactly, is it?"

Father hesitated, an odd look crossing his face. He glanced at Lady Pahame, who smoothly stepped in to answer my question.

"His name is Baxley. He and I knew each other, long ago. Before I married my late husband, Lord Pahame, may he rest in peace. It's been a long time, but perhaps Baxley will remember me. At the very least, it would be lovely to renew our acquaintance again."

A typical patron, then. One whose curiosity over what-might-have-been overcame their good sense to let the past — and all its forgotten potential — lie. I had to hope this commission would not end in tragedy, but Lady Pahame seemed to be more grounded than most of the patrons who sought my services.

"Two days, then," I said. *Like I really have a choice*, I added bitterly, but this time I was careful to keep my mouth closed and my thoughts firmly my own.

Absently, I bowed to Lady Pahame, even as my mind raced through the personal preparations I would have to make. While I trusted my father, a former Seeker, to oversee everything, there would be certain tweaks I would need to make to suit my own preferences. It was *my* commission, after all. As much as I would have hated to admit it, my heart was pounding with anticipation. I loved the excitement of seeking — I just hated the usually inevitable sad outcome of a job well done.

Lady Pahame inclined her head in acknowledgement, including not just me, but my sister and father as well. "Thank you," she said simply, and walked past us and out the parlor doors, leaving a faint scent of lavender in her wake.

Chapter Three

THE NEXT TWO DAYS PASSED in a flurry of activity. I spent most of my time interviewing potential hires to accompany me on my upcoming trip.

After the Rosemary fiasco, I had sworn — to my friends, if not my family — that I would never take another seeking commission again. My regular team had taken me at my word and had moved on to other work, and were now unavailable. And, if they were pressed into honesty about the matter, they would have admitted that they, too, had had their fill of my commissions. Since my jobs tended to start and end in heartbreak, my crew also tended to have high turnover. Very few people had the stomach to handle all the sadness, even if they were well paid in the end.

My final interviews were two friends who apparently had extensive experience in the field. Rhyss was a tall, gangly redhead who claimed to be the muscle of the duo. Farrah, a half fey, half human woman with dark skin and striking purple eyes and hair, had some magical ability to heal and also claimed to be good in a fight.

"We need something to do, now that the Seeker we usually support is out of commission," Rhyss said.

"Out of commission?" I repeated, horrified. "Do you mean he or she died? Or worse?"

Since Seekers *had* to use their gift once they came into their powers, or eventually go mad, it was important for those in a Seeker family to ensure that those powers were either active or dormant in their respective hosts. An unchecked Seeker ability would prove catastrophic, given enough time. When Seeker children came of age and were ready to take on the family responsibilities, the previous generation would pass down the Seeker mantle in a formal ceremony. Usually it was a parent, but sometimes a grandparent, aunt, or uncle, who transferred responsibility. While some parents were sad to release their duty, others were relieved to be free of that lifelong burden. Their gift remained intact, but they no longer had the compulsion to use their ability all the time, or live under the fear of the consequences if they resisted using it.

Rhyss laughed at my horrified expression, but Farrah poked Rhyss in annoyance. "Don't scare the man," she said. "We actually want the job, remember?"

She turned to me. "Our friend — and former employer — moved to Calia," she said, naming another kingdom in the Gifted Lands, our closest neighbor just to the north of Orchwell. "He rarely takes on seeking jobs anymore. He has other duties that take up his time, and he doesn't really need the money."

"But how does he avoid the madness?" I asked, curious. "Unless he's already entrusted his duty to his children?"

"No, he doesn't have children," Farrah said.

"Yet," Rhyss chimed in.

Farrah, seeing my confusion, explained further. "We used to work with Beyan, the dragon Seeker. When he married Jennica, the Crown Princess of Calia, that seemed to keep the madness at bay. I think, somehow, the marriage satisfied his compulsion to seek out dragons. He hasn't had any issues for, I believe, close to a year."

I nodded, now understanding. I had heard of the events in Calia the previous year, including the unexpected news that Calia's princess was also a dragon shapeshifter. Privately, I envied Beyan's neat solution to the problems that came with being a Seeker.

Farrah seemed pretty sharp. Maybe she would know ...

"That's fascinating," I said nonchalantly. "Do you know, is that the only way one would be able to 'get rid' of the Seeker gift? As it were."

Farrah looked thoughtful. "I'm not sure. We'd worked with Beyan for a long time, and since I grew up with him, I was invited to attend the formal ritual that transfers the official Seeker role within families. It's usually passed from a parent to a child — in this case, from father to son. The strength of the Seeker gift can vary from child to child or between generations." She bit her lip as she concentrated harder. "From what I know, there are times when a worthy individual, not in a Seeker family line, has been granted a Seeker's gift. But it's very rare, and it's dangerous. I don't know all the details, but if you can become a Seeker that way, then by the same logic, you could lose your Seeker status by doing the opposite of ... whatever that spell or ritual entails."

I leaned back in my chair, impressed. "It sounds like you both know exactly what you're doing, and how to handle yourselves. Are you able to leave tomorrow morning?"

Rhyss and Farrah exchanged satisfied looks.

"We're always ready to go," Rhyss said. "We could leave tonight, if you wanted."

"Tomorrow will be just fine," I said, smiling at his enthusiasm. "Meet me at the gates just after sunrise."

"You don't want a reference?" Farrah said. "It's a tight deadline, but if we send word immediately to Calia, we might get a letter back in time before we leave tomorrow ..."

"No need," I said, trusting my instincts that these two were reliable. My instincts rarely failed me ... usually. "If our travels take us to Calia, you can see if your friends would put us up for the night." I laughed. "Sleeping in a palace ... that would be a more than adequate recommendation."

Chapter Four

THE DAY OF DEPARTURE dawned misty and cold. Even though the late autumn sun weakly pierced the lazy clouds floating in the sky, I still shivered slightly under my woolen traveling cloak as I waited on horseback for the rest of my group to arrive.

My horse whickered softly. I leaned down and patted her neck. "Easy, girl," I said in a low, soothing tone as I kept an eye out for Rhyss, Farrah, and Lady Pahame.

Mother and Father had still been abed when I rose to get ready to leave. Only a few servants had been up and about, preparing the household for the day. A simple breakfast had been spread out for me in the kitchen.

As was our tradition, my sister had woken up early as well. She always saw me off on the start of my journeys, waving at the door as I reached the manor gate.

Now I stood at the gates of Orchwell, which were just opening in the early dawn light. As people began moving through the gateway, I heard someone call my name. Looking to my right, I saw Rhyss and Farrah riding toward me, each on their own horse. I waved at them.

As they approached, I looked my new team over. They were carrying so little; short swords at their belts, with identical knapsacks and one small bedroll each affixed to their horses' saddles.

I must have been gaping, because Rhyss was quick to reassure me. "Don't worry, we're completely prepared for anything that might happen."

"I'm not worried," I said. "It's just ... my former team knew how to travel light, but you've definitely done them better."

"Oh, hey. Thanks." Rhyss beamed.

"But I'm surprised." I indicated the lone swords they each carried. "That's all the weapons you're bringing? I mean, you don't need to bring a lot, but if something got lost or damaged —"

"Farrah's got her bow in her bag. And as for me, this is the only weapon you can see. It doesn't mean it's the only weapon I'm carrying." He grinned.

"I truly am impressed," I said sincerely.

Farrah rolled her eyes. To me, she said, "Now you've done it. I'm going to have to listen to Rhyss brag over and over about how clever he is. How *impressive*."

Before Ryhss could retort, two more cloaked people on horseback joined us. One rider drew forward.

"And I am impressed at how punctual you and your team are, Kaernan," Lady Pahame said, looking over our little group. "Usually I'm the first one to arrive to any gathering. I hope this bodes well for our search."

I made a half-bow of respect. "Welcome, Lady Pahame. I'd like to introduce you to your traveling companions, Rhyss and Farrah. Rhyss, Farrah, this is Lady Adallia Pahame."

"Please, call me by my given name, Adallia," Lady Pahame told us. "I find it easier — and safer — to not use my title when I travel."

"Of course, Lady ... I mean, Adallia," I said.

"Good. Then let us depart. The sooner we begin, the sooner we can return." She turned her mount to face the wider road beyond Orchwell.

"But ... ah ..." I stopped, flustered. I looked from Adallia to the rider behind her. It seemed rude for Adallia to leave without saying goodbye to her unknown companion, but Seekers never brought miscellaneous people on a commission. And I couldn't figure out a polite way to say that to Adallia.

Adallia turned slightly to follow my gaze. "Oh, my apologies for not introducing you. That's my daughter, Delphine. She will be coming with us. Let's go."

Without any further explanation, the noblewoman spurred her horse forward and started down the road, Delphine right behind her.

"But —" I said to their rapidly departing backs. Cursing under my breath, I spurred my mount after her.

Behind me, I heard Farrah comment to Rhyss, "This will be an interesting trip."

THIS WAS THE FIRST time I had ever had someone along who wasn't either my patron or a member of my team, and it made me feel awkward and uneasy. Often a patron — and especially my patrons — wanted to keep their purposes private, and they were the ones who balked at traveling with anyone besides their hired Seeker. I couldn't exactly demand that my patron leave her daughter behind, but I worried Delphine would be a hindrance to completing this commission.

Delphine had her mother's striking looks and near regal bearing. However, she was a much more outgoing and friendlier soul than her hard-to-read mother. I guessed she was roughly the same age as me. She was inquisitive about everything, and not shy to strike up a conversation with any of her companions.

Like her mother, she also insisted that we call her by her first name only, dropping the formalities of her station. Not even a few hours out of Orchwell, she became fast friends with Rhyss and Farrah. She tried several times to draw me into conversation, but I couldn't keep up with Delphine's rapid chatter.

While Delphine was quizzing Farrah and Rhyss about the far-off places they had traveled in the Gifted Lands, I brought my horse to ride alongside Adallia.

"Adallia," I said. "I know you talked a little about who you are searching for when we first met, but with all the last-minute travel preparations, we unfortunately didn't have time for a longer interview. So I thought, before we get too far into our journey, we could discuss more about your commission? We've got a little bit of time before we hit the crossroads and have to decide whether to go north, or west."

Adallia looked taken aback. "I thought the letter I sent your father when I asked him to help me made everything clear."

There had been a letter? "My father didn't share your message with me," I said, wondering why my father had put me at a deliberate disadvantage in my search.

Adallia stilled and didn't say anything for several moments.

"Oh."

It came out soft and uncertain, surprising me. To me, Adallia was an unmovable pillar of a woman.

"All right then. If your father didn't see fit to share my letter with you ..." She trailed off, thinking. "As I told you when we met, I am looking for a man named Baxley. We started as childhood friends, and then eventually became sweethearts."

Her expression grew distant, her voice wistful. "We adored each other, but there were too many things working against us. His family felt I was beneath him, as he came from a very long and cultured line of Seekers. My family is one of the few in Orchwell without the Seeker ability. We were modestly well off, but did not have the fame or fortune that a Seeker lineage would have given us.

"Baxley didn't care. He was willing to marry me regardless. But then —" Adallia's face darkened at the memory "— my family fell into immense debt. My father was threatened with imprisonment or a lifetime of servitude. To lose him would have devastated us even further. With four younger siblings, my mother wouldn't have been able to earn a living and take care of us all. I was able to bring in a little money with the odd seamstress job, but not enough to take care of my family.

"A nobleman came to our door one day, offering to help us out of our debt. It seemed he had seen me in the marketplace and decided he must wed me. My family's misfortune only made his suit stronger. If I agreed, he would help us.

"I had no choice. Baxley's family had threatened to disown him if we were to marry. My family needed my father alive and free. I couldn't have condemned my family to poverty or worse because of my own desires. Lord Pahame and I wed within a week of his offer. My family's debt was paid off in full shortly after the wedding."

She sighed. "We had a happy enough life together, I suppose. Our daughter, Delphine, was the best thing to come out of that union. But now that my daughter is grown and my husband is gone ... well, I often wondered what might have been."

Adallia turned slightly in her seat to glance at her daughter, who was still talking animatedly with Rhyss and Farrah. When Adallia turned back to me, the warm smile on her face was genuine.

"What happened to Baxley?" I asked. Obviously, Baxley and Adallia had lost track of each other, but it would help to have any known details, and to know exactly how cold the trail was.

Adallia's face clouded over. "Right before the wedding, we met late at night, in secret. He begged me to reconsider, asked me to run away with him that night. I was tempted ... but I couldn't destroy my life and my future that way. Nor could I destroy his. He left, vowing to always love me.

"He disappeared right after the wedding. He didn't attend, of course. It was a small affair anyway, for family only. But he just ... vanished ... from Orchwell. No one knew where he had gone."

"Not even his family? His friends?"

"They were just as baffled as anyone else. Even his entire family, including his own brother, had no idea. They had been close growing up, but I understand his brother mightily disapproved of the idea of Baxley and I together. Anyway, his family woke up one morning and Baxley was gone. They tried to find him, but they were unsuccessful. I suspect that Baxley, familiar with traditional Seeker methods, somehow made it impossible for anyone to find him in that manner. After a year's fruitless search, his family gave him up as completely lost. Or dead."

I could tell it hurt Adallia to relive these memories, but I would be remiss as a Seeker if I didn't ask about and explore every option. "But you didn't. Why search now?"

Adallia toyed with a bracelet on her wrist. "Baxley and I exchanged tokens while he was still in Orchwell. This —" she held out her wrist, showing off a simple gold bracelet with a bright red carnelian jewel in the center "— is a bloodstone."

I gaped at the bracelet.

Adallia smiled at my recognition. "Ah, then you know what this is."

"Yes," I said, awestruck.

"Then you know that they are literally formed from the blood of a person. It reflects the health status of the one to whom it is linked. If Baxley was in trouble, the red color would grow darker. If he was dead, it would turn black, and crack in two." She showed off the stone again. It shone a vibrant blood-red, and was still completely intact. "I know it's been over twenty years, but he's still alive."

My mouth still hung open stupidly as I stared at the delicate piece of jewelry Adallia so casually wore on her wrist. Bloodstones were extremely rare, if only because the cost to make them was so prohibitive that only the richest people could afford them. The physical cost to creating one also took a toll on the person linked to the stone.

And yet ... Adallia's possession of that stone should make my job childishly easy.

"May I see your bracelet, Adallia?" I asked.

She hesitated. "I rarely take it off. I don't like to be without it."

"Please," I said. "It will make our journey go that much faster."

Adallia nodded in understanding. She brought her horse to a stop. I did the same. Behind us, Delphine, Rhyss, and Farrah halted their mounts as well, curiously looking on.

Adallia slipped the bracelet from her wrist and carefully handed it over to me. It sparkled in the palm of my hand, the sunlight glinting off the carnelian in the bracelet's center. I closed my fist around the bracelet. Adallia gasped and made a motion to grab the bracelet back.

"It's okay," I reassured her. "I'm not going to break it. Just give me a moment."

Adallia pursed her lips but put her hand down. I stopped paying attention to her as I concentrated on the bracelet in my hand.

It was so small and delicate, a stark contrast to the self-possessed woman who carried it close to her person daily. And yet, for all its seemingly frail nature, I could sense the wild, erratic pulse deep within the jewel's core.

I had thought that such a personal artifact would give me all the answers I needed immediately. I was therefore surprised to find that the bloodstone resisted me, refusing to give up its secrets. I opened my eyes and frowned at my fist. That shouldn't be. A bloodstone, crafted from the very essence of the person I was seeking, should have yielded some answers. Namely, who I was searching for, and their exact location.

But those answers didn't come. I closed my eyes again, sinking my thoughts deeper into the bloodstone. Very faintly, I felt a tug.

Inspecting the faint pull closer, I just got one overwhelming feeling. I reopened my eyes and found my eyes were scanning the horizon to my left. West.

To the west of Orchwell lay the countries of Rothschan and Bomora. Some of my commissions had taken me to Rothschan, or just beyond, but I had never been as far as Bomora. "West" was a very broad direction. We could be wandering for weeks.

Blinking as I recollected myself, I saw the curious stares of my traveling companions all around me. I shook off the last remnants of the deep concentration I had been in, opened my still clenched fist, and handed the bracelet back to Adallia. She secured it around her wrist, breathing a barely audible sigh of relief once it was back in place.

"We go west," I told the inquisitive faces. I frowned, thinking again of how little information the bloodstone had given me. "I didn't really learn anything beyond that. But we should at least travel west to Rothschan ... perhaps even further, all the way to Bomora."

"Oh!" Rhyss perked up. Now it was my turn to give him a quizzical look.

"Bomora is my home country," Rhyss explained. "I haven't been back in several years. Beyan's commissions never really took us out that way — it's not typical dragon country. It would be wonderful to go back, even for just a short visit."

"That's perfect, then," I said. "We have someone who knows the area who can help us get around."

Rhyss straightened in his saddle, puffing his chest out proudly as Farrah rolled her eyes.

She clicked her tongue, and her horse started moving again. As she passed me, she said pointedly, "I blame this, and whatever else comes as a result, completely on you."

I could only stare at her retreating back in confusion before spurring my own mount forward.

Chapter Five

AS OUR GROUP CONTINUED west, the days fell into a simple, steady rhythm. The days were for traveling, engaged in easy conversation to while away the time. Nights were for eating, resting, and the occasional entertainment from someone in the group. Rhyss and Farrah were full of stories from their previous commissions with a former dragon Seeker. Looking up in the sky, seeing the majestic creatures winging overhead, I was in awe of Rhyss and Farrah's adventures.

Adallia had her own unique stories, as she had grown up outside of Seeker society in Orchwell. Delphine, normally so effervescent, was shy about her talents, but as time went by, she relaxed enough to treat the group to her beautiful, clear soprano.

Rhyss and Farrah traded off the hunting and cooking duties for the party. Occasionally I would help, but I was more than happy to let the pair take point. While both Rhyss and Farrah were competent at their jobs, Rhyss turned out to be an excellent cook — something that, when I remarked upon it, caused Farrah to give me such a fierce look that I resolved to keep quiet about it from that point on. It didn't stop the self-satisfied grin from spreading across Rhyss's face though, nor did it stop the barely audible huff of annoyance from Farrah.

I shook my head at the memory of the incident. I couldn't understand those two. They got along well, if getting along well together also included constant verbal jabs and lots of sarcastic back-and-forth commentary.

Then again, it wasn't like I had a lot of experience with relationships, friendship or otherwise. Most relationships I had seen ended in misery. It did, after all, come with the nature of my gift ....

"Is everything all right?"

I looked up, startled out of my thoughts, to see Delphine studying me curiously. "Oh. Yes, I'm fine."

Delphine sat down next to me with little regard for the dust that would gather on her dress. I was surprised at how well she and her mother had adapted to life on the road. In my experience, the higher the station in life, the more complaining a person did. It only added to the overall misery of my commissions.

"What were you thinking about?" Delphine asked.

I chuckled. "Remember a few nights ago, when I told Rhyss how much I enjoyed his cooking but then Farrah got mad?"

Delphine laughed along with me. "Oh, that. That *was* pretty funny. What else were you thinking about?"

My mirth died mid-chuckle. "It doesn't matter."

Delphine's smile faded. "I didn't mean to offend you."

"You didn't." It came out a little too quickly to be sincere. "Why do you ask?"

She paused. "It's just ... I've never seen such an array of emotions on your face before. You're usually kind of ..."

When she didn't continue, I asked, "What? I'm kind of what?"

Delphine shrugged. "Kind of closed off. You're very hard to read, did you know that?"

Now it was my turn to shrug, mostly to hide my discomfort. Delphine was surprisingly perceptive. "I don't mean to be ... but I guess I'm not surprised I come across that way. My sister is definitely the more outgoing of the two of us."

"Your sister? Is she older or younger?"

"Younger, by five minutes. She's my twin."

"Wow." Delphine turned a wide-eyed stare on me. "You're so lucky."

"I suppose so. For the most part it's great, having a twin. But sometimes it can be a little trying." Like during Father's non-stop constant comparisons between Kaela's superior seeking abilities and my own unwanted skills.

"No, really," Delphine insisted. "I'm an only child. It often gets lonely. And ..."

Delphine looked around our campsite. Farrah and Adallia were several feet away, busy chatting over meal preparations. Rhyss was just returning to camp, a pair of rabbits dangling from his hands. He joined the women where they sat, pulling out his knife as he settled in to skin the rabbits.

With everyone else suitably preoccupied, Delphine leaned toward me and lowered her voice. "Mother has always been super protective of me, but it's gotten worse since

Father died. I feel like I have to carry the weight of all her hopes and dreams."

She stopped, embarrassed. "I'm sorry. I don't mean to burden someone I barely know with all of this. Mother says I need to learn to hold my tongue." Delphine started to get up.

I surprised myself by putting my hand out and touching Delphine's arm to stop her from leaving. "No, it's all right. I don't mind. I ... I understand."

Delphine settled back next to me, turning her rich brown eyes on mine. I tried not to squirm under her scrutiny. She definitely had her mother's ability to pierce someone's soul with a single glance. "You do?"

"Yes." I looked away, watching the rest of our companions making dinner on the other side of the campsite.

"Tell me. If you like. If it helps."

I looked back at Delphine. There was no hidden agenda in her face. Not the disapproval of my father, nor the disappointment of my mother. Not even the encouragement tinged with sadness that I often felt from my sister. Delphine had no preconceived notions of how I "should" be, or any biases about how I actually was.

And, maybe in some respects, she was also a kindred spirit. It seemed she would at least understand the pressures and the loneliness I often dealt with in my profession as a Seeker.

"Well," I started slowly. "I've been feeling that same weight my whole life, but it really came to light when I accepted a commission for a noblewoman named Rosemary …."

I found myself telling Delphine the whole story. Once I opened that floodgate, I couldn't stop the deluge of words that poured out. The disastrous commission, the trial before the Council of Seekers, and the cold aftermath — I left nothing out.

"ROLAND WILL WANT TO see me, I know he will. It's just that he doesn't know how to find me. That's why I need your help."

Lady Rosemary's eyes shone a little too brightly as she finished her impassioned plea to hire my Seeker services to find her lost love, Roland. She had a typical broken hearts story: two lovers, torn apart for whatever societal reason, and now, oh-so-many years later, she wanted to find him and hopefully reunite with him.

She was surprisingly young, probably no more than nineteen or twenty. Much younger than the people who normally sought my help. In our brief interview, she had seemed a little too excitable, a bit too romantic. But I had dismissed it, thinking it was just her youth speaking.

I agreed to the commission, and we set out immediately to find her man. As in, within the hour, at Rosemary's insistence. I didn't even have time to gather my team, but Rosemary had wanted us to go alone anyway.

Our time together was probably the shortest I've ever had on a commission — just three days. But it was enough time for me to get the feeling that Rosemary wasn't being completely open with me about the circumstances of her parting with Roland. *But*, I thought, *that doesn't matter. It's their personal business, theirs alone to know. I just need to do my job.*

But on the third day, everything changed.

We found Roland alone at his house on the outskirts of Orchwell, while his wife was at the Sunday market with their child.

Rosemary rushed up to the stunned Roland and threw her arms around him. "My love, my darling! We'll never be apart again!"

Roland pushed Rosemary away, none too gently. "R-Rosemary? What are you doing here?"

She laughed shrilly. "Roland, my love, I've found you at last! Now we can be together again. Isn't that wonderful? You, me, and our boy. Our family."

Roland blanched and quickly stepped back into his house, trying to shut the door in Rosemary's face. Rosemary immediately stuck her foot out, keeping the door wedged open, but her slight frame wasn't enough to fully force the door open against Roland's weight.

Meanwhile, I stood a few paces away, watching the power struggle between the two estranged lovers with dispassionate eyes. I had completed enough of these love-lost commissions to know it was better to not get involved after I had located the person I was hired to find.

Through the half-closed door, Roland said loudly, "Go home, Rosemary. Your place is not with me, as I told you years ago. I have my own family now, a lovely wife and a little girl."

"But your son —" Rosemary began.

"He's not my son!"

"He is! I haven't been with anyone before or since I was with you."

"So you said when you came to me heavy with a child you insisted was mine. All I saw was evidence of your unfaithfulness."

Rosemary began crying. "How can you say that, Roland? You knew it was your child. How can you deny him?" Her eyes grew wild. "It's *her*, isn't it? *She's* the reason you won't acknowledge your own son."

She began babbling, her voice growing louder and more frantic with each word. "He's a beautiful boy, Roland. He looks just like you. He's two now, and he always asks me about you. His father. I don't know what to tell him, that's why I hired this man here to find you." She pointed wildly at me. I tried to shrink back into the foliage surrounding Roland's house. "Because I tried to find you on my own, and I couldn't, and I realized you must have been using magic somehow to hide from me. Did you hire someone to place a charm on this house? On you? It doesn't matter. Roland, our boy deserves to know his father. I deserve to have you back in my life. I've missed you so, my love ..."

Rosemary's unhinged monologue had caused her to ease up on her original task of forcing her way into Roland's house, and Roland took advantage of her distracted air to firmly shut the door, nearly severing her foot in the process. As she jumped back, we heard the inside locks slide into place.

Rosemary banged on the door. "Open up!"

But no matter how she pleaded, screamed, or threatened, Roland did not open the door.

I watched the sun change positions in the sky as Rosemary kept up her relentless knocking. I watched as her hands grew bloody from her abuse and her beautiful face turned into a mess of tears and snot she refused to wipe away.

And then, I watched when Roland's wife and little girl — no more than a baby, really — returned home to see a crazy Rosemary on the front steps of their house.

I held out my hand towards Roland's wife, warning her not to come closer. She paused, a question in her eyes, but waited just out of Rosemary's sight.

Rosemary's energy finally seemed to be fading as I carefully approached her. Gently, I put my hands over hers, stopping her from banging on the door any further. I kept my voice low, much as I would speak to a wounded animal. Which, indeed, she was. "Rosemary, I'm sorry it turned out this way. But I think it's time to leave."

Rosemary turned to me, her eyes glazed over as if in a trance. She looked down at her hands, uncomprehending. "My hands. Why are my hands all red?"

"It doesn't matter, we'll get you somewhere you can rest, get some food, and we'll put some bandages on those hands. Doesn't that sound nice?"

Rosemary nodded, but then her gaze sharpened as she spotted something over my shoulder. Glancing behind me, I saw Roland's wife, holding her baby girl, staring at Rosemary in shock.

I turned back to Rosemary as the words tumbled out. "Don't pay her any attention, Rosemary, just keep your eyes on me."

Slowly, Rosemary turned her gaze back to me.

"That's it," I soothed. "Now, we're going to walk away from here, just keep looking at me, don't worry about anything else around us ..."

I was so focused on keeping Rosemary calm that I didn't even notice her slim hand shooting out to grab the dagger at my belt. The light of the setting sun glinted off the silver blade as she plunged it deep into her heart.

Somebody screamed. Was it Rosemary? Roland's wife? Me? I wasn't sure.

I barely caught Rosemary before she tumbled to the ground. Blood bloomed from the dagger in her chest, mingling with the darker, dried blood on her hands.

As I sank to my knees cradling the dying woman, she whispered to me, "Help ... my son ... find ... his father."

Things after that went by in a blur. I recall bringing Rosemary back to Orchwell, but I was too heartsick and ashamed to attend the lady's funeral. Her young son was now a ward of the Crown, as she had been disowned by her family when she had become pregnant. It was probably the best outcome for the boy; if he worked hard, he could become a squire when he was old enough, and maybe one day serve the kingdom as a knight.

If Rosemary's son wanted to find his father, he could do so on his own, when he was a grown man. Or Roland could take the initiative and seek out the boy himself. I wanted nothing more than to distance myself from the whole sorry affair and was secretly glad I would be unable to reunite them, at least through magical means. And thankfully, neither the Crown nor the Council of Seekers seemed inclined to force me to do so by more mundane methods.

After Rosemary's death, I had been called before the Council of Seekers to recount my time with her. I hadn't been sure why — surely I wasn't going to be imprisoned for her death? After all, I had just been doing my job. While I should have had better instincts about the woman — I should have trusted my intuition about her and refused the commission — the Council ultimately decided that my limited experience as a Seeker meant I was innocent of any wrongdoing, and thus did not merit my powers being stripped.

Although that didn't stop the whispers around town, or the averted eyes as I walked down the street. I sometimes thought that being rendered giftless would have been the kinder option, instead of carrying the horror of this woman's death around with me everywhere I went.

But even if the Council called me innocent, and the people of Orchwell could forgive me, I had yet to forgive myself.

ONCE I FINISHED MY story, I stared into the fire. I could feel the heat of Delphine's gaze on me, but I was afraid to meet her eyes, not wanting to see the inevitable judgement there.

I felt slender fingers lightly touching mine. I looked down at Delphine's hand on top of my hand, cautiously offering comfort.

"You're not a monster."

Her quiet words touched my heart more than my father's yelling ever did. Now I looked at her fully, startled by the intensity in her face. "That's kind of you, Delphine. But I'm sure the people I 'help' would say otherwise."

She shook her head, as if she was trying to shake off my negativity. "You have a gift, Kaernan. You may not think of it as such, but it's a rare and beautiful gift all the same."

"Beautiful?" I snorted. "Yes, like disease or famine is beautiful."

"You laugh, but it's because you're too close to the subject. You get to show people the big what-might-have-been question of their lives. Instead of slowly going crazy with wondering, the people that seek your services can actually see the outcome of their romantic choices, and either finally rekindle it or put it to rest. Not everyone has the means to have your help, and if they do, then they lack the courage to face the true answer." Her hand gripped mine tightly now, as if she could infuse her convictions into me through sheer strength. "Kaernan, you help people face their deep, hidden regrets. Because everyone carries regrets."

I had often thought it was best to just let the past lie dormant, and not face the what-ifs. But Delphine's passionate words gave me a different perspective. Maybe, sometimes, it *was* better to know the possibilities instead of to live in ignorance.

Maybe, as the Seeker, I needed to find a way to guide my patrons to their answers in a way that also helped them put the past to rest.

We sat there frozen in front of the fire, our eyes locked on each other.

From across the camp, Rhyss called, "Hey, you two! Dinner is ready."

Farrah and Adallia looked our way. Delphine quickly unlaced her fingers from mine and stood up, but not before I caught the frown that darkened Adallia's face. It passed quickly, smoothing out into a more neutral expression. But I was acutely aware of it, just as I was still very aware of Delphine's warm hand holding my own just moments earlier.

Chapter Six

WE SOON REACHED THE town of Meira, the halfway point between the kingdoms of Orchwell and Rothschan. As we approached, Farrah asked me, "Kaernan, do you want to stop here for the night? Or just grab a quick meal and press on? There's plenty of daylight left for travel."

I turned to Adallia. "Whatever suits our generous patron."

Adallia smiled ruefully. "I'm afraid my body isn't used to such rough accommodations. I, for one, would love to sleep in an actual bed tonight. And since I *am* paying for this trip …"

We all laughed, Adallia's words settling the matter. I would never have said it aloud to the others, but I was privately pleased to stop overnight in the town. A good meal and a comfortable bed would be a nice respite from camping on the hard ground and eating Rhyss's good but now rather repetitive cooking.

We turned our horses toward Meira. Their ears perked up and they stepped faster, as if they, too, were looking forward to the brief break from being on the road.

At the town's entrance was a modest stable where we could lodge the horses. While Farrah, Rhyss, and I busied ourselves with the horses and our gear, Delphine ran outside the stable immediately after turning over her mount's reins to a young stableboy who had come to greet us. Adallia smiled and shook her head, but stayed behind to help us distribute the gear.

Delphine didn't turn around as we exited the stable. She was openly gaping at Meira, every line in her body full of suppressed excitement to go exploring.

"Have you ever traveled beyond Orchwell?" I asked her.

She shook her head, her eyes still drinking in the town. "No, never."

"I think you'll find Meira interesting, then. As a midway point, it gets many goods from both Orchwell and Rothschan, and some of the other kingdoms as well."

Delphine finally turned toward us, looking at her mother with pleading eyes.

Adallia laughed. "I knew stopping for the day was the best choice."

I pointed at an establishment just inside the town, where a simple wooden sign depicting a cat standing on its hind legs hung above a green wooden door. "When you're done with your exploring or shopping or whatever it is you want to do, come back to this place, the Dancing Cat. We'll be able to stay here tonight."

Adallia eyed the inn doubtfully. "Are you sure? We should probably make sure it's not full. I'm sure a lot of people come through here daily."

"I'll go check while you walk around the town, but I'm not worried. The owner, Ravon, is a friend of mine. I stay here often on my travels, and he's always been able to accommodate me."

Adallia nodded at me, then at her daughter. Together, she and Delphine walked away from us, down the cobblestone main street of Meira, farther into the town.

"Is there anything you need us to do?" Farrah indicated Rhyss and herself.

"Thank you, but I think I'm good," I said. "If you two want to go look around, feel free."

"Great," Farrah said. "We'll see you back here tonight, then."

She and Rhyss took off in the same direction that Adallia and Delphine had disappeared, at a much more leisurely pace.

I watched them go, then I opened the door to the Dancing Cat and stepped inside.

Since it was only early afternoon, the inn was empty save for one patron: an old, grizzled man sitting by himself as he loudly scarfed down his late lunch. He finished up quickly, belching as he stood and pushed by me. I wrinkled my nose as he passed, catching the mingled scent of alcohol and body odor. I tried not to breathe in too deeply, but as he opened the inn's door and stepped into the afternoon sunshine, I started coughing.

The innkeeper, a stocky middle-aged man, was wiping down the tables with an old rag. He cocked his head when he heard the commotion at the door, but didn't bother to look up as he continued to clean.

"Kitchen's closed until this evening. Come back in a few hours if you want a meal."

"While your meals are always excellent, I actually wanted to inquire if you had any rooms available for tonight.

And," I added with a laugh, "I promise to actually pay my tab this time, so you don't have to scold me."

This time the innkeeper did look up, recognizing my voice. When he saw me, he smiled.

"Kaernan Asthore." He promptly left the rag on the table, hastily wiping his hands dry on his half-apron as he walked around the tables toward me.

"Ravon, it's good to see you." I held out my hand to shake his, but instead Ravon grabbed my hand and pulled me into a big hug. Even after all the many times I'd stayed at the Dancing Cat, Ravon's boisterous shows of affection always surprised me. I think it was because my family wasn't very physically demonstrative with each other, with the exception of my twin sister.

Ravon held me at arm's length to beam at me broadly before releasing me completely. "Kaernan, it's been far too long. Where have you been keeping yourself? Usually I'd see you every few weeks while you're on a commission of some sort. I missed my favorite customer! Although perhaps your travels have been taking you in other directions?"

I fidgeted under his open, earnest smile. "Ah ... no. I just haven't been traveling as much lately."

Ravon's eyebrows shot up. "Oh? Has business been —"

I cut him off before he could finish his question. "I'm actually on a commission right now. I wasn't joking when I said I needed some rooms. At least two, although if you have more my traveling companions might like that."

Ravon looked around the room, and then behind me, trying to locate these invisible traveling companions. "How many are in your group?"

"Three women, two men. Ideally four rooms, I think, if you have them."

He nodded absently at me, deep in thought.

"Most of my rooms are taken already," he said apologetically. "There's a fair that starts in town in two days, and we have some out-of-town merchants and other visitors who came to Meira early to secure places to stay. But I have three rooms still open."

"That sounds good," I said. "When my companions come here later this evening, I'll see what they prefer. If someone else comes in needing a room, I'm sure it's no hardship if we use just two rooms instead."

With that matter settled, Ravon walked back to the table he had abandoned earlier and resumed cleaning. "Talk to me while I work, Kaernan," he said. "What have you been doing lately, if you haven't been working as much?"

I didn't say anything, not wanting to lie to my friend but also not wanting to disclose the story of my disastrous last commission. When the silence stretched out too long, Ravon stopped his cleaning again to look at me.

"Kaernan? Everything all right?"

"I ... uh ..."

"It's okay if you don't feel comfortable talking about it," Ravon said.

I shrugged. "My last commission ended poorly." What an understatement. "It ... turned me off to seeking for a while."

Ravon's eyes narrowed as he studied me. "I remember when you came through here last, you were with that wispy near-ghost of a woman. Rosie?"

"Rosemary."

He started wiping down the table again, with such a deliberately casual air I knew he was trying to figure out the best way to say what he was thinking. Plus, he had already cleaned that spot on the table at least two times. "I heard something a while back ... something about the Council of Seekers holding a trial recently in regards to a botched commission ... and the poor soul on trial nearly getting stripped of their abilities." That spot on the table was now beyond clean; he was going to wear a hole in the wood soon if he wasn't careful. "You wouldn't happen to know anything about that, now would you?"

I paused, then took a deep breath. "Yes. That was my trial." Then, to cover my nerves, I added, "I think you can move on to a different part of the table now."

"What?" Ravon blinked, shaking his head to clear it. "Ah, yes. Of course." He began cleaning another, noticeably dirtier, part of the table.

"How did you hear about it?"

"The trial, you mean?" Ravon looked at me from the corners of his eyes.

"Yes."

"I'm an innkeeper, in one of the busiest way stations between Orchwell and Rothschan," he said simply. "People are always eager to share the latest stories. And the Council rarely holds a trial. It was big news."

He was right; unfortunately the whole sorry event, from Rosemary's death to the trial, had been the talk of Orchwell. I had hoped that word of the event wouldn't have spread beyond Orchwell, but that was just my own naive, wishful thinking.

Ravon finished with the table. Straightening up, he tucked the rag into the waistband of his half-apron. "You all right, Kaernan?"

"Sometimes I wish the Council *had* taken my abilities away."

"You don't mean that."

"Yes, I do. It would have made my life so much easier."

Ravon quirked his mouth, giving me an odd little half-smile. "Maybe. Maybe not."

"What does *that* mean?"

The innkeeper leaned against the newly cleaned table, looking at me intently. "If I may speak freely?"

I nodded.

Ravon said, "It's easy to think that, since all you know is being a Seeker. And as I've seen you here over the years, I've seen the toll it's taken on you, on your mind, your heart. It's a heavy burden you bear, Kaernan. But you're a strong person. You're still finding your way. There's nothing wrong with that."

I dropped my gaze. Although we had gotten to know each other over my years of travel, it had always stayed at a superficially friendly level. I hadn't realized Ravon was so insightful.

He coughed, pulling my attention back to him. His tone changed from a kindly elder to a neutral businessman. "You said your friends will be here later today? By sunset, do you think?" I nodded. "I'll make sure your rooms are ready by then. The kitchen will be open for dinner by then, too."

I nodded again, glad to be back in familiar emotional territory. "Perfect. I ... we ... will see you then."

I shouldered my pack and headed out the door, feeling Ravon's appraising gaze on my back as the inn's door shut behind me.

Chapter Seven

I SPENT THE NEXT FEW hours wandering around Meira, alone with my thoughts. I watched the preparations for the fair that were taking place all around the town without really seeing them. Occasionally I'd see other members of my group also out exploring — Meira wasn't *that* large of a town — but I did my best to avoid them.

At one point, I spotted Delphine, who lit up when she recognized me. I was far enough away that I could pretend I didn't see her, and I deliberately turned away, feeling vaguely guilty. I quickly began walking in the opposite direction.

"Kaernan!"

I ever-so-slightly picked up my pace.

Light footsteps, coming at a run, sounded behind me. Someone reached out to tap my shoulder. "Kaernan, wait!"

I stopped, suppressing my disappointed sigh. Steeling my features, I attempted some sort of a smile before turning around. "Hi, Delphine. I ... didn't see you."

"It's all right," she said, turning on that bright smile of hers. "Can I walk with you?"

"Of course." What else could I say? I looked over her shoulder. "Where's Adallia?"

Delphine put her hand on my arm, indicating I should lead. "Mother was feeling tired, so she went ahead to the

Dancing Cat. I think I've walked around the town three times already, but I didn't want to stop. I wanted to see everything, over and over again."

I laughed at her infectious enthusiasm. "You really didn't get out much, did you?"

"No." She didn't sound upset, just matter-of-fact. She looked around us, beaming. "But I am now."

"Well, even though you've seen the town three times over, is there anywhere you'd like to go? Anything you'd like to see?"

"Just the Dancing Cat. I'm ready for dinner. I walked around and around so much I couldn't remember which direction it was in."

We headed back to the inn, where we found Adallia and Farrah already seated at a table. The place was beginning to fill up; I was glad that the two women had the foresight to come back early and hold seats for all of us. Delphine slipped into a chair next to her mother, while I sat across the table from them, next to Farrah.

"Where's Rhyss?" I asked.

"Upstairs, in one of our rooms," Farrah said. "The innkeeper said we had our choice of two or three rooms for all of us?"

"Oh, yes," I said, remembering. "It's really your preference, Farrah. If you want your own room, you have that option."

Farrah hesitated. I immediately understood what she was trying to figure out how to politely ask me. So I added quickly, "I don't mind the extra expense."

She smiled. "Then I'll take it. It will be nice to have a bit of privacy tonight. You hardly ever get any while on a job."

I nodded in complete understanding as Rhyss bounded down the stairs, nearly barreling into another patron who was headed upstairs. The portly man stepped back, startled, to make room for the gangly bundle of energy that was hurtling past him.

"Sorry!" Rhyss said to the man in passing, not sounding sorry at all. He joined us at our table, sitting on Farrah's other side, as Farrah and I exchanged meaningful glances.

"If he starts snoring, you can hit him on the shoulder to wake him out of it," Farrah told me.

"Hey!" Rhyss said.

"I'll keep that in mind, thank you," I said to Farrah.

"Hey!" Rhyss said again, a little louder.

"Or just turn him on his side, that should do the trick," Farrah said.

"Hey!" Rhyss practically yelled.

We both looked over at him. "Yes?" we both said in unison.

"I'm right here!" Rhyss said, indignant. "And I don't snore."

Somehow, Adallia, Delphine, Farrah, and I were able to exchange a four-way glance. An exasperated Rhyss stood up, saying, "Sheesh, I know when I'm not wanted. I'm going to go get a drink."

Rhyss left. Our entire table burst into laughter.

"Oh, my," Adallia said. "I didn't think this trip would end up being so entertaining."

"It's just too easy to tease him," Farrah said. "But he never takes it to heart, he knows it's just friendly ribbing."

Rhyss returned, holding a tray full of drinks.

"Does Kaernan not pay you enough?" Farrah asked.

"Funny, you," Rhyss said good-naturedly. He served the drinks all around the table, starting with Adallia and her daughter. "Just for that, I'll keep your drink as well as mine."

Farrah tried to swipe a drink off the tray, but Rhyss easily moved the tray out of her reach. Skirting around her, he offered me a drink.

"Okay, I'm sorry," Farrah said. "And thirsty. Now can I have my drink?"

Rhyss took his seat beside Farrah again, setting the tray down. She grabbed one of the two remaining drinks and took a quick swallow before he could stop her. Rhyss picked up the last drink and sipped at a more leisurely pace.

"They're a bit short-handed back there," Rhyss said, waving a hand toward the kitchen area. I could see Ravon and his helper, a frazzled-looking young woman, hurrying back and forth from the kitchen to various tables, trying to fill orders as fast as possible. "I offered to bring our drinks back so they didn't have to worry about it."

"That was very kind of you," Adallia said. Rhyss shrugged, seemingly nonchalant, but the two spots of pink on his cheeks betrayed his pleasure at her compliment.

Adallia turned to me. "You're the Seeker. What do you expect we'll do, once we get to Rothschan?"

I shrugged, a little uncomfortable. "Seeking isn't a precise science. It's not a science at all, really. Your bracelet was more helpful in figuring out which way to go than my abilities. When we get to Rothschan, I'll have to ask around, try to pick up Baxley's trail. Where he was last seen, where he could have gone, if he ever even was in Rothschan. Things like that."

Adallia looked disappointed. "I guess I thought, what with you being a Seeker, finding Baxley would be ... instantaneous."

I laughed. "If that were so, madam, I would have found your Baxley within ten minutes of our first meeting. I am not a bloodhound, although if I was, it would make my commissions much easier. Much of what I do is good old-fashioned investigative work. The rest of it is ... well, I'm not even sure how to describe it."

"I understand your sister Kaela is one of the finest Seekers in your family, in a long time."

I nodded. "My father has already turned over all his commissions to her, and was able to retire earlier than he expected."

"Good for him," Adallia said. I refrained from saying that while early retirement may have been good for my father, it wasn't good for *me*, as it meant he had more time and attention to devote to showing his disapproval of me.

"If you and your sister are able to seek out perfect love matches, why are neither of you married? Or at least betrothed?" Delphine asked.

Adallia gasped at her daughter's rudeness. "Delphine, that is an extremely inappropriate question to ask. Apologize immediately."

Delphine looked down at the table. "I'm sorry, Kaernan."

"It's all right," I said. "It's actually a more common question than you realize."

Delphine looked up at me, the question still in her eyes.

"The truth is, our Seeker abilities do not work on us," I told her.

"Really?" That one word from Delphine was tinged with a healthy dose of skepticism.

"The Asthores have never been able to use their abilities on themselves, or anyone else in their immediate family," I said. "I suppose we could seek for people distantly related to us, but to my knowledge we never have. It's only been for non-family."

"You mean no one in your family has never at least tried to use their seeking ability on themselves?"

"Oh, some in my family have tried. But it's like running into a brick wall, mentally. And, depending on how stubborn my ancestor was, it hurts as much as running headlong into that same brick wall. So for the most part, we don't try. It's not worth it."

Delphine pursed her lips as her brows drew together. "So, what you're saying is ... your family can find other people's true loves, and yet can't find their own?"

I nodded. "Yes, that's exactly it."

She laughed. "The irony of it! All those Asthores, with this amazing gift, having to choose a random love match like everyone else."

"Everyone has the choice of who they want to be with. We just help people make better choices, if they want our services."

Ravon the innkeeper came by at that moment holding a tray laden with steaming bowls and dishes for our table.

"Let's see, who ordered the lamb?" he asked. At the end of the table, Rhyss lifted his hand. Ravon placed the dish in front of Rhyss.

The wonderful smells coming from Ravon's tray suddenly reminded me that I was starving, and my stomach growled loudly. Across the table from me, Delphine laughed, drawing Ravon's attention briefly. He looked confused for a minute, staring at her as if trying to place her face in his memory.

Delphine stared back, a little wary and confused herself.

Adallia sat up, suddenly looking like she had a steel rod in her spine. With an equal amount of steel, she addressed Ravon. "Excuse me, but can you tell us why you feel it necessary to stare at my daughter like that?"

I leaned forward, reaching out a hand toward Adallia. "I'm sure he doesn't mean anything by it, Adallia."

"*Lady* Pahame." She corrected me as she waved a hand at me impatiently, indicating I should keep my mouth shut. Still glaring imperiously at Ravon, she said, "This man has a mouth, I'm sure he can speak for himself."

Rhyss and Farrah exchanged glances, but didn't say anything. Delphine's eyes darted back and forth between Ravon and her mother, wondering what would happen next. I half rose out of my seat, ready to do ... something. I didn't know how I would diffuse the situation between my employer and my friend, but I knew I had to try.

Ravon shook his head and blinked, bowing his head toward Delphine and then Adallia.

"Forgive me, my lady," he murmured in Delphine's direction. "I thought I had perhaps seen your face before."

"I don't see how, considering she's never traveled this way before," Adallia said, thawing a bit but not quite mollified.

"Again, forgive me," Ravon said. He finished passing out the dishes and hurried away.

Dinner discussion abandoned, we began eating. It really was delicious, but tucking into the food was also a good excuse to avoid talking about the awkwardness that had preceded the meal. It was easier to focus on our food and avoid looking at each other.

While I ate, I looked around the room. Back at the kitchen area, I could see Ravon occasionally looking over at our table, in between various tasks. He looked ... worried. And perhaps a little scared.

Delphine and Adallia finished eating before the rest of our table, placing their napkins on the table and waiting patiently for Rhyss, Farrah, and me to finish our meals.

"No need to hurry," Adallia told the three of us.

Delphine opened her mouth to say something, but instead a big, cracking yawn came out. "Sorry," she said sheepishly.

"There's nothing to apologize for," I said. "You've had a very full day."

"I'm feeling tired too," Adallia said. "Perhaps we should retire for the night, Delphine."

It wasn't really a question.

Obediently, Delphine stood. "Goodnight, everyone."

Her mother stood as well, nodding at Farrah, Rhyss and me. "Goodnight. Enjoy the rest of your dinner."

"If it helps, feel free to sleep in tomorrow," I said. "We don't need to leave right away. If we can be on the road by mid-morning, that would be fine."

Adallia nodded. "We'll see how we both feel, but thank you."

Mother and daughter left, making their way around the various tables and up the stairs to the inn's rooms.

With the noblewomen gone, the mood at the table lightened considerably. Farrah pushed her dish across the table and switched seats so she could talk to Rhyss and me comfortably. "Ah, it's so nice to have all this room," she said as she settled into her new seat. "I was getting squished over there between you two."

"That was extremely uncomfortable," Rhyss said. Farrah made a face at him. "I wasn't talking about you. I meant earlier. I really thought Adallia — or, excuse me, *Lady Pahame* —was going to make a scene of some sort, she was so incredibly offended."

"She's very protective of Delphine, of course. But that did seem a bit much." Farrah turned to me. "Do you have any idea why she was so touchy?"

I shook my head. "I don't know Adallia very well. I think she's an old friend of my father's, but it must be a very old connection indeed, since I had never met her before this commission."

Ravon came back, holding another full tray of food. "Are you all finished? Is everyone ready for dessert?"

"Dessert?" I asked, confused. "We didn't order any more food."

"No, it's on the house. As an apology for my offense earlier." Ravon put the tray down, distributing the new dishes. The dessert looked delicious: an apple compote with fresh cream on top. As Ravon looked around the table, he realized we were missing part of our group. "Where did the lady and her daughter go?"

"They were tired, so they went up to bed," I said. "Lady Pahame was most likely just exhausted from the days of travel."

"If you say so." Ravon glanced toward the stairs, the worried look back on his face.

"I'm sorry they'll miss the dessert," I said. "It looks wonderful. And thank you for the gracious thought, even though an apology wasn't necessary."

"I'm not sorry," Rhyss said. He pulled a second dessert dish toward him, joining the compote already in front of him. "Can't let it go to waste."

Farrah snorted. "You eat like an ice dragon preparing for its winter hibernation. How does your stomach not explode?"

"I stay active," Rhyss said, sticking a spoon piled high with compote and cream into his mouth.

Ravon gathered up the empty dishes and dirty silverware and left. Farrah snorted again but didn't respond, as she was busy eating her own dessert. I picked at my dessert, distracted by thoughts of Ravon's agitation and the earlier scene between him and Adallia.

"Hey."

Even though Ravon had said the dessert was complimentary, I resolved to give him some extra money the next morning for his trouble. And as an apology, of sorts, from me.

"Hey."

Perhaps I should ask Delphine if she had any thoughts on how to handle any similar situations in the future. After all, she would know best what her own mother was like ....

"Hey, Kaernan!" A slender finger was poking my arm. Repeatedly. And hard. It was Rhyss.

"Ow!" I said, rubbing at the spot where he had mercilessly dug in. "What?"

Rhyss waved his spoon over at the fifth and untouched dish of apple compote. It was just out of his reach, on the other side of my half eaten dessert. "Are you going to eat that, or can I?"

Chapter Eight

OUR ENTIRE GROUP DID end up sleeping in the next day. Rhyss, Farrah, and I stayed up late into the night, talking over the remains of our dessert. And Farrah was right — Rhyss did snore, and that kept me up part of the night as well. Funny how I had never noticed it while we were camping on the road, but then again, there were other sounds that filled the night and perhaps masked the sound of his snoring. Or maybe sleeping in a comfortable bed brought out the snores in Rhyss.

Despite all of that, I was surprised to find that I was the first of our group to rise. I quietly got ready for the day, stuffing my things into my pack and bringing it downstairs to the empty main room of the inn.

I saw the frazzled young woman from last night, cleaning up the room. "Is Ravon around?" I asked her. She pointed toward the kitchen.

As I approached the kitchen door, a voice called out, "Who's that coming?"

I recognized Ravon's voice. "It's Kaernan," I called back.

The door swung open easily at my light push.

Ravon was elbows deep in suds, cleaning the last of the dishes from last night's dinner. "Kaernan! Come over here and talk to me while I finish these up."

I put my pack down on a stool near the door and walked over to Ravon. "Need any help?"

"No, no! Like I said, I'm nearly done. Just keep me company, it will help the time go by faster."

Despite his protests, I grabbed a towel and started drying the cleaned dishes. "I'm sorry about what happened last night," I said.

"Oh, no, don't be. I'm sorry I offended your companion."

I'd known Ravon for years, and I knew he was not a predatory or lascivious sort. Delphine and her mother had nothing to fear from him on that count. Still ... "Why were you so preoccupied with Delphine?" Realizing that Ravon wouldn't know my companions' names, I amended, "The young lady."

Ravon didn't say anything for a moment as he concentrated extra carefully on cleaning a bowl. When I was sure he had scrubbed the bowl at least three times, I coughed delicately. Ravon sighed, rinsed the bowl, and handed it to me. I dutifully wiped it dry, watching his face the whole time.

Ravon plunged his hands back into the sudsy water and fished around for a bit. There were no more dirty dishes. He sighed again as he pulled his hands out of the water and held out his hand to me. I placed the towel in his hand and he dried his hands off.

Throwing the towel on the counter, he ran his hands through his hair in agitation. He hadn't quite dried his hands off — there were now a few suds in his hair. He didn't notice, though. He opened his mouth, closed it, then pursed his lips.

Now *I* was getting worried. I'd never seen Ravon anxious. "What? What is it, Ravon?"

Ravon looked over at the kitchen door, making sure it was shut. With his voice lowered, he said, "When I saw your friend, I thought I had seen her face before. I wasn't sure why. But late last night, after the inn had closed for the night, I remembered why."

He pulled a folded piece of paper from his apron pocket and handed it to me. "Some riders from Orchwell came by the day before you arrived. They're looking for this person, and offering a substantial reward."

I took the wrinkled paper from Ravon and carefully unfolded it.

It was a medium-sized poster, listing the substantial reward Ravon had mentioned. By the order of the Orchwell Council of Seekers, and sanctioned by our King and Queen, the poster listed one thousand gold for the capture of, or information leading to the capture of, the person pictured.

Wanted for murder.

My heart stopped.

Looking up at me from the flyer was the beautiful face of Delphine.

Chapter Nine

THE LEAFLET SHOOK IN my hands, betraying my confusion and fear. "The riders ... are they still around?"

Ravon shook his head. "No. They stopped here to eat, but they were eager to press on. They just gave me this poster and asked me to post it by the door, especially since the fair starts soon, so many people would see it and word would spread. I stuck it in my apron pocket and forgot all about it. Until I saw your companion's face."

My mind, spinning with questions, refused to focus. I grabbed on to the last thing Ravon said. "So you recognized Delphine from this picture. But you didn't post this paper yet, and I didn't see any other leaflets posted around the town yesterday. So it might be safe to say no one else knows about this, yet?"

"Not here in Meira, to the best of my knowledge. The riders left town right after they finished eating."

"Where were they headed, do you know?"

"Rothschan. I overheard them talking while they were eating, and they mentioned wanting to reach Rothschan within two days, but they weren't sure if they wanted to go beyond Rothschan or return to Orchwell."

I frowned, thinking. The riders were already well ahead of us, and would probably reach Rothschan today. There was no way we could overtake them, and we could very well be riding into the kingdom only to be met with Delphine's face plastered on every wall and post.

And then, of course, there was the other thing. The most important thing...

"Is she?" Ravon's voice was barely above a whisper.

I looked down again at the leaflet. Delphine's face, unusually serene and grave, looked back at me. I nearly didn't recognize her; I was so used to her smiling, laughing countenance. I guessed the picture on the leaflet must have been copied from a formal family portrait.

"I don't know," I finally said. "It's hard to believe it, from what I know of her. But ... this commission is for her mother, not for her. I didn't even know she was coming on the trip until the day we left. If she really did kill someone ... then it makes sense that she would come along. It's a convenient excuse to leave Orchwell."

Convenient in more ways than one, I realized. Instead of fleeing into the night and having to fend for herself as a lone traveler, she could take advantage of the protection traveling with a Seeker's trained team would give. We'd see her safely to her destination and she would blend into a foreign land, with no one the wiser.

Now that I had this information, what should I do? Should I confront Delphine and Adallia? Perhaps confer with Farrah and Rhyss first? Or stay quiet but observant? I racked my brain, trying to remember if there had been any important news or splashy gossip that had people buzzing before I had left town on this commission. Orchwell could be a little gritty at times, but a supposed murder would definitely have been the talk of the kingdom.

But my own troubles had occupied most of my days, and I had been a recluse for several weeks, not wanting to go out and run into anyone I might know. My sister, who would normally be the most well-informed person in our family, had been away on her own commission for weeks, and would have been behind on kingdom news. And my parents weren't the type to gossip.

For now, I decided, I would keep the news to myself. If Delphine truly was a murderer, then it would be unwise to let her know I knew her secret. And I obviously couldn't bring it up to Adallia without Delphine becoming aware. Adallia was fiercely protective of her daughter; it wasn't hard to conclude that Adallia probably had known of the situation and was trying to save her daughter from it.

So was this commission a front, then? Was this whole journey nothing more than a sham, a plausible excuse to escape justice? Or did Adallia truly desire to find her man, this Baxley, and the timing just happened to work out perfectly? If it was the latter, I was in luck. If the two women were planning on harming me or my team in any way, they wouldn't be able to do it until after Baxley was found. They needed our skills to find him safely.

But after the commission was completed, what then?

I folded the paper up and carefully placed it in the inside pocket of my jacket. It weighed heavily on me, like I had just put a bunch of rocks in my coat pocket instead of a feather-light piece of paper.

"What are you going to do, Kaernan?" Ravon's eyes searched my face anxiously.

"I don't know, Ravon. I really don't know."

Chapter Ten

AFTER BOLTING DOWN some leftover bread that Ravon generously provided from last night's meal, I settled our group's tab with the innkeeper and then headed to the stables to prepare for the day's upcoming travel. I wanted as much time to myself as possible, to think through what I had just learned and hopefully clear my head.

Taking the brush from the confused young boy, I waved the stablehand away and turned my attention to my horse. The mundane process of grooming soothed me as I continued to mull over the information Ravon had given me.

I had just finished grooming my horse when Farrah and Rhyss arrived, Adallia and Delphine a few paces behind them.

"Ravon said you'd be here," Delphine said. Her tone implied, *Why didn't you wait for us?*

"The weather looks like it will hold for a few days," I said, looking up at the cloudless sky to avoid her eyes — and her unspoken question. "We can take our time getting to Rothschan without having to worry about rain."

"That's good to know," Delphine said, eyeing me curiously. I'd have to be careful around her; she was a sharp one.

Farrah and Rhyss saddled their horses while the stablehand helped Adallia and Delphine with their mounts. Once we were all ready, we turned our horses west, on the road that would lead us to Rothschan.

As we rode, my mind worked furiously, trying to figure out the best course of action. Traveling at a normal pace, we would reach Rothschan in about three days. I estimated the Orchwell messengers had two days' head start on us, which meant they were most likely in Rothschan already. I supposed we could go around the city, but Adallia's bracelet had given me a strong sense that some, if not all, of our answers lay in Rothschan. So we — or at least, Adallia and I — had to go to Rothschan.

I was riding in the lead, with Adallia behind me. I was glad I was at the front, as no one would be able to see the troubled thoughts marching across my face. Delphine and Farrah were riding side by side, comparing stories about their home countries. Farrah, half Fae and half human, was originally from the kingdom of Shonn before she had moved to Orchwell when she was a child. As Delphine had never traveled beyond Orchwell, she found Farrah's stories fascinating, and was peppering her with rapid fire questions. Rhyss brought up the rear.

So, it wasn't really worth it to rush and try to make it to Rothschan. My mind turned to what to do about Delphine. I had visited the military kingdom of Rothschan a few times, always on business. It wasn't a place that encouraged visitors, although, like the other kingdoms in the Gifted Lands, it had a fascinating and rich history of its own. One thing I did know — the people of Rothschan tended to be cold and logical, with little room for shades of gray in their predominantly black-and-white thinking. If Delphine's face was indeed plastered all over their country, then anyone who spotted her wouldn't hesitate to arrest her and turn her over to the Orchwell authorities.

Or worse. After all, the poster hadn't specified that Delphine had to be recovered alive.

Which meant that, ultimately, I would have to confront Delphine and Adallia about the murder charge sometime before we got to Rothschan.

Terrific. I had three days to figure out how to casually work this revelation into conversation. *Excuse me, Delphine, but have you killed anyone lately?*

Somehow, I didn't think this was going to be easy. Or go over well.

Chapter Eleven

AS IT TURNED OUT, IT was a lot easier to bring up Delphine's situation to the group than I thought. But it wasn't because there was a clear opening to talk about it. Instead, circumstances ended up forcing my hand.

We had been on the road to Rothschan for two full days and had settled into our makeshift camp for the night. All through the night I kept trying to figure out how to bring up the wanted poster that Ravon had given me. While we were unpacking our horses? While we were cooking dinner? While we were cleaning up and getting ready to go to sleep? I suppose I could have said something at any point in the evening, but I was just too cowardly. I didn't want to destroy the easy camaraderie our group had. I didn't want to think about what Rhyss, Farrah, and I would have to do if we needed to restrain Delphine and, presumably, her mother.

And I didn't want to know the true answer to the question, was the sweet and bubbly Delphine actually a murderer?

So I kept my mouth shut, all the while silently berating myself for my cowardice. Rhyss offered to take the first watch, with Farrah to relieve him. We banked the fire and settled into our bedrolls, and soon I could hear the light snoring and deep breathing of my companions that signaled they were asleep.

I lay there in the darkness, staring up at the few stars that I could see peeking through the dark tree branches overhead. Finally, I fell into a fitful sleep, still fretting about the paper with Delphine's face that was an unwanted weight in my pocket.

I HELD THE WANTED POSTER at arm's length as I studied it intently, willing Delphine's unmoving face to give up its secrets. As I continued to stare at her portrait, one of her eyes suddenly winked at me. A smirk played at her lips.

"Delphine?" I croaked, surprised at the picture's sudden movement. I was taken aback by the knowing expression on Delphine's face, so unlike the person I knew.

Her smirk deepened. Her arms reached out from the paper and grabbed my arms, drawing me into the poster.

The world around me melted into an odd grayish cream color, devoid of any scenery. The horizon was a darker gray, fading into a black void. The air had a slightly sooty, wood-and-metallic tang to it. I raised my shirtsleeve to my nose, breathing shallowly through the fabric to avoid the odd taste the air left in my mouth.

I turned to my companion, my voice muffled. "Delphine? What is this place? Why did you bring me here?"

She smiled and started to say something, but then suddenly gasped. The smile slipped from her face as her eyes grew wide and fearful. She started struggling against something unseen, something that was pulling her backwards.

"Dephine? What's wrong?" I asked, but she continued to slide away from me. She thrashed her head violently from side to side, but it looked like whatever had ahold of her wouldn't allow her to speak.

I attempted to move after her, but my feet wouldn't cooperate. Whatever unknown force was taking my friend away from me had also pinned me in place.

"Delphine!" I screamed.

She had a brief moment of reprieve from her invisible captor, just enough time to say, "Come find me, Kaernan!"

And then, still struggling, she was dragged into the blackness on the horizon, and was gone.

MY DISTURBING DREAM about Delphine jarred me out of my slumber. I woke up feeling unusually ... heavy. It was hard to wake up, like when you stay up too late and then fall asleep, only to wake still feeling exhausted. I fought through the mental fog that was wrapped around my brain and sat up, extremely groggy.

Nearby, Farrah and Rhyss sat up in their bedrolls, trying to blink away the remnants of sleep as well. Farrah looked at me curiously. "Kaernan, are you all right?" Her voice was oddly muffled.

I shook my head, but it felt like I was trying to do so underwater. And it made the dull throbbing at the back of my skull worsen.

"No," I said. Even my words came out slow and fuzzy, like my tongue was wrapped in cotton. "I had a bad dream that someone ... some *thing* ... took —"

"Delphine? Where's Delphine?"

I turned my head — carefully — to see Adallia looking around, wide-eyed. She seemed disoriented, too, and sounded just as cotton-tongued as I did.

"Maybe she went to relieve herself?" I suggested.

"No ... no," Adallia said. "She knows not to stray from the group unless she tells one of us where she's going first."

Rhyss groaned, drawing my attention. He was holding his head, wincing in pain. He caught me looking at him. "I feel like I do the day after we celebrate a successfully completed commission, without the fun of actually drinking in celebration."

Farrah frowned. She reached out and touched Rhyss on his temple. In just moments, he brightened considerably as his headache lessened. He beamed at his friend. "Thanks, Farrah."

She was still frowning, her brow now furrowed in deep thought. "Not a problem." Her expression grew more serious. "Your headache was a result of something magical, not natural."

Now we were all looking at her. "What do you mean?" I asked. "Didn't you set up the magical wards last night?"

She nodded. "I did, like I do every night. You hired me for my magical abilities; I wouldn't have forgotten something so basic to my job."

I nodded as well. I hadn't meant to sound accusatory, but I had to explore every angle.

Fortunately, Farrah didn't seem offended, just thoughtful. "Everyone seems to be feeling disoriented, even though we got a good night's sleep. Actually, we're all feeling that way *because* we got a good night's sleep. Well, maybe not *that* good. It feels like ... I think someone cast a sleeping powder on our group in the night."

"But how?" I asked. "I thought your wards protected against that sort of thing."

"Against magical attacks, yes," Farrah said. "But not against physical attacks or magical items. No wards can do that. That's why you should always set a watch."

She turned to look pointedly at Rhyss, who wilted under her glare and sheepishly looked away. "Sorry," he said. "I *was* watching ... but the next thing I knew, I was waking up with the rest of you."

"It's okay," I said. "From what Farrah is saying, it doesn't sound like there was much you could have done."

"No, Farrah's right, I'm usually more competent than this. I should have —"

"It doesn't matter what you should have done," Adallia interrupted impatiently. "What matters is what we do *now*. And in this whole time we've been talking, my daughter hasn't returned. Do you suppose ... do you suppose she's been taken?"

"Oh, no," Farrah said, in an attempt to comfort Adallia. "Why would anyone want to take your daughter?"

This was it. Now I *had* to say something. I picked up my rolled up jacket, which had been serving as a makeshift pillow. Reaching into the inside pocket, I drew out the crumpled piece of paper and smoothed it out.

"I think I know what may have happened. Adallia, I need you to be honest with us. Does this state the truth about your daughter?"

Chapter Twelve

I OPENED THE PAPER and showed it first to Adallia and then the rest of the group. There was a small, surprised gasp from Farrah, and Rhyss stiffened in shock. They both turned wary eyes on Adallia and subtly shifted their weight, ready to take action.

The noblewoman didn't notice. Upon seeing her daughter's likeness, Adallia burst into tears. "Yes. And no! I don't know. It can hardly be called a murder. It was self defense. We think. We're not sure. It happened the day I went to meet your father to ask him to take this commission."

"*What* happened? What are you talking about?"

Adallia was crying uncontrollably. Farrah and Rhyss exchanged glances, and Farrah shifted her hand from her weapon to her pocket, where she fished out a handkerchief and handed it over to Adallia. Adallia took the small cloth square, ineffectually mopping at the tears streaming down her face.

"While I was meeting with you and your family, my daughter was meeting with her magic tutor, Lord Olivera. He was a good friend of my late husband's, but I never liked him much. He was always a little too ... interested in our family's affairs, more so than seemed polite. But my husband trusted him, so I tried to give him a chance.

"My daughter has recently come into magical powers, something very unexpected. I thought of sending her away to Calia to perhaps enroll in the new magical college there, but I was reluctant to let her go. She's my only child, you know. I convinced myself that she would need some sort of rudimentary foundation in magic before she could attend. There aren't many magicians in Orchwell, as you know. Lord Olivera offered to teach her, and, although I tried, I could think of no good reason to turn down his offer. Especially since he was wiling to teach her for free, and after my husband's death, we've had to be careful with our family's finances. We've already had to sell off a few family heirlooms, and most of the household servants are gone, as we couldn't afford to keep paying them.

"It wasn't so bad, at first. Delphine was learning quickly, and I was hopeful she would be able to leave for Calia within a few months. I was always home for her lessons, so Lord Olivera was always on his best behavior. Indeed, everything seemed to be going just fine.

"But on the day I went to see Lord Asthore about my commission, Lord Olivera came over unannounced to meet with Delphine. He claimed he was leaving for an extended trip and wanted to get an impromptu magic lesson in with Delphine before he left. In actuality, he tried to force himself upon my daughter."

Adallia twisted the damp handkerchief in her hands, agitated at reliving the memory. Farrah, Rhyss, and I were a captive audience, our initial wariness forgotten, replaced by an intense sympathy.

Adallia continued, "When I came home, my daughter was sitting on the floor disoriented, having just regained consciousness. Lord Olivera was also on the floor, not moving. When she came to, Delphine wasn't sure what had happened. All she knew, after she told me what had happened between them, was that she was frightened, and wanted to protect herself ... then she blacked out, and when she woke up, Lord Olivera was unconscious."

"Was he ... dead?" I breathed, unwilling to interrupt Adallia's story, but desperately wanting to know.

"No," she said, "but he was barely alive. I called for the doctor right away, who determined that Lord Olivera must have had a heart attack. My daughter and I didn't see it necessary to correct his diagnosis. The doctor didn't think he would live through the night ... nor wake up. Lord Olivera's servants came to take their master back to his estate. My daughter and I made plans to leave Orchwell, with this trip providing a terrific excuse to flee.

"On the morning that we left Orchwell, Lord Olivera was still alive, but still unconscious. He must have died later that day for this poster to go out so fast. I can only guess that, before he died, he woke up long enough to name Delphine as his attacker."

A thick silence fell over our group. None of us bothered to ask Adallia why she and Delphine hadn't spoken up about what had really happened with Lord Olivera. Without the protection Adallia's late husband, Lord Pahame, could have provided, the two women were vulnerable in Orchwellian society. Their status as nobles protected them to a certain extent, but not necessarily against other nobles. And not against one as powerful as Lord Olivera had been.

Rhyss broke the silence. Carefully avoiding looking Adallia's way, he said to me, "What do you think happened to Delphine, then?"

I shared everything I had learned from the innkeeper Ravon, concluding with my thought that Delphine's picture had already been widely shared in the kingdom of Rothschan.

"We're not too far away from Rothschan now," I said. "I've heard that bounty hunters abound in the area, because they know that Rothschan justice will turn a blind eye to any, ah, unorthodox methods they may employ."

Adallia began crying again. "Who knows what evil things could be done to her in the name of 'justice' — we need to find my daughter immediately!"

"I agree, but running headlong into Rothschan won't help us find your daughter any faster," I cautioned. "And who knows? Whoever took her may have decided to head straight back to Orchwell. But we've wasted enough time here; let's break camp and discuss what to do as we travel."

Suiting my actions to my words, I stood up and quickly began packing my bed roll. The others followed suit, shaking off the last of the magically induced grogginess. Rhyss handed out some travel rations for a quick breakfast as Adallia, having finished her own packing, started to clean up Delphine's part of the camp. I stopped her, reaching out to touch Delphine's things. A moment later, I came out of my Seeker trance and addressed the group.

"We need to keep heading west. I have no doubt that Delphine has indeed been taken to Rothschan."

Chapter Thirteen

I HAD HAD THE OPPORTUNITY to travel to Rothschan before, since my various commissions sometimes brought me there. It wasn't a place that warmly welcomed travelers, unlike some of the other countries in the Gifted Lands. Perhaps the kindest thing I could say about the country of Rothschan was that it was very well-maintained, and its citizens were polite and fair.

Too fair, sometimes. To the citizens of Rothschan, a wanted poster was pretty much irrefutable evidence that the person featured on it was guilty, no matter the actual circumstances. Which meant that, even if she were to escape her captors, Delphine would find little sympathy or help around here.

As we traveled, we discussed our course of action. To find Delphine, we would need to know who, exactly, had taken her. But how would we uncover that information?

"If it's a matter of money, I'm prepared to pay any ransom," Adallia declared. "One thousand gold is a large sum, but I'll match it. Double it, if I have to. Even if I have to sell everything I own to do it. Anything to get my daughter back."

"I understand your sentiments, Adallia, but perhaps don't speak them so loudly. Or at all," I cautioned. "It would not be good if the kidnappers were to learn of your connection to Delphine. They would surely exploit it and use it against us."

"Then how do you suggest we get my daughter back?" Adallia snapped.

Rhyss and Farrah looked at me. I frowned, knowing — and hating the knowledge — that as the leader of our group, proposals on things like how to retrieve kidnapped maidens fell to me.

"I don't know," I admitted. "I've never faced anything like this before. But I'm sure something will come to mind soon."

I hoped.

As we drew closer to Rothschan, we noticed several trees with Delphine's wanted poster hastily tacked to them. Adallia savagely attacked one poster while Rhyss and Farrah took down the others. They folded the papers and stuffed them into their packs.

"They'll make great kindling later," Rhyss said, and was rewarded with a sad smile from Adallia.

We still hadn't come up with a good plan, though. The only things we could agree upon were to keep our eyes and ears open for any unusual news, and that we would stay in Rothschan for as long as was necessary until Delphine was recovered.

Hopefully alive.

The unspoken thought hung in the air among all of us.

DESPITE OUR MAGICALLY-induced late start, we made good time to Rothschan's capital city and arrived just after midday.

Compared to the noisy bustle that always marked Orchwell's gates, entering Rothschan was a subdued, orderly affair. Back home, it was common to see children playing games such as tag, peek-a-boo, or hide-and-seek as their parents waited in line to enter the kingdom. Here at Rothschan's gates, there was none of that playfulness. Families huddled together quietly as they waited, as if the unseen weight of the place made them afraid to be noticed. A crying baby was sharply and quickly hushed into silence. Even the livestock waited quietly, instead of the normal vocal exhalations and weight shifting that was common among animals.

As if by unspoken agreement, we all dismounted and drew together, trying to appear as orderly and well-behaved as the others standing in line, unwilling to draw too much attention to ourselves.

Despite the long line, we made it through the gates fairly easily and surprisingly fast. Once we were a few paces away from the guards — and out of their earshot — my companions turned to me expectantly.

"Rhyss and Farrah, why don't you stable the horses," I said. I handed my horse's reins to Farrah. Rhyss took charge of Adallia's mount. "Take your time there; maybe you'll be able to pick up some news if you linger. Adallia and I will walk around and see if we can find out anything as we wander. I know it's not much of a plan, but ..."

Farrah put her hand on my arm sympathetically. "It's not a bad idea either."

"And it's the best we've got," Rhyss said.

I pointed toward the city center, where stone benches outlined a magnificent fountain. Several people were relaxing by the falling water, enjoying a brief respite in their busy day. "How about we meet over by the fountain, right around sunset? Maybe by then one of us will have some information to share with the rest of the group. Or we'll have a better idea of what to do next."

Rhyss and Farrah nodded and set off toward the stables with the horses.

Adallia and I started walking down the stone streets of Rothschan, headed toward the merchant's district. I had a vague idea that if we did some shopping, or at least pretended to, we might be able to glean information from the shopkeepers or other patrons.

Adallia didn't question where we were going, just kept pace with me as I set our direction. After a few moments, Adallia touched my arm to get my attention. "Kaernan, do you notice anything odd?"

I slowed my pace as I looked around. "I don't think so," I said. "It looks like Rothschan always does — very clean and very quiet."

Adallia shook her head. "You said that news of Delphine had preceded us by at least a day or two. And we saw a few fliers on the way here. So I would have expected Rothschan to be plastered with her face. But ... there are no pictures posted anywhere."

Looking around more carefully this time, I noticed what Adallia already had seen. She was right. The kingdom's walls and doors were devoid of any wanted posters.

"Perhaps they are only allowed to post papers within the shops?" I said.

"Perhaps," Adallia replied dubiously.

At that moment, we came to a freestanding wall with a shallow wooden overhang. The wall had a myriad of papers tacked to it: a community message board.

We stopped to look at the various posts. Notices for shops in the area, or announcements of items for sale by random citizens. One poster heralded a special event happening in a few weeks' time. But there were no pictures of Delpine hanging on the board.

"You know, Adallia, I think you're right. There is something strange about this," I said.

"Your innkeeper friend was sure those messengers were headed this way?"

"Yes. He said they weren't sure if they would continue west or double back to Orchwell, but they definitely mentioned that Rothschan was where they going."

"Hmm. Well, in that case, I suppose we should —"

Adallia gasped, interrupting herself mid-sentence. Moving lightning-fast, she twisted her right arm and clamped her hand down on a small, thin wrist. Adallia moved slightly, revealing a slight girl of about seven or eight.

"Impressive," I said, a slight question in my voice.

"You forget I wasn't born a noble," Adallia said. "When it comes to being safe on the streets, there are some things you don't forget."

"As well you shouldn't," I said, looking down at her captive. "And who do we have here?"

The little girl was trying — unsuccessfully — to remove her wrist from Adallia's grip. Looking around wildly, she said, "Please let me go! I promise I won't try anything anymore. Just let me go and don't tell anyone I was here."

I felt a quick flash of sympathy for the child. Pickpocketing was rare in Rothschan, because the penalties for even the smallest crimes were extremely harsh. She and her family, if she had any, must be very desperate indeed.

"You're making more of a scene thrashing about like that," Adallia said. "And how can I trust your word, that if I let you go, you won't try to steal from me again?"

"I *said* I wouldn't, lady, and —"

The girl stopped in shock as she got a good look at her captor's face. Her tone changed from petulant to one of awe.

"Wow. I know you! How did you get away from them?"

Chapter Fourteen

ADALLIA NEARLY DROPPED the girl's wrist in surprise. "You know me? Get away from who? What are you talking about?"

The girl babbled on, "No one ever gets away from them, how did you do it?"

Adallia shook the girl's wrist to get her attention. "I just came to Rothschan today. I don't understand what you're saying."

The girl stopped, her eyes narrowing as she studied Adallia's face. "Oh ... you're not her. But you look just like her. But older."

Adallia looked like she didn't know if she should be offended or hopeful at this observation. Before Adallia could say anything, I stepped in. In my most soothing voice, I asked the girl, "What's your name?"

The girl turned her big brown eyes on me, giving me the same appraising look she had given Adallia. I must have passed muster, because she nodded to herself. "I'm Juneyen."

"Juneyen. That's a pretty name."

"It was my grandma's," Juneyen said proudly.

"I see. Juneyen ... you saw a woman yesterday? Who looked just like this lady here?"

Juneyen nodded. "But come to think of it, I guess it wasn't the same person." She jerked the wrist that Adallia still gripped. "Because you're here and that can't be right. No one ever gets away from them."

I could feel a headache beginning to form. Did Juneyen always talk in circles, or was it something special just for Adallia and me?

I decided to try a different approach. "Juneyen, what do you think of *them*?"

She looked around cautiously and dropped her voice to a whisper. "They're scary. If they take you away, then no one ever can find you ever, ever again."

"This woman they took yesterday ... would you want to help her get away from them, then?"

"Yes," the girl said. "She seemed really scared, I felt really bad for her. But I can't help you."

"Oh." I pursed my lips, frustrated by the dead end.

"But maybe my mama could."

I perked up. "Do you think she'd be willing to help us?"

Juneyen shrugged. "I don't know, but you could ask her."

"Well, okay, then." I exchanged a look with Adallia. "We'll see you home, and if your mother is in, we'll ask her for help."

"Okay," Juneyen agreed. Adallia dropped the child's wrist, and we were both surprised when Juneyen slipped her hand into Adallia's. "Come on."

Juneyen confidently led us through the streets of Rothschan. We walked through the merchants' district, which had been our original destination, and into a more residential area of the kingdom. The houses were uniformly modest, making me wonder if any of the wealthier families lived within the kingdom's capital city or if the outward appearance of prosperity was frowned upon.

We stopped at a row house that looked just like its neighbors. There were some small things that set it apart, however: a small green wreath hanging on the door, and a black cat sitting in the window. When it saw us approach, it yawned, stretched, and then jumped down, disappearing from our view.

Juneyen dropped Adallia's hand to push open the door. She shooed back the cat, who was now trying to wind around her legs in greeting. "Scoot back, Scout. We've got visitors."

Satisfied the cat wouldn't try to run out the door, Juneyen waved Adallia and me inside. "Come on in."

The little girl bounded toward the back of the house. "Mama? Mama!"

I quietly closed the door behind me, taking in the worn, faded curtains, the holes in the furniture, the discolored paint on the walls that highlighted where pictures must have once hung. The bookshelves pitifully boasted just a few books and knickknacks, most of which were old, broken, or chipped.

As Juneyen came skipping back to us, we could hear footsteps hurrying after her.

"Junie, how many times have I told you not to yell?" A woman came into the room, wiping down a bowl with a stained and ragged linen towel as she walked. "Unless it's a matter of extreme impor —"

Her voice trailed off as she saw Adallia and me standing by her front door. "Oh my goodness," she said as she took us in.

Juneyen pointed at us. "Mama, I met these fancy-looking people today."

"I take it you are Juneyen's mother?" I asked.

The woman nodded mutely, her big grey eyes wide. She pushed back a tendril of hair that had fallen out of her messy bun. Her upswept hair revealed the gray that was beginning to feather her otherwise dark tresses. "Yes, that's right."

"We met your daughter earlier today, at the community board. We're visitors to Rothschan, and —"

Juneyen's mother gripped the bowl and towel in one hand, and grabbed her daughter's arm in the other. Shaking Juneyen's arm slightly, she asked her daughter, "What have you done?"

Juneyen howled in protest. "Nothing, mama."

"I told you not to do that anymore! You promised me you wouldn't! You know what the penalties are if you're caught."

"But, mama —"

Still holding tightly to her daughter's arm, the woman pushed Juneyen behind her protectively. "Please sir ... madam ... my daughter is just a child. I'll make sure she's duly punished here at home. Only please don't report her to the authorities."

"My dear lady, we —" I tried to reassure her, but she cut me off.

"We don't have much, but if it's money you came for, name your price."

I spread my hands out in a conciliatory gesture. "No, no, mistress. You have it all wrong. That's not why we're here."

Juneyen's mother eyed me suspiciously. "It's not?"

"No."

"Then my daughter *didn't* try to pickpocket either one of you?"

"Well ... she did, but —"

Juneyen cried out again as her mother swung around to confront her. "When will you learn, Junie?"

Raising my voice to be heard over the child's wailing and her mother's scolding, I said, "We're here for information, not extortion. We're not going to report your daughter to anyone. We were hoping you could help us."

The woman stood warily, still holding her daughter behind her as she slowly took our measure. "What is it you want, then?"

"Apparently a young woman was brought through the streets the other day, someone who looks like me." Adallia stepped forward. "Juneyen kept saying the young lady was taken by *them*, but cannot or will not say exactly who 'they' are. She said you could name the young lady's captors, and I hope you will. The person they have taken is my daughter."

The other woman's face instantly changed from wary to sympathetic. "Oh, my dear lady," she breathed. "I am so sorry."

Now that her mother was distracted, Juneyen wriggled out of her mother's grasp. Her mother shot her a stern look. "Don't think you're off the hook, young lady. You're still to be punished for even *thinking* of pickpocketing again. And you know any punishment I give you is still way more lenient than anything that would happen if you got caught."

Juneyen hung her head, knowing she was obviously in the wrong. Her mother knelt down and gave her a hug. "I'm glad nothing bad happened to you. Go put the kettle on to boil, so we can have tea with our guests."

Giving her daughter the towel and bowl she had been holding, she pointed toward the kitchen.

Juneyen disappeared, and her mother indicated we should sit. Adallia and I sat on a small, worn loveseat near the window while her mother perched carefully on a wooden chair in the corner.

"Well, I suppose we should start over," the woman said. "My name is Carissa, and you've met my daughter Juneyen. Welcome to our home."

"I'm Kaernan, and this is Adallia," I said, deliberately leaving out titles or affiliations. I was aware that, even in our simple, dusty traveling clothes, we still appeared more well-off than Carissa and Juneyen, and I didn't want to draw any more attention to that fact than was already apparent.

Carissa nodded toward us, her gaze soft as she concentrated on remembering.

"Juneyen mentioned seeing a young woman taken through the streets of Rothschan yesterday." Carissa leaned forward, reaching out to take Adallia's hand. Surprisingly, the noblewoman allowed the other woman to touch her. "My dear woman, I'm afraid that Hauster has your daughter. And if that's the case, then you may never see her again."

Chapter Fifteen

"HAUSTER? WHO IS THAT?" For having just been told that her daughter might be permanently lost to her, Adallia's voice was remarkably steady.

"Hauster is not a who, not exactly," Carissa said. "It's a clan, one of the clans of Rothschan. Although they're now considered on the fringes of respectable society."

"Bounty hunters?" I asked, wanting to confirm my earlier hunch.

Carissa nodded. "One of their many specialities, but in truth, their main one."

Juneyen walked back into the room, this time holding a plain wooden tray laden with a white china teapot and four small white cups. Carissa stood up and took the tray from her daughter, placing it on a nearby table. She began pouring tea in the little cups, handing one each to Adallia and me. As she poured a third cup, Juneyen piped up, "I want some tea! I brought a cup and everything."

"All right, but if you're having tea, you'll have to sit in your own chair, as is proper," her mother said.

Juneyen frowned. "Can I sit in your lap when I'm done?"

Carissa started to laugh, and then tried to cover up the laugh with a cough. "Juneyen, what am I going to do with you? You need to learn to be a young lady someday."

"Does it have to be today?"

Carissa didn't even try to hide her laughter this time, nor did Adallia and I. She handed her daughter a nearly full cup of tea. "I'm not in *that* much of a hurry for you to grow up. Here you go, and yes, you can sit in my lap when you're done."

Juneyen plopped down on the floor and began drinking her tea. She slowly lowered her cup when Carissa gave her a pointed look. Sheepishly, she stood up, climbed onto an empty chair, and began drinking her tea again, this time slurping loudly. Carissa gave her daughter another pointed look. Juneyen swallowed her sip of tea and quieted down.

Carissa took her own cup of tea and resumed her seat. Once she was settled, I leaned forward. "Tell us everything you know about this Hauster family."

She shrugged. "There's not much to tell. Although they often employ some questionable methods, because they're one of the oldest families in the kingdom, they get away with pretty much anything. The Crown turns a blind eye to them, but that's because the Crown has employed them from time to time."

So we wouldn't get any help from any of Rothschan's leaders or law enforcement. Not the best news, but still helpful to know.

"Do you know where we can find them?" I asked. Carissa shook her head. But then:

"Yes."

We all turned to look at Juneyen, who had finished her tea and jumped up to put the empty cup back on the tray. She climbed into her mother's lap and settled in contentedly.

"Juneyen, how can you possibly know where ...?" Carissa's voice trailed off.

Her daughter looked down at the floor. In a small voice, she said, "I ... followed Jondan."

"Juneyen, I told you not to seek him out. To stay close to home. To stay safe."

Juneyen's eyes filled with tears. "But I miss him. I want him to come home."

Carissa stilled, her face changing to emotionless stone. I shifted, wanting to ask what was going on, but Adallia lightly grabbed my arm and gave me the smallest of head shakes. *No, Kaernan. Leave it alone.*

The moment passed, but not before Adallia and I saw the intense pain that flashed across Carissa's face. She took a deep breath.

"You plan on rescuing your daughter, no matter what?" Carissa asked.

Adallia nodded emphatically. "Of course. I could never forgive myself if I had the power to save her, and did not use it."

Carissa said sadly, "Some things are beyond even a mother's love, sometimes." Carissa regarded her daughter, who was busy wiping away the tears now spilling freely down her face. "Juneyen."

The little girl looked up, sniffling.

"Juneyen ... you want to help, don't you?"

The girl nodded.

"If you promise to be *extremely* careful, I will allow you to help these people. Take them to ... wherever it is you saw Jondan, and come right home. Don't go inside any buildings, just lead these two there and come right back. Can you do that?"

Juneyen nodded again, her sadness replaced by excitement. "Should we go now?"

I shook my head. "We actually came with two others. We need to let them know what's going on before we make any plans."

"After you meet up with your friends, why don't you bring them back here?" Carissa suggested. "If you need a place to stay, I've an empty room you can sleep in. And Juneyen can sleep with me, so that's a second room if you need it."

"Thank you. That's a good plan."

"You'll need a plan if you're going to try to save your friend from the Hausters. Go, find your friends, and come back quickly. The sooner you go, the sooner we can all come up with a plan together."

Chapter Sixteen

I LEFT ADALLIA WITH our new hosts while I went to find the rest of our party. Even though it wasn't quite sunset, I found Farrah and Rhyss waiting at our meeting spot.

Farrah shook her head as I approached. "Sorry, Kaernan. We couldn't find out anything." She looked around. "Where's Adallia?"

"It's all right," I said. "Come with me; we've secured a place to stay for the night. Adallia's back there."

"We're not staying at …?" Rhyss indicated an inn near the city gates, one of three in the area.

I shook my head. "No, we'll be staying with a local. I'll fill you in as we go."

We hurried further into the city. Keeping my voice low, I told my friends how Adallia and I met young Juneyen, and what had transpired afterward. The tale took the entirety of our walk. Reaching the row houses, I looked for the one with the green wreath on the door and briskly knocked on it.

Juneyen opened the door wide, taking in the new people I had brought with me. "You're back!" She motioned toward the back of the house. "Come on!"

This was getting to be familiar. I smiled and shrugged at Farrah and Rhyss, shutting the door behind us. We made our way to the kitchen, where Juneyen was now playing with

Scout the cat on the floor. Carissa was stirring something in a pot over a fire, while Adallia stood at the counter. Adallia's hair had been pulled back into a hasty bun, with her sleeves of her traveling dress rolled up. And she was ... cutting vegetables?

"Adallia?"

She turned when I said her name. There was a smudge of flour in her dark hair. "I'm glad you made it back safely. And I hope you're all hungry."

"I didn't know you ... enjoyed cooking." I corrected myself before I said what I was actually thinking, which was, *I didn't know you could cook.* Rhyss and Farrah did the majority of our cooking on the road, and as a noblewoman I didn't expect Adallia to spend her time in the kitchen. Then again, I often forgot Adallia's background as a commoner.

She smiled wryly, as if she knew what I was thinking. "I find it somewhat comforting," she said. "And now that it's just my daughter —" her voice caught slightly "— and me, I take over some of the cooking duties so we don't have to pay the servants as much."

"It smells wonderful," Farrah said. "I, for one, am definitely hungry. And it will be nice to have something else besides Rhyss's idea of dinner."

"Hey!" Rhyss said, nudging Farrah in mock anger. She laughed. They both knew that Rhyss was an excellent cook.

"Do you need any help?" I asked, aware of how much we were imposing on our host.

Carissa waved away my offer. "We've got it well in hand."

She lifted the wooden spoon from the pot, tapping it against the side to shake it clean. Placing the spoon on a table nearby, she wiped her hands on a towel tucked into her waistband and then held out her hand toward Farrah. "I'm Carissa, and that's my daughter Juneyen over there playing with the cat. Welcome to our home."

Farrah, and then Rhyss, shook Carissa's hand, introducing themselves in turn. She waved them toward the plain wooden table that sat in front of the fire, indicating they should take a seat.

But instead of sitting, the pair sprung into action. Rhyss grabbed a pitcher and some cups, taking them to the table and filling them. Farrah opened a random drawer and rooted around in it, producing enough spoons for everyone. She joined Rhyss at the table. I slowly followed suit, marveling at their ease to fit into any situation, and mentally kicked myself for not helping out as well.

Dinner was soon ready: a savory chicken and biscuit stew. For a while, the cozy kitchen was filled with the sounds of people happily eating.

As the meal wound down, the dinner talk turned from pleasantries to crafting a plan to breach the Hauster stronghold. From the rumors of the family's holdings, and from what Juneyen had seen, stronghold was an apt description. The family used to live in a mansion in the city like the other wealthy families of Rothschan did, but as they grew in size and reputation, they had built a secret fortress somewhere on the outskirts of the kingdom. The former Hauster home was now used as a way station of sorts for messages or people connected to the group.

But if their location was so secret, how did Juneyen know where they were?

Carissa cleared a space in the middle of the table. She reached into her skirt pocket, drawing out a worn, folded piece of paper. Opening it, she placed the paper in the newly cleared area. I saw a beautifully done sketch of four people — two middle-aged adults, a young man, and a little girl. Recognizing Carissa and Juneyen, I realized this must be a drawing of their family. Except, so far, we hadn't met anyone besides Carissa and her daughter. Who were the two men in the picture, then?

"It's a lovely drawing," Adallia said politely.

"Thank you," Carissa said, her eyes sad as she looked at the picture. "My niece has a talent for it, don't you think? I always encouraged her artistic abilities; she's gifted enough to be painting portraits for kings and queens. But her mother — my sister — thought it was a waste of time, and didn't like me 'egging her daughter on in frivolous pursuits,' as she put it. It caused some problems between us. Now my sister and I don't talk, and we haven't for several years. I don't know if my niece is still creating art, but I somehow doubt it."

"I'm sorry to hear that," Adallia said gently. "It's always sad when families don't get along. And your sister, is she your only sibling?"

Carissa nodded, still gazing at the picture.

"Forgive my rudeness, Carissa," Adallia said. "But, is that ...?"

Carissa nodded in answer to Adallia's unfinished question. "Yes. That was my dear Thann, rest his soul. He passed away a little over a year ago, in a riding accident. His horse spooked and threw him."

"I'm sorry," Adallia said. The rest of us nodded in agreement or murmured condolences.

"He was a good husband, and father. When he died, he took pieces of all of us with him. But my eldest, my Jondan, he ... never quite recovered. Money has always been tight, but we got by. After Thann's passing, Jondan kept getting into trouble. Trouble with the law, trouble with those who didn't follow the laws. Eventually he landed in trouble that he couldn't get out of — unless he completely surrendered to it. Which he did. He went to serve the Hauster family two months ago."

Carissa studied the drawing for a few silent moments. None of us dared interrupt her thoughts, although I could tell, as I looked around the table at my friends, that we all had questions we were bursting to ask her.

Finally, she looked back up. She pushed the picture toward Adallia.

"Take it," Carissa said.

"But ... it's your family picture. I couldn't possibly take such a keepsake away from you. And I have no need for it."

Carissa pushed it more forcefully toward the noblewoman. "You do have need of it. It will help you when ..." She took a deep breath and met each of our eyes in turn. "When you go to rescue your daughter and friend, please, I beg you all, please do one thing for me. Save my son."

Chapter Seventeen

IT WAS STILL DARK WHEN I awoke, although a quick look out the slightly cracked window showed the hazy pink of twilight. Soon the sun would rise, and we needed to be in place by then. I shook Rhyss. "Wake up!"

Rhyss came awake immediately, which was surprising considering he was the deepest sleeper in our group. Perhaps he was excited about this important and risky task we were about to undertake. I know I was. Although *excited* wasn't really the right word for it. Worried, apprehensive, nervous ... those were probably more accurate to what I was personally feeling.

We dressed in the dark quickly, not bothering to take the time to light a candle or lamp. In the room next to ours, we could hear Adallia and Farrah moving about as well.

Rhyss and I gathered our packs and left our room, but not before I left a sizable purse of coins under the pillow for our host to eventually find. Carissa had told us not to worry about paying her for the rooms and meal — recovering her son would be payment enough. But I didn't want the woman to stress about money more than she was already, and I didn't want little Juneyen to be tempted to try to pick pockets again, either. At least our money would keep them for a little while.

We met Adallia and Farrah in the main room of the house. They also had their bags in hand, as we all knew we would not be returning to Carissa's.

Adallia handed me a small bit of cloth. It was a hair ribbon, in a bright and cheerful yellow. Adallia said, "It's Delphine's. I found an extra one in her bag."

I nodded, grateful for Adallia's foresight. As unexpected and unusual as it was, Delphine was now a second 'lost love' of Adallia's I was to find, so having something of Delphine's on hand would definitely help.

A sleepy-eyed Carissa joined us, pressing some food into my hands. "For all of you as you travel, since there's no time for a proper breakfast."

"Thank you, Carissa."

Juneyen bounded in, the most alert of all of us. "I'm ready! Are you all ready? I'm ready, let's go!"

Her enthusiasm buoyed my spirits. Perhaps, like Juneyen, I should just view this situation as a grand adventure instead of a dangerous endeavor.

Carissa drew her daughter aside and spoke to her in a low murmur. The rest of us busied ourselves with preparations that were already finished, not wanting to intrude on their private moment.

Carissa kissed Juneyen on the forehead and gave her a hug. "Be careful, be watchful, and listen to our new friends. When it's time for you to leave them, come straight back here."

Juneyen nodded solemnly, throwing her arms around her mother for a second hug. Carissa held her tightly for a moment, then released her and motioned her toward the door. Juneyen pulled it open, running down the street a little bit before coming back. "Come on, don't you want to get going?"

She was right; it was time to go. We said our farewells to Carissa, and my friends started to follow Juneyen down the street. I lingered just a little longer with our host, who was dabbing at her eyes.

"We'll bring them back," I promised.

Carissa smiled at me through her tears. I turned and followed the rest of the group. Behind me, I heard the click of the door as Carissa closed it against whatever the day would bring.

JUNEYEN LED US CONFIDENTLY through the streets of Rothschan. Before leaving the confines of the kingdom's capital, we stopped at the stable to collect our horses. We planned on hiding our packs somewhere and tying the horses nearby, hoping that they would stay hidden and safe in the forest until we were ready to leave. Carissa had told us very few people ventured into the forest, as it wasn't a throughway to any of the other kingdoms in the Gifted Lands.

The morning traffic was starting to flow through the gates, and we easily slipped through, unremarked by anyone.

Next to me in the growing light of sunrise, Rhyss yawned. "I really hope we get to sleep in tomorrow. Do you think —"

"Shh!" I waved him to silence. The cool morning breeze had blown a bit of conversation back to us from the people on foot just ahead of us, and I wanted to hear more of what they were saying.

"I don't know how we'll get all the cleaning done in time, what with Penyon sick and Alea out for a while," a man was complaining. "You know how it is on Ceremony days."

"Shut your mouth and save your breath for walking faster," his female companion retorted. "We should have hired some horses."

"We already lost pay when Alea was forced to stop working," the man said. "We can't afford to spend what little we have on horses, not when we have two perfectly good legs."

"That will fall off before we even get to the stronghold because of how fast we have to walk to get there on time," the woman retorted. "And Alea did pretty good, working right up until she had the baby." She sighed. "We're all so close to finishing our contracts, I don't want anything to go wrong. Had I known that working for the Family would be little better than slavery ... well, starving to death might have been better than indentured servitude."

Rhyss and I exchanged a look. Spurring my horse ahead of the man and woman on foot, I blocked their path.

"Excuse me," I said.

"You're not excused," the woman said frostily. "Get out of our way, or you'll make us late for work."

"That's actually what my friends and I wanted to ask you about."

On their own horses, Farrah, Rhyss, and Adallia, her arms encircling Juneyen sitting in the saddle in front of her, had come up behind the couple while I was conversing with them and now had them surrounded. The man and woman looked around warily, noticing the others.

"Let us pass. You don't want to make enemies of our employers," the man said.

"Would those employers be the Hauster family?" I asked.

Neither of them would meet my eyes, which was all the answer I needed.

"I'd like to offer you something." I held up a small leather pouch. "An incentive to take the day off, if you will."

Their eyes lit up as they heard the sound of the coins shifting within the bag. The woman eyed me, one eyebrow raised. "That's very generous of you, Mister ...?"

"My name is irrelevant. I just ask that you both stay well away from the Hauster compound for two or three days, starting today. This should be more than enough to cover your wages for the days lost." I tossed the bag at the woman.

She opened it, quickly assessing its contents, then shut the bag immediately, her eyes wide as she looked at her companion. He nodded ever so slightly, and she nodded back decisively, a decision having been made between them.

She turned to me, amazed. "This is enough for at least a week's worth of wages. And not just for me and my friend here, but for the other two cleaners who couldn't join us." But although the amount I was offering them was more than generous, I could still sense their hesitation.

"What's the issue?" I asked the woman.

"What will we do when we have to return to work? You must have an extremely compelling reason to not show up for a day's work for the Family. And the punishment for offending the Family is most severe — anything from garnished wages, to an extended contract, or imprisonment ..."

"Or worse," the man whispered.

I looked at Rhyss, who shrugged back at me. *Thanks for your help.*

"We ... we'll say that you and your team have come down with a very contagious disease, and have been quarantined," I said, thinking furiously. "By the order of the Rothschan government. My friends and I have been sent as replacements, we'll handle the work in your team's name, and our labor will count towards your contracts. Hopefully that will keep you from getting in trouble when you do return back to work."

The woman nodded as I outlined my plan. "Yes, that will satisfy the Hausters. We'll do as you ask."

"And keep your silence, as well?"

"Yes."

With that, my group pulled their mounts back, allowing the couple to slip free. They turned and hurried back toward Rothschan, not bothering to look back as they whispered to each other about their good fortune.

I spurred my horse into motion, the others following suit.

"I hope you knew what you were doing back there," Rhyss said.

"I hope so, too," I said. "That was most of the money I brought for this trip."

"Really? What will we do for the rest of our travels, then?"

I shrugged. "It is amazing what a famous family name and a good reputation for paying off one's debts in a timely fashion can do for a person."

Rhyss grinned in response.

Now that the sun had risen in full, we were able to see each other's outfits clearly for the first time.

"Wow, is that what you're wearing?" Farrah teased Rhyss. "It looks like you got dressed in the dark."

"I *did* get dressed in the dark," he pointed out. "As did you."

Farrah looked down at her outfit ruefully. "Don't remind me." She laughed, the rest of us joining in. It helped lighten some of the tension we were all feeling.

Last night, when we had talked through possible plans to infiltrate the Hauster stronghold, one thing kept coming up: We all needed disguises of some sort. Our traveling clothes, purchased in Orchwell, easily marked us as foreigners. Carissa still had clothing from her son and her late husband, and she had used those to outfit Rhyss and me. For the ladies, Carissa had generously given them some of her own clothes.

When Carissa had suggested we take her family's clothes, I had been worried. How could someone else's clothing possibly fit any of us? But in Rothschan, they apparently favored loose fitting clothing styles, quite different from Orchwell's more tailored fashions.

They also favored dull, plain colors. We were all dressed in various shades of brown or cream, with maybe a splash of gray here and there for variety. The Rothschan red that was famous throughout the Gifted Lands was probably only worn by the nobility, as the average citizen wouldn't be able to afford expensive dyes. Nor would they want to draw attention to themselves, I thought, remembering Carissa's anxiousness over her daughter's proclivity for pickpocketing.

I glanced over at Juneyen, who was happily chatting to Adallia as if we weren't walking into certain danger. I wished there was a way we could make sure she would get home safely, but the girl had assured us she would be fine.

Leaving the main road, we turned into the bordering woods. Soon we were immersed in the tall trees, with no real landmarks around us. Juneyen confidently led us on as the sun rose steadily overhead.

We had been riding for nearly an hour, I estimated, when Juneyen looked around the forest, puzzled.

"What's wrong?" I asked her.

Juneyen shook her head, confused. She pointed at an oak tree that was split open, a bright orange stripe of exposed bark running down its length. "We should have cleared the trees by now. We passed that tree some time ago. But here it is again."

"It's okay," Adallia soothed the little girl. "I'm sure this landmark will help jog your memory."

Juneyen looked ready to cry. "I thought this was the last marker before we left the forest," she said. "But I don't remember, entirely. I had just been following my brother and I guess I didn't pay as good attention as I thought."

Before her tears could spill in earnest, I reached out and touched her shoulder. "Don't worry, Juneyen, it really will be okay."

"But we're lost," she wailed. "And if we don't find our way soon, you'll miss your chance to get in, and —"

Adallia hugged her, hoping to reassure her. Drawing back, I reached into my shirt pocket and pulled out Delphine's yellow hair ribbon. It shimmered like a little ray of sunshine in my hand. "Juneyen, you've done so well getting us this far. Let's see if I can get us the rest of the way there."

Farrah and Adallia took charge of the little girl, fussing over her and trying to cheer her up. I was grateful for their help; I didn't think I was that great with children, and their distracting Juneyen would allow me to focus on the ribbon — and finding Delphine.

Holding the ribbon between my fingers, I sent my awareness into the object. Every Seeker has a different way of tapping into his or her abilities. For me, I often had to use an item as a focus. Preferably an item that belonged to the person I was seeking, but something that had a strong association to the person could work as well.

Delphine's spare ribbon radiated the cheer and exuberance of the woman that owned it. It helped that Delphine had such a strong personality, and that the trail was only a few days old. I could feel the echoes of her personality within the ribbon. And yet, when I tried to sense in what exact direction those echoes were coming from, I found ... nothing.

I frowned. That was unusual. I should get some sort of feeling, some hint of a general direction. What could be going on?

Rhyss saw my expression. "Is something wrong, Kaernan?"

I turned the ribbon over and over in my hands as if it might suddenly reveal Delphine's whereabouts. "I can sense Delphine ... but I can't sense *where* she is. And that's not normal, not for me."

Adallia looked worried. "If we're lost, and *you* can't find my daughter, what can we do?"

"I know I can find her," I said stubbornly. "But something is blocking my seeking abilities, and I don't know what it is or why it's doing it."

Farrah looked over at me. "Something's blocking you? Something magical?"

"It must be," I said. "I can't think of anything else that would hinder a Seeker."

"What does it feel like?"

I concentrated on the ribbon again, trying to pinpoint the feeling of nothingness. "It's like running into a wall, but one that surrounds me on all sides. Like I'm in a box, or a cell. I can sense who I want to find, but whichever way I turn, I can't figure out where the source is coming from. Like it's coming from all places, and no places, at once."

Farrah nodded thoughtfully. "It sounds like this magical cell is trapping you within its walls, and while you're in it, it's somehow able to mute your Seeker abilities," she said. "I'm not strong in defensive magic; I can't just blast you out of there. But what I could do is create a shield around you, on all sides, that would prevent the cell's magic from touching you. Perhaps that might allow you to tap into your seeking abilities again."

My fist tightened around the ribbon. "Let's do it, Farrah."

Everyone dismounted, and Farrah and I handed our horses' reins to Rhyss and Adallia. Taking my elbow, Farrah guided me over to a fallen log. "Sit down," she said. "It will make it easier for me, since you're so much taller than I am."

I sat down on the log. "Now what?"

She put one hand on my shoulder, and her other hand on my forehead. "Give me a few moments to get into place, magically speaking. Count to one hundred, slowly, and then repeat what you did earlier when you were first trying to find Delphine."

"All right."

Farrah closed her eyes, holding incredibly still. She began softly murmuring under her breath. Not wanting to break her concentration, I silently mouthed the countdown. *One ... two ... three ...*

As I continued my meticulous counting, Farrah kept up her barely audible chant. When I reached forty-two, Farrah stopped speaking, but seemed to be deeper into her spell. At seventy-three, she swayed a little, but still held on tight. A small sheen of sweat glistened on her brow.

Rhyss moved a little closer, ready to catch Farrah in case something happened with her spell casting. I could feel her shaking, ever so slightly, but still she held on, both physically and mentally.

I had reached one hundred. I unclenched my fist, staring at the small bit of silk laying in the palm of my hand. Holding it between my thumb and forefinger, my eyes went soft as I sent my awareness into the ribbon once more.

This time I could sense three different things. There was Delphine's presence, tethered to her hair ribbon and thus floating around me somewhere. There were the four walls surrounding me, hemming me into a neat little prison cell with its ability to mute my Seeker abilities.

The third thing I could feel was much closer to me. It was a shield of some sort, also surrounding me on all sides. Inside this tight bubble the air felt much better. Lighter, and more natural. This was Farrah's creation, and it really was a beautiful thing.

However, I could feel the dark energy of the prison just beyond it, and knew that Farrah's spell wouldn't hold for long. I would have to hurry. And although I was a skilled Seeker, I didn't necessarily like working under pressure.

I worked on sorting through, and then separating, the different energies surrounding me. That sense of Delphine — I wanted to keep that. That feeling of calm and protection that Farrah's shield was giving me — that, too, I would keep. That sense of nothingness from the cell's magical atmosphere outside the shield — that had to be pushed aside somehow. I knew it was there, but if I didn't give it as much focus as I gave the first two feelings, then maybe I would be able to get my work done. And figure out how to find Delphine.

I sent my senses along the Delphine energy, while trying to pull Farrah's shield around me like a blanket. I could feel Farrah pouring more and more of herself into the shield, trying to keep the void at bay. Following Delphine's sense was just like following a dancing ray of light: happy, warm, and cheerful. It danced west, then north, then ran back east.

I was getting a bit dizzy trying to follow its happy but erratic movements.

The nothingness smacked up against the shield's slick surface, sliding off as it failed to gain purchase.

Delphine's energy kept flitting back and forth. I turned this way and that, trying to keep it in my view.

The nothingness hit the shield again, just above and to the right of me. It didn't fall off this time. Instead, it stuck firmly to the shield, slowly eating away at it.

Cursing mentally, I willed Delphine's energy to calm, and show me where I needed to go. Perhaps my seeking skill was bolstered by my urgency, for Delphine's energy responded by slowing down. It still weaved this way and that, but showed signs of actually straightening its path.

I was nearly there ....

And then the nothingness broke through the shield.

Chapter Eighteen

THE SHIELD CRACKED under the full weight of the nothingness. The force of its attack absorbed both the rest of Farrah's shield and Delphine's energy. I squeezed my eyes tightly shut against the magical onslaught as I was pushed out of my seeking trance, back into the forest, where I found myself breathing heavily as my heart beat a crazy, uncontrollable tattoo. There was something rough and wooden underneath my cheek, and I was propped up against whatever it was. As I tried to open my eyes, I realized I was now sitting on the dusty ground, slumped against the log I had been sitting on earlier. Overly bright stars danced at the edges of my vision. I groaned and slowly blinked, hoping the stars would fade quickly.

Next to me, just on the other side of the log, Rhyss was holding Farrah, who was both shivering and sweating simultaneously. Her ebony face was unnaturally pale. Her eyes were rolled back in her head, but her chest was steadily rising and falling.

Rhyss shook Farrah, gently. "Farrah? Farrah, wake up!"

Adallia and Juneyen stood nearby. Adallia was holding the girl by the shoulders, either in an attempt to soothe her or to keep her from running toward Farrah. Juneyen's eyes were wide and frightened.

My heartbeat and my breathing began to slow a little as I tried to get them both under control. I was still a little woozy, though, and didn't want to lift my head just yet. Still panting slightly, I asked, "What happened?"

From where she stood, still holding Juneyen, Adallia said, "We're not sure. You were in your Seeker's trance, and Farrah was holding you, doing her spell, when suddenly she flew backward one way, and you pitched forward and tumbled off the log. It was like something had punched Farrah, and flung you aside."

"That sounds about ... right," I said. My breathing was still a little labored.

Farrah's eyes fluttered. Weakly, she asked, "Did it work?"

Rhyss smiled. "Farrah! You're all right! Thank the gods."

Farrah rolled her eyes, wincing with the effort. "You know how much that annoys me."

"I'll visit every god's temple if it means you're okay. And I'll make you come with me."

"I think I liked it better when I was unconscious," Farrah said. She sat up, aided by Rhyss. She tried to swat him away, but he refused to let go of her.

From where I sat still slumped over the other side of the log, I said weakly, "I'm fine too, thanks for asking."

Rhyss said guiltily, "Sorry, Kaernan."

I moved my head to look at him and instantly regretted it. My vision still swam, and everything was overly bright. I was going to have a monstrous headache, I was sure of it. Groaning, I put my head back down on the log.

"You need some healing," Farrah said.

"You are not in any condition to provide it," Rhyss told her firmly.

"But Kaernan will need —"

"No," Rhyss insisted. "If you're going to do any more magic, at least wait a while so your magical reserves can replenish."

"But, Rhyss, you know that —"

"Rhyss is right," I interrupted, forcing myself to raise my head and push through the pain. "I'm feeling much better already. You need to save your energy — and your magic — for more important matters. And you took some damage yourself. Probably more than I did, since it was your shield between me and that ... nothingness."

"Are you completely all right? Or are you just saying that to make me feel better?" Weak as she still was, the force of Farrah's stare was enough to make me look away. She nodded in satisfaction. "I thought so. Once we get to the Hauster stronghold, I'll heal whatever still ails you. You'll need to be in top condition before we go in."

Neither Rhyss nor I could argue with her logic, so I simply said, "Agreed."

Rhyss produced a waterskin from his pocket and gave it to Farrah, who drank greedily from it. I sat up, sliding back onto my original seat on the log. A small strip of gold caught my eye. It was Delphine's hair ribbon. It must have fallen out of my hand as I slipped off the log.

I picked up the hair ribbon.

Farrah finished drinking and passed the now considerably lighter waterskin back to Rhyss. Already she was getting color back in her face.

Adallia asked me, "You know what happened out here. What happened to the two of you when you were seeking?"

I briefly explained about trying to pin down Delphine's essence so I could accurately find her, and how Farrah's shield had fallen under the nothingness.

Adallia said, a tinge of worry in her voice, "Well? Were you successful? Do you know which way we should go?"

I looked at the yellow ribbon in my hand. Rubbing the fabric between my fingers, I could sense a faint echo of Delphine in the distance. "Yes, I do."

Chapter Nineteen

I STOOD UP, A LITTLE unsteadily, and held the ribbon at arm's length as if it was indeed, physically tethered to Delphine. I started toward the direction I felt her essence calling to me. I turned around to face my companions. "This way."

Adallia reached down and grabbed Juneyen's hand, the two of them moving after me. Farrah stood up, brushing herself off, with a concerned Rhyss hovering behind her.

"Are you sure you're all right?" Rhyss asked.

"I'm fine," Farrah said, sounding both exasperated and appreciative. "You can carry me if my legs give out, how's that? Come on, we don't have much time."

She was right. The time I had taken to search for Delphine, twice, plus dealing with the aftermath, had taken up way more more time than I had intended. We'd have to hurry, and hope that my hunch was correct.

I followed the faint call I felt through Delphine's ribbon, and my friends followed me. As we continued onward, the sensation of Delphine's energy steadily grew stronger, boosting my confidence that we were headed the right way.

Now that we had a clear direction, we made surprisingly good time, despite everything that had happened to delay us. We reached the edge of the forest, staying hidden in the protection of the trees. The forest gloom that we had been wandering through was suddenly replaced by the full light of day, making all of us blink rapidly or wince as our eyes adjusted.

Before us was a small meadow, dominated by a hill in the middle. And that was it. No buildings, no people, not even any animals dotted the landscape.

I looked down at the yellow ribbon I still clutched in my hand. Delphine's presence was strong here. Confused, I looked at Juneyen. She was smiling.

"This is it," she whispered.

"This?" I whispered back, confused. Why were we whispering? "There's nothing there, Juneyen."

"Yes, there is," she insisted. She pointed at the hill. "The Hauster family lives in there."

I turned to look back at the hill again, this time seeing it not as a natural feature on the land, but as a hidden fortress for a clever crime family. The more I studied the landscape, the more I realized that the area had been carefully cultivated, so there was a clear line of sight from the hill to the forest. Anyone trying to approach the hill, from any side, would easily be spotted. "How do we get inside?"

"I didn't see exactly where the door is," Juneyen said. "My brother caught me following him and made me stay in the forest, so I wouldn't be seen. He said it wouldn't go well for either of us if *they* saw me with him."

She pointed to her left, to another line of trees that outlined the clearing. The trees on that side crowded the meadow a little more than the rest of the forest.

"Jondan kept to the trees until he got over there," she said. "Someone met him as he came out of the forest ... and then he disappeared. I didn't even get to say goodbye." Her voice was heavy with hurt. "He just told me to stay in the forest and go home and walked away without looking back."

My heart twisted, knowing the little girl would have to watch more people she had come to care about do the exact same thing. But if all went well, it would be worth the short-term heartbreak.

I knelt down and quickly hugged Juneyen. "You're a very brave girl," I told her. "Thank you for everything you and your mother have done for us."

Standing, I tousled her hair fondly and passed her a small pouch. "But we need to get going, we're cutting it too close as it is. Get home safely, Juneyen."

We found an area where we could hide our bags in some bushes and tied the horses to the nearby trees. As I turned to lead the group toward the fortress, Juneyen put a hand on my arm to make me pause. She slipped a brown-and-black, braided leather bracelet from her wrist and pushed it over my hand, onto my wrist. "My brother gave this to me before he ... left me behind. Please give it to him if you find him."

"Of course."

"And, *fahteynann*."

"What?" I resisted the urge to say, *Bless you*.

"*Fahteynann*," Juneyen repeated. "I don't know what it means, but I heard my brother say it before he went with that person into the hill."

I smiled. The girl was more clever than even she knew. "Thank you," I told her again. This time when I turned to leave, Juneyen didn't stop me.

The four of us made our way quickly and quietly to the far side of the clearing, toward the clump of trees Juneyen had pointed out to us. I repeated the odd word, *fahteynann*, under my breath, working on committing it to memory so it would sound effortless when I had to say it. I was sure it was a password of some sort to gain entry into the compound. I just hoped they didn't change passwords often, or our mission would be over before it ever got started.

In short order, we were at the clump of trees on the far side of the clearing. Looking across the meadow, I could see Juneyen still hiding just inside the forest, watching us. I waved at her, both to comfort her and also to indicate she should leave. She nodded in understanding and waved back before turning and quickly leaving. I counted to twenty to give her some time to get away, then glanced around at my friends. No one said anything, but I could tell from their set faces and grim expressions that they were ready for whatever came next.

Taking a deep breath, I stepped out of the trees and into the sunlight, the other three at my back. Immediately, something detached itself from the side of the hill and approached us. It was a man dressed in green and brown, tall and imposing. He was camouflaged so well that he really had looked like he was part of the hill. I glanced around warily, wondering how many more people were stationed nearby.

When I looked back at the man, I was looking at him down the length of a long, sharp sword.

Chapter Twenty

THE GUARD'S DEEP VOICE shattered the quiet. "State your purpose."

"Cleaning staff," I said. Did my voice just shake? I hoped not.

The guard looked at the position of the sun in the sky. "You just made it. Cleaning staff is usually here right after full sunrise."

"It's my fault, sir," Farrah spoke up from behind me. "Morning sickness, something fierce. The others were kind enough to wait for me to feel better."

He nodded, accepting her excuse. But he didn't move. He just stared at us expectantly, his sword still at the ready.

What was ...? *Oh, yes.*

"*Fahteynann,*" I said.

The guard lowered his sword and stepped aside, allowing us to pass. Striding forward, the others hard on my heels, I self-consciously reached out toward the hill, near where the guard had originally been standing. Fortunately, I didn't have to fumble around for too long — my hand found a hidden door handle, cleverly concealed to look like it was part of the natural formation. The disguised door swung open, and my companions and I disappeared into the torch-lit gloom of the Hauster fortress.

The door shut behind us.

Immediately I was struck by the interior of the Hauster fortress. Smooth rock walls lined both sides of the hill's interior, creating an impressive hallway. The hallway was fairly well lit, but not by lamplight, or even torchlight. Instead, there were small pinpricks of light, just above our heads, that seemed to glow from within the rock walls. They cast a cool, even light along the hallway without heat or smoke.

Farrah curiously touched the wall, examining the lights. "Faerie lights," she breathed in awe. "We had these in my home growing up, but that's only because my mother was Fae. It's not common to see them in other places."

"I didn't think the Hauster clan was Fae," I said.

"I don't think they are," Farrah agreed. "They must have paid a handsome price for this."

"Or someone owed them an enormous debt," Rhyss said.

We fell silent, contemplating the implications.

None of us had any idea where to go now that we were actually in the stronghold. Neither Juneyen nor Carissa had ever been inside, so they hadn't been able to provide us with any information. Delphine's hair ribbon was tucked away in my pocket, but I didn't want to try seeking her out again until we were in a safe location. Standing in the middle of an open hallway in a potentially hostile hidden stronghold did not count as *safe*, in my mind.

I turned around to see my friends staring back at me, just as unsure as I was. I shrugged. "Well, let's clean," I said. I picked a direction and started walking.

We hadn't gone far when we were stopped again. Instead of meeting a sharp sword, we were met with an equally sharp voice.

"Well, it's about time you all got here! The Ceremony's in just a few hours, and the great hall needs to be prepared for it. Not to mention the master's private chambers could use a good cleaning. But see to the great hall first, that's much more important."

Everything about the woman addressing us was severe: the perfect bun of brown hair piled atop her head; her crisp gray and cream dress; and the stern expression on her face as she looked us over. Our faces evidently betrayed our confusion, because she added, "Don't know where the great hall is, do you?"

As one, we mutely shook our heads.

She looked us over suspiciously. "Where's the usual team?"

I mumbled the story we had concocted earlier to excuse the regular cleaners' absence.

She sighed in annoyance. "Spare me from having to constantly train new hires. It's one level down. There's a closet nearby where you'll find brooms, rags, buckets and other things to clean with. After you're done cleaning the room, start setting it up for the Ceremony. The kitchen is on the same level close to the great hall; Cook or someone else there can help you out if you need water. The private rooms are on the level below. Any questions?"

"Uh, where ...?" I spoke up hesitantly, cursing the fact that I seemed to become the group's official mouthpiece.

The woman sighed again and pointed down the hallway. "Stairs are on the right, over there. You should be using the servants' staircase, but this one's closer. And make sure you're on hand for the Ceremony, but stay out of sight."

"Uh, the Ceremony ...?" The servants we had bribed had mentioned this Ceremony, but we hadn't asked them for details.

The woman looked, if possible, even more annoyed. "The Ceremony. You don't know what the Ceremony is? When a commission is fulfilled and the bonds of those captured are magically transferred from the Family to the one who commissioned the hunt? Sometimes justice is meted out on the spot. It can get a bit messy. Now, then. Any *other* questions?"

"No. Uh. Thank you."

"Hurry along, then," she said, waving us away. She continued on, muttering under her breath.

Taking the woman's words to heart, we hurried along the hallway. The faerie lights lit our path, showing off what seemed to be a mansion created within a hill. Along the stone corridor were several wooden doors, some plain, some with ornate carvings. Beautifully embroidered tapestries on the walls spoke to the Hausters' great wealth. Even the workmanship of the stronghold's interior suggested careful craftsmanship, and not something made roughly or haphazardly.

At the end of the hall, we found the staircase the severe woman had indicated. The stairs led us down to another level, where we saw several more doors dotting the new hallway. The entrance to the great hall was easy to spot. Its doors were taller than the other doors around it, and were decorated with ornate carvings along the edges.

I cracked open the door while Rhyss kept lookout. Thankfully, there was no one in the great hall. Farrah had found the closet the woman had mentioned and was taking out buckets and brooms. She handed out various items to us, and we entered the great hall, shutting the door behind us.

"Now what?" Rhyss said. His words echoed off the stone walls.

"Now, you clean," Farrah said. "I heal Kaernan, and then he can search for Delphine."

"It must be nice, having special abilities," Rhyss grumbled good-naturedly. He started attacking the floor with the broom Farrah had given him.

Adallia took a section of the room behind me to start cleaning. Farrah touched my arm, closing her eyes as she concentrated on pouring healing energy into me. By now, I had recovered somewhat from the failed shield spell outside the compound, and fortunately Farrah didn't need to expend too much magic to help me.

After completing her magic, Farrah released my arm and then reached for a broom to start working on another part of the great hall. Before she could walk away, I stopped her. "Wait a minute before you start working. You need to recover, too."

Farrah smiled at me gratefully as she sank down on a wooden bench nearby.

I took a rag and empty bucket and moved to the back of the room, positioning myself on the floor so if anyone casually looked in, it would look like I was scrubbing the floor. In actuality, I had Delphine's yellow ribbon in my hand again, using it as a focus as I tried to search out her location in the compound.

It was odd. I knew that Delphine was here, and yet I couldn't get any clearer sense than that. It was almost as if the hill itself were dampening my abilities. But that couldn't be right; I'd never heard of anything that could block or hinder a Seeker's ability. Well, until just a few moments ago. I shuddered mentally, not wanting to repeat Farrah's and my little experiment.

And yet, I couldn't pinpoint Delphine's exact location. All I could feel was a general sense that she was here, somewhere. It was maddening, to know that I was so close and have the answers just out of reach. The more I tried, the more I could feel something pushing back against my seeking. A headache was starting to bloom at my temples.

A hand on my shoulder made me jump.

"I'm sorry," Adallia said. "I didn't mean to startle you, but I was getting antsy. Have you found Delphine?"

I shook my head. "I know she's here, but for some reason, I can't tell exactly where."

I held out the yellow ribbon to Adallia, offering it back to her. She shook her head. "Keep it for now. Perhaps you'll have your full abilities back later, and then it will be useful."

Adallia gently pushed my outstretched hand back toward me. As she did so, her bracelet tumbled down her wrist, the inset bloodstone brushing against my fingers.

I gasped aloud. My fingers instantly felt like they were set ablaze.

Adallia stared at me. "Kaernan, what is it?"

"Your bracelet ..." I started. "It's Baxley. He's here."

Adallia gasped as well. "Baxley? Really? You're sure?"

I had a very strong sense of his presence. I had suspected he could be in or near Rothschan, from my first impressions long ago. But now I knew, with absolute certainty, that Baxley was here, in the Hauster fortress.

"As sure as I am that your daughter is here as well." At Adallia's intensely inquisitive look, I added, "But, just as with Delphine, I can't tell exactly where in the fortress he is. All I know is that he's here."

The hope that lit Adallia's face could have illuminated all of the great hall. "We'll have to save him too, then. Get Baxley, get Delphine, get Jondan. Get out."

I nodded in agreement even as my stomach twisted in knots. *I really hope it will be that easy.*

Behind us, someone coughed discreetly to get our attention. Adallia looked up as I turned to see Rhyss, a small clump of dust and dirt piled up next to his now still broom.

"What's the plan, then?" he asked me. "If you're not sure where Baxley and Delphine are, should we wander around the stronghold and hope we get lucky? Not to mention we need to find Jondan, too, and who knows where he could be around here."

"We could split up and try to find them," Adallia said.

Rhyss shook his head. "We know these people are powerful, and smart. You don't become a crime family in Rothschan — and somehow survive in this kingdom — without being tough. I don't think any one of us would want to be alone if we got into trouble while we're in their domain."

"Rhyss is right," I said. "But I'm not sure what we should do to find any of them. Farrah, maybe you can help me understand this, since you're better versed in magic than I am. Why am I not able to use my Seeker abilities fully here, yet you're able to use your healing magic?"

Farrah, who had regained her strength and had been industriously arranging the wooden benches, looked thoughtful. She straightened up, stretching her back. "My guess is that your Seeker talents are in direct competition with the Hauster family's goals. Since you *are* in their territory, *and* we've seen already there's a liberal use of magic to keep this place going ... they must have some sort of magic over this compound that doesn't allow people who have similar skills to utilize them here. It makes sense; it would help deter any other bounty hunters ... or Seekers ... from easily taking the people they've captured."

I frowned, thinking over her words. "Fine, then, I can accept that I'm at a big disadvantage here. But if I can't use my Seeker ability, then what are we going to do?"

Farrah laughed. "Stop fretting. We already know where to find all three of the people we're looking for."

"We do?" I asked her.

"Remember the woman from upstairs, the one who sent us down here? She mentioned some sort of event happening in a few hours — the Ceremony. It sounded like most people here, if not everyone, will be in attendance. At the very least, we know Delphine will be, because she's one of their captives. I'd guess Jondan, too, since he's in their employ. And if Baxley is a captive also, which he most likely is, then he'd be at this Ceremony too."

Adallia, Rhyss, and I all paused, thinking it over. "You're right," I said. "It's perfect, they'll all be in the same place at the same time. But how do we get them out of here, safely, in front of all those people?"

Farrah shrugged. "I have no idea. I was hoping you'd come up with something brilliant. But we have plenty of time to figure something out."

"We do?"

Farrah opened her arms wide, indicating the room around us. "We're still under cover, and we still, technically, have a job to do. May as well do it right. Maybe we'll find something out while we're acting as cleaners."

I groaned. "I nearly forgot."

She handed me an empty bucket. "Here you go. Have fun snooping. And cleaning."

Chapter Twenty-One

EMPTY BUCKET IN HAND, I strode to the entrance of the great hall, intent on finding the kitchen. Rhyss paused in mid-move of a table, grinning at me. "Are all of your commissions this glamorous, Kaernan?"

I shook my head, an answering grin spreading across my face. "I wish they were. I could get used to this."

Indeed, I mused as I closed the heavy wooden doors behind me, I was rather enjoying myself on this commission. For once. I could handle potential murderesses and captured damsels much easier than weepy, spurned lovers.

At least, I hoped I could.

I walked down the hall, keeping my eyes open for any room that looked like a kitchen. I could hear noises coming from an archway nearby, and the smells that came from that direction also seemed promising.

Fortunately, as the woman upstairs had promised, the kitchen was very close to the great hall, just two doors down. It made sense; if the great hall was where the family met for dining and communal gatherings, having the kitchen nearby would make things easier for both the family and their servants.

Tentatively, I poked my head in the doorway. Evidently the cleaning staff wasn't the only group that was busy preparing for the Ceremony. The kitchen was abustle with servants dressed in dark blue jackets running to and fro.

Most were prepping items for a big communal meal of some sort: the tables were covered over in trays laden with fruit, brown bread, or meat. There was an incredible amount of meat: chicken, beef, mutton, pheasants, and duck. I even spied a peacock, beautifully arrayed on its tray. My family was wealthy, but we had never boasted a spread this grand, even when my parents threw their lavish parties. I doubted even the King and Queen of Orchwell ate this extravagantly.

If the servants weren't preparing the food for the Ceremony, then they were fetching things for the authoritative woman standing in the center.

She was calling out orders every which way, pointing her wooden spoon at various people as she yelled a command.

Seeing me, the woman paused mid-order, pointing her spoon at me. "You there, what is it?"

"You're Cook?"

"I am. What do you need?"

I held the empty bucket in front of me like a shield. She nodded and pointed toward a wall in the back of the kitchen. "Over there." She resumed her constant flow of orders.

I approached the back wall that Cook had indicated. Confused, I just stood there, stupidly staring at the wall. Did Cook mean I should go outside for water? But there was no door or handle that I could see. Besides, we were underground.

Noticing my confusion, Cook pointed her spoon at me. "What are you waiting for? Get your water and go. There's enough going on around here without you getting underfoot."

I waved my empty bucket toward the wall. "I ... I can't find the door?"

Cook stepped from her place in the kitchen's center to walk over to where I was awkwardly standing. The room suddenly got very quiet. I was acutely aware of the eyes of everyone in the room fixed upon Cook and me.

"There is no door, silly," Cook said as she approached. "We're underground, inside a hill; where would you go?"

"I thought ... I mean, I'm sure there's a well nearby, or a stream ...?"

"We don't have time to go running to some stream that's a mile away to get water whenever we need it. Plus that would be a surefire dead giveaway of our location. You're new, aren't you?"

Cook peered at me closely as I nodded. I tried to remain calm under her scrutiny. I could only hope she was so stressed and busy with all the preparations that she wouldn't remember any details about me later.

She sighed heavily. "You'd think Patrice would have briefed you before sending you off on your own. Well, I suppose that's the best way to learn. Here, now."

Patrice must have been the woman we ran into when we first entered the fortress. From her demeanor and the things she had said, I guessed Patrice must be the head housekeeper or something similar. I refrained from commenting on my group's encounter with Patrice. Instead, I focused on what Cook was pointing at on the stone wall.

At first I couldn't understand why the boisterous woman was pointing at a rock that was jutting out of the wall. Then I realized that what I thought was a rock was actually a small spigot. Cook took the bucket from my unresisting hands and put it on the ground, turning the spigot slightly. A steady stream of water came gushing out, spilling into my bucket. Cook turned the spigot back the other way, showing me how to stop the flow of water. "That's how you turn it on, and off. Any questions?"

My amazement must have shown on my face, for Cook snorted in suppressed laughter at me. "Like I said, we're underground. Where would you go?" She shook her head, walking back to the center of the room as she resumed calling out orders. The kitchen activity quickly picked up behind me.

It seemed like such a little thing, but seeing that spigot was another reminder of how rich, and powerful, the Hauster family must be. Few families could afford to have indoor water; it was too expensive to pay for the piping system and upkeep to have it. Even in Orchwell, which was by and large a prosperous kingdom, only the royal family had indoor water, and even then, it was only in certain parts of the castle. It was much easier to just send servants to the central fountain to get water, or, if you couldn't afford to employ servants, to fetch it yourself.

It made sense that this criminal family would want to keep their underground bunker as secret as possible. But then ... how deep did corruption run in Rothschan, that even the kingdom's engineers were willing to provide aid to the Hauster fortress while turning a blind eye to their activities?

For the first time, I wondered at how easily everyone had accepted my group, a bunch of supposedly new servants. Loyalty was to be prized, of course, but if not ... it was easy enough to get rid of people that were, in essence, supposed to be overlooked.

I shivered, but it wasn't from the cold, dank air that permeated the underground kitchen.

From her place at the center, Cook called out to me, "Did you forget how to use the tap already?"

I shook my head. I slowly turned the spigot, marveling at the water gushing into my bucket. As the water neared the top, I quickly spun the spigot back the other way, watching as the flow of water slowed, then stopped completely.

Hefting the now-full bucket, I left the kitchen, nodding at Cook in thanks as I left. I carefully made my way back to the great hall where my friends waited.

"Wow, that was fast," Rhyss commented when I opened the heavy wooden door. "We expected you to be gone much longer."

"We debated following you with the other buckets, just to make things go faster," Farrah added. "But we weren't sure it was wise to split up the group more than we had to."

"No, you're right," I said, putting the bucket down. "Not unless we can learn something from splitting up, but there doesn't seem to be a lot of activity on this level. Besides what's going on in the kitchen."

"Did you learn anything of import?" Adallia asked.

"Not in regards to tonight's event. But I did learn that the Hauster clan has more money and people in their pocket than we originally thought." I told them about the underground compound's indoor water supply.

"So that's why you returned so quickly!" Farrah said.

I nodded. "Unfortunately I wasn't there long enough to really overhear anything, though."

"It's all right," Farrah said.

"It is?"

She smiled. Pointing at a stack of empty buckets, she indicated the expanse of the great hall. "We've got a lot of cleaning to do. You really think one bucket is enough for all this?"

I groaned. Farrah was right, and it would allow us to go back to the kitchen and try to gather information. But still, I was not looking forward to hauling multiple buckets back and forth between the kitchen and the great hall.

Farrah plucked two buckets from the stack and handed it to me. I took it, grimacing. Surprisingly, she grabbed the remaining two empty buckets as well. "I'll go with you while Rhyss and Adallia work on the great hall. Two sets of ears might be more useful."

"Thanks," I said gratefully.

"Hey, why do we have to stay behind and clean?" Rhyss complained.

"Would you rather haul buckets of water back and forth?" Farrah pointed out.

Rhyss pointedly picked up the full bucket I had brought back to the room, waving us away. "You make an excellent point, as always, Farrah. You two better get going. I have cleaning to do."

Chuckling, Farrah and I took our buckets and left the great hall.

Chapter Twenty-Two

LADEN WITH OUR EMPTY buckets, Farrah and I entered the bustling kitchen. Cook was no longer standing in the middle of the room shouting orders. Instead, she was industriously working in one corner of the kitchen.

Everywhere I looked, there was some activity happening. Several people were busy kneading dough or tending the massive oven at the back of the kitchen, while others were busy roasting the meats or carving them up. One servant had the thankless task of constantly running for more wood to keep all the kitchen fires burning.

Occasionally Cook would look up, a queen surveying her kingdom, and yell out a correction or order to one of the servants scurrying about. As Cook tended to use her extremely large, extremely sharp butcher knife to point at whoever she was yelling at, I made a mental note to give her a wide berth.

I led Farrah to the back wall where the water supply was, putting a bucket down under the spigot and turning it on. Impressed, Farrah raised her eyebrows at me, but didn't comment out loud.

I finished filling the bucket, moving it out of the way so Farrah could put another empty bucket in its place. Lifting the unwieldy, full bucket, I grimaced. "I don't think I should try to carry two of these at the same time. Not if I don't want to spill this all over the place."

Farrah took the bucket from me, testing its weight. "I agree. It's probably best if one of us stays here to fill the buckets, and the other person can carry the full buckets back to the great hall. Would you prefer to go, or shall I?"

I didn't relish the idea of hauling huge buckets of water back and forth, but I also felt it would be unchivalrous to make Farrah be the one to carry everything. "I'll take them back. You can stay and fill."

She nodded, a slight smirk on her face as if she knew what I was thinking. "All right. Thanks."

I took the bucket back from Farrah and carefully threaded my way through the busy kitchen and into the hallway.

Even though the kitchen wasn't far, it took me twice as long to get back to the great hall. Balancing the heavy bucket meant I moved rather slowly. I didn't want to spill any water and have to clean both the great hall *and* the hallway.

When I returned to the kitchen, I saw Patrice and Cook in a deep discussion. Farrah had filled another bucket, leaving the full bucket in its spot under the spigot. Patiently standing by the wall, when she saw me enter the room she raised her hand in greeting as I walked over to her.

Quizzically, I looked at the other two empty buckets. In the time I had been gone, I would have expected at least two buckets to be ready, if not all of them.

Farrah followed my gaze. "I didn't want them to get in the way of anyone working here," she said, indicating the hustle and bustle of the kitchen.

That made sense. I supposed. As I grabbed the handle of the full bucket to take it away, Farrah commented in a low voice, "I'm not in a hurry to get back and clean, are you? Feel free to take your time coming back here."

Farrah smiled. I blinked. Then, what Farrah was trying to convey clicked in my head. "Oh!" I said, feeling stupid. "Yes, of course."

Even without Farrah's coded instruction, I still would have taken a while to go to and from the kitchen. This new bucket felt like it was even heavier than the first one had been. Was my mind playing tricks on me, or had Farrah filled this one higher than the last?

When I got back to the great hall, I was surprised to see Rhyss, Adallia, and Patrice standing outside, talking. More accurately, Patrice was talking, and Rhyss and Adallia were nodding and keeping their mouths firmly shut.

Patrice saw me and waved me over. "Where's the other one?"

Realizing she must be referring to Farrah, I said, as I put my heavy pail down, "She's in the kitchen, filling buckets."

"Oh, good," Patrice said. "When you three get to the kitchen you can tell her to stay there and make herself useful, along with the rest of you."

My blank look obviously annoyed Patrice, because she huffed impatiently, "Cook needs more help in the kitchen. The great hall can keep for now. So, get to it."

My friends and I looked at each other and shrugged. I turned to head back to the kitchen, Rhyss and Adallia falling in step behind me.

A pointed cough stopped me before I could take my first step.

I turned around to see Patrice glaring at me. "Well?"

I looked around, confused. "What?"

Patrice pointed at the bucket I had placed on the floor. "Take that back with you."

I groaned inwardly. Picking up the full bucket of water, I resisted the temptation to dump its contents over Patrice's head. It would probably have been useless anyway; I doubted mere water would have wiped the smug expression off of her face.

I started my slow way back to the kitchen, Rhyss and Adallia kindly keeping pace with me instead of walking faster. We could hear Patrice's rapid footsteps fading as she walked down the hallway. I stopped and looked over my shoulder just in time to see her disappear down the stairwell at the end of the hallway. I sighed, putting the stupid bucket down for a short rest.

"Hey!"

I looked up. Farrah was coming toward us, carrying the rest of the buckets in her hands.

"Go back," Rhyss said. Realizing how ominous that sounded, he amended, "Patrice's orders. We're supposed to be working in the kitchen now."

"I know," Farrah said. "That's why I'm out here; I'm supposed to put these buckets away and then head back to the kitchen for further instructions."

"Lucky us, coming on the one day they're so short staffed," I grumbled.

"Lucky indeed," Farrah agreed cheerfully. "It's going to be the reason we can rescue Delphine."

Chapter Twenty-Three

FARRAH QUICKLY FILLED us in on what she had overheard in the kitchen while Adallia and Rhyss had been in the great hall and I had been running back and forth between them and Farrah.

"Delphine, along with some other captives, is being held one level down. Tonight's Ceremony has taxed the entire household staff; all the servants have been doing three times as much as their normal duties."

"And no one's complaining?" Rhyss asked.

"They're complaining, all right, but quietly. They've been promised that their contracts will be shortened, or cancelled entirely."

"Contracts?"

"Remember that couple that Kaernan paid off? They mentioned something about being indentured servants. Some of the other servants talked about the same thing. It seems the Hauster family is quite the 'employer' in these parts for those who have fallen on hard times."

"Ah."

"Anyway, while I was waiting one of the guards came by and said that dinner was supposed to be served early, when could Cook have it ready? She was annoyed, but promised that she'd send some people down soon. After he left she grumbled that she really didn't have anyone to spare. Patrice came by then, and I'm assuming then she went to the great hall to send you over to the kitchen."

Farrah hurried over to the closet and put away the empty buckets she had been carrying.

"What about this?" I said, nudging the full bucket with my foot. I really didn't want to have to carry the thing back to the kitchen just to carry the empty container back out, but I also didn't want Patrice to find it and hunt me down over it.

A wicked gleam appeared in Farrah's eyes. "Allow me."

She hefted the bucket, doing her best not to spill any water, and placed it in the back of the closet.

"Someone is either going to love you or curse you when they finally find that," Rhyss commented, but he was chuckling.

"That's usually the case when people are dealing with me," Farrah quipped as she closed the closet door.

On our way to the kitchen, we passed other servants headed down the hallway back toward the great hall, bearing crisp, clean linens.

Time was running short. The Ceremony would begin soon, and Delphine, Jondan and Baxley were depending on us.

We hurried to the kitchen where the activity level had increased to a frenetic pace. Before the kitchen had hummed with the meal preparations for the upcoming Ceremony, but now that the event was nearly upon them, several servants were busy putting the finishing touches on the food trays, artfully arranging them before they were whisked away by other people waiting to take them down the hall.

Seeing us enter, Cook pointed her knife at us. "If you don't need anymore water, then get out. It's crazy enough here without you."

"No," Farrah said, holding her hands out in placation. "We're here to help, if you need us."

"Oh, good," Cook said. She pointed her knife at two plain wooden trays lying askew on one side of the room, away from the hustle and bustle. One tray held a large pot and ladle. The other tray held a bunch of wooden bowls and spoons. "Guards are complaining because they want dinner early. Like feeding them or the prisoners is priority right now. Take that downstairs, and make sure to portion it out equally because there isn't any more, nor do we have time to make extra."

She turned away, muttering to herself. "Guards get paid better than we do, even if they *do* have the same contracts. It's so not fair, we work harder than any of them. Easy to wave around a sword, it's much harder to feed a bunch of people."

While Cook was complaining, we moved toward the trays. Cook stopped us, saying, "Not all of you. It doesn't take all of you, and besides, I could use the extra hands up here. You, and you —" she pointed at Adallia and me "— take the trays down. The other two, help with setting up the great hall."

I exchanged quick glances with my friends. How could we attempt a rescue if our group was going to be split up?

But there was nothing for it. We'd just have to take the trays down and see what information we could gather.

Maybe a solution would present itself while we were down in the prison area. I hoped.

Adallia and I picked up a tray each and left the kitchen. More and more of the kitchen staff were filling the hallway, scurrying to and from the great hall. Adallia and I headed past them, toward the staircase we had originally used. A petite woman carrying a large silver bowl filled with fruit called out to us.

"Here, where do you two think you're going?"

I turned, trying not to spill the contents of my tray. "We're headed downstairs to the prison level."

"I can see that," she said. "But you're going the wrong way. Servants' stairs are back there." She jutted her chin in the opposite direction.

"Oh, uh, thank you." Adallia and I started in the direction the woman had indicated. As we passed her, I heard her mutter something about "having to constantly break in new ones."

We hurried down the hallway, looking for the stairs while trying not to be too obvious about it. We needn't have worried; the staircase was at the very end of the hall.

As we descended the staircase, Adallia whispered, "How are we going to get Delphine out, and then get the others without raising suspicion?"

I whispered back, "I have no idea. I think the only thing we can do is find Delphine, make sure she's all right, and let her know we're here. If she's aware that we've come to get her, then she'll be watchful for a chance to escape." I hoped. I worried about what state Delphine might be in if — when — we located her.

"I understand. As a mother, I just want to run down there and grab my precious girl out of their clutches ... but I understand the need for caution as well."

I stopped, forcing Adallia to halt behind me. I turned to her as best as I was able in the cramped stairwell. "Adallia, that reminds me. We know Baxley is also here. Did you see him among the servants, at all?"

"No."

"He might be on this level then. In fact, it's quite likely he's one of their prisoners. Keep a sharp eye out, and let me know if you spot him."

"Of course."

We continued our descent, exiting the stairs into another rock-hewn hallway. This hallway wasn't as nicely done as the two upper levels had been. Well, if it was only meant to secure prisoners, the family certainly didn't need to expend the money or energy into making this floor look pretty.

Just a few feet from the stairs' entryway were two guards. One was perched precariously on a stool, head lolling back on the wall behind him. Opposite him stood another guard, whose equally slumped posture suggested boredom. The second guard's head swiveled toward Adallia and me when they heard our footsteps on the stone floor.

I said, "Cook sent us down with food for you and the prisoners."

The guard on the stool perked up immediately, sitting up straight on his stool. "It's about time! I was about ready to eat my boot."

"That would have been a sight," the other guard said, chuckling. "I thought you were sleeping over there."

"I was not! I was just deep in thought."

"Don't know what you could be thinking about. There's nothing *to* think about when you're on duty down here. Besides, I don't think you ever had a deep thought in your life."

"I have plenty of deep thoughts!"

"Watch that you don't drown in them." The second guard laughed, pleased at his joke.

"Hey —"

I coughed politely, trying to cut through their banter. "Uh, if you don't mind ...?"

The guards settled down and each grabbed a bowl and spoon from the tray Adallia carried. Carefully, I balanced my tray while Adallia shifted her tray to her hip and ladled out the gruel into each of their waiting bowls. While she did so, I studied the guards.

The standing guard carried a key ring with several metal keys at his belt, which I assumed were for the cells on this level. Unfortunately, he also seemed to be the sharper of the two. While we fed the prisoners, Adallia and I would have to think of a way to distract or disarm him.

"There's barely anything in here," the seated guard complained. "I'm pretty sure I can see the bottom of my bowl."

"It's not that bad, quit exaggerating," the guard who was standing said.

"Cook said this was all they could spare," Adallia said apologetically.

The seated guard snorted, busying himself with eating. The standing guard rolled his eyes and waved us through. As we continued down the hallway, we could hear them loudly slurping behind us.

Although this level consisted mostly of prison cells, not every cell was occupied. We walked through slowly, taking our time as we gave out food so we could observe as much as possible. The prisoners we did see looked surprisingly healthy. It could be that they were newly caught, as Delphine was. Or, the more cynical part of me realized, it could be that the Hausters wanted their commissions to be well taken care of, so as to fetch a higher price when the patrons came to claim them.

As we distributed food to the prisoners, I would eye Adallia carefully for a reaction. Each time she shook her head at me. *No, this isn't Baxley.* But my sense of his presence was still very strong, and I was sure he was here. If he wasn't a prisoner, where could he be?

Near the end of the hallway, we finally found Delphine.

In the furthest corner possible from the cell door, she sat on a pile of dirty straw, her knees pulled to her chest, her head against the stone wall. As we approached, her eyes flicked over to us with a disinterested glance.

"Supper's here," Adallia said.

Upon hearing her mother's voice, Delphine's eyes kindled. She quickly stood up, mouth opening to speak. Adallia gave the smallest shake of her head, putting her finger to her lips to warn Delphine to be careful with her words.

I glanced over Adallia's shoulder to where the guards were at the other end of the hallway. The one standing was still eating; the seated guard was now sleeping in earnest.

Delphine came to the front of her cell to get her food.

As Adallia handed a bowl to her daughter, she said, "Hold this steady, now." She grabbed the ladle from my tray and scooped out a generous amount of gruel. As she turned to drop the food into Delphine's bowl, she moved closer and whispered, "Are you well?"

Delphine nodded, eyes wide.

"We're going to get you out here." Delphine's eyes lit with excitement, and Adallia reluctantly whispered, "Not yet, but soon. Be watchful for when."

Adallia handed a spoon to her daughter. Aloud, Delphine said, "Thank you." The look in her eyes told us her gratitude was for more than just supper.

"Of course, dear," Adallia said. Mother and daughter held each other's gazes for just a moment. A small frisson of hope passed between them.

Chapter Twenty-Four

RELUCTANTLY, ADALLIA turned away and started walking back the way we had come. I gave Delphine a brief nod and small smile before following Adallia down the hallway.

As we walked, we gathered any empty bowls the prisoners had pushed through the bars of their cells.

When we reached the guards again, the man in the chair was snoring loudly. His companion alternated between giving him disgusted glances and looking longingly into his empty bowl. In the sleeping guard's lap lay his empty bowl and dirty spoon.

Adallia carefully reached down to pluck the dirty dishes from the sleeping guard's lap. She quietly placed the items on her tray. Turning back to me, she caught the eye of the guard who was standing on the opposite wall.

"Would you like more?" she asked him sweetly. "We have a little bit left, we may as well use it all up."

"That would be great," the guard said immediately. Adallia scooped the remaining gruel into his outstretched bowl.

"Wait," she said, when he was about to take his bowl back. She grabbed the pot from my tray and upended it, tipping every last drop into the guard's bowl.

"Thank you," he said. He stuck a spoonful in his mouth, then made a face. "It's gone a bit cold, but when you haven't eaten since the early morning, everything tastes good."

"They keep you that busy, then?" Adallia asked.

"Yes," the guard said around a mouthful of gruel. He swallowed. "We're lucky Cook even remembered us today, what with the Ceremony happening later."

"Everyone keeps talking about this Ceremony, but no one's really told us what to expect," Adallia said. The guard looked at us curiously as he stuck another spoonful of food in his mouth.

"We're new," she explained unnecessarily. "The head of household — Patrice? — just sent us right to work without telling us anything else about, well, anything."

The guard shook his head sympathetically. "They're like that around here. You get used to it. Just keep your head down, do your work, and eventually you pick up enough not to get in trouble."

"Well, what *should* we expect?" Adallia asked. "So we won't do something foolish during the Ceremony."

The guard waved his spoon toward the prison cells. "We'll bring them all up for inspection for our 'honored guests'. There's not too many this time, just the four prisoners. The Hauduare does some sort of magical ritual or something, then there's a party afterward celebrating a successful hunt. The guests can stay for the celebration, or they can take their prisoner and leave. Most choose to stay, though; there's enough food and drink the lighten the mood of even the sourest attendee."

His tone was casual enough, as if he had seen a good share of Ceremonies happen and could care less about the event. But there was a glint in his eye that gave me pause. Perhaps he didn't agree with his job as much as he made it seem like he did.

"Hauduare?" I asked, trying to match the guard's casual tone.

"The Hauster family's leader," he clarified, giving me a curious look. I cursed myself mentally for being so careless in my questions. I had been to Rothschan enough to know that their family leaders were referred to by title, comprised of the first part of the family name, and *duare*, an old Rothschan word for the number one. While everyone in the Gifted Lands now spoke a common language, each country had their own native language, rarely used outside their areas.

"It's a good thing there's only four prisoners," Adallia said, changing the subject. "It might be hard to keep any more in line during the Ceremony. Although, I guess it doesn't matter, it's probably too hard for them to break their shackles anyway. I'm guessing they're also magically bound?"

"In a way, yes," the guard said. "Magic is tricky here. Sometimes it works, sometimes it doesn't, depending on the type of magic."

He shrugged. "I don't much about it. All I know is, when the prisoners are brought in, they're magically bound to the Family, and to the hill. That's why the Ceremony exists, to release the prisoners from their magical ties to the Family so they're able to leave. Otherwise, they wouldn't be able to leave the area, no matter what they tried. Putting them in cells is really just to keep them out of the way. It wouldn't do to have the prisoners wandering around the estate, getting underfoot."

He shoveled more food in his mouth, allowing Adallia and me to exchange the briefest of glances. Farrah's guess — about why my Seeker abilities were dampened here but she was still able to heal me — was correct, then. Too bad this guard couldn't give us more insight on exactly what kinds of magic would work, though. Without knowing specifics, Farrah, our group's magic user, could be at quite a disadvantage.

"It sounds like quite an event," Adallia said. "Now that we know a little more about it, I think we'll be able to serve the Hauduare and his family a lot better."

"I wouldn't worry about it," the guard said. "You'll figure it out fairly quickly, once things get underway." He finished the last of his gruel, licking the last of it off his spoon before sticking the dirty utensil in the empty bowl.

I reached out to take his dirty dishes. As I did so, the long sleeve of my shirt fell back, exposing the leather bracelet Juneyen had placed around my wrist earlier in the day.

The guard saw the bracelet and immediately grabbed my wrist, none too gently. His eyes flashed dangerously. In a low, urgent voice, he asked me, "Where did you get this bracelet?"

I glanced at Adallia, who had moved to the guard's side. *What should I tell him?* I tried to ask her with my eyes. Her face held no clear answers for me. Her eyes were wide, and she shook her head ever so slightly.

The guard's face was just inches from mine. His grip on my wrist tightened as he repeated his question. "Where did you get this bracelet from?"

"Why do you want to know?" I asked through gritted teeth.

"You have ten seconds to tell me," the guard said, equally fiery. "If you don't tell me, nothing will stop me from gutting you right here where you stand and raising the alarm about your companion. So, you decide how much a lie is worth to you. You have five seconds, now."

"A little girl gave it to me for safekeeping," I said.

"The girl's name?"

I didn't respond. His free hand moved to the weapon at his side.

"Juneyen," I ground out. "The little girl who gave me the bracelet is named Juneyen."

The guard's face changed from one of anger to one of shock. "How do you know her?"

Adallia tensed, looking ready to jump in between the guard and me. I warned her away with my eyes. No sense in drawing the guard's ire against both of us.

"I ... ah ... met her in the town square. She introduced me to her mother, who asked me to seek out her son when I told her I would be working here. Juneyen gave me this bracelet to give to her brother, who is somewhere in this compound."

The guard grew still, his gaze becoming soft as his thoughts turned elsewhere. Adallia and I exchanged glances again, unsure of what was happening or what I should do next.

I moved slightly, hoping that the guard's grip on my wrist would loosen now that he was distracted. My movement caught his attention, and he turned his gaze back to me again.

His grip had slackened slightly, but he still held my wrist firmly in his grasp. Any sudden moves on my part would most likely incite him to attack me.

I asked, "What does this matter to you, anyway? It's just a little girl's trinket."

The guard's eyes flashed. In anger? No. In pain. "It's not just some little girl. Juneyen is my sister."

Chapter Twenty-Five

BEHIND THE GUARD, ADALLIA gasped. It was the smallest sound, but it was enough to grab the guard's attention. He turned his head slightly. "You know my sister?"

There was no point in pretending ignorance now. Before Adallia could say anything, I spoke up. "Yes, we both do." I nodded my head toward Adallia. "She was with me when I met Juneyen. Juneyen was quite fond of her."

"She's a darling child," Adallia said, her tone placating and slightly defensive.

The guard snorted. "'Darling' isn't the word I'd use for her. She must have been on her best behavior when she met you two."

My expression must have betrayed my thoughts, because the guard said, "No?"

"It was a rather memorable meeting," I said.

The guard laughed. "Knowing my sister, I can imagine how things might have gone." Releasing my wrist, he turned his grip into a handshake. "I'm Jondan. But then, you probably already knew that."

"Well met, Jondan," I said. "I'm Kaernan. My companion is Lady Adallia Pahame."

Jondan's eyebrows shot up at "Lady," but he merely took Adallia's hand and bowed over it.

I slipped the leather bracelet off my wrist and held it out to Jondan. He stared hard at it for a moment, his eyes bright. He then reached out and took it from my outstretched fingers, pushing the bracelet over his hand and onto his wrist with a sad smile. He backed up a step so he could look at both Adallia and me. "Thank you."

"Of course," I said. Next to me, Adallia nodded her head slightly in acknowledgment.

Jondan peered behind us, to his fellow guard on the opposite wall. The other guard was still asleep, his snores echoing loudly against the stone walls. Jondan shook his head in amusement.

"Well, for once Bertan's bad habits are useful," he said. He lowered his voice as a precaution, even though it seemed unlikely Bertan would wake up anytime soon. "So, I'm guessing you're not really servants." It was more a statement than a question. "You came here only to deliver this bracelet to me?"

When neither Adallia nor I answered immediately, Jondan said, "I thought as much. Will you say what your true purpose is, then?"

Adallia looked at me as if to say, *If you think it's best, go ahead.*

"You know we're trustworthy." I indicated Jondan's bracelet. "How do we know the same of you?"

"You don't," he admitted. "Just my thanks and my word that I won't turn you both in."

"No offense, but it doesn't seem like much to go on."

"I know. But I'm glad you've come. You've given me back my resolve. I've been trying to figure out how to leave this place. Perhaps, with your help, I can finally escape."

Adallia breathed a sigh of relief. "Oh, good, that makes things much easier."

Jondan gave her a quizzical look. "What do you mean?"

There was nothing for it, I reasoned. He already knew enough to expose us, so I figured we might as well tell him everything.

"We're here to free one of the prisoners," I said. "The girl in the cell at the end of the hall."

"Oh?" Jondan said.

"My daughter," Adallia said.

"Oh." Jondan nodded in understanding.

"We're also here to find and free someone else," I added. "A man named Baxley. He'd be a bit older, closer to ... ah ... close to ..."

"Close to my age," Adallia said. An amused smile played on her lips as she looked at me. "You're welcome."

"My apologies, my lady." I said sheepishly.

"No apologies are necessary."

Jondan frowned. "I don't know anyone here by that name. I've only been here a few weeks, but I've met everyone who lives or works here. In general, the Family prefers to have the same servants in their employ all the time, and they either pay handsomely for that privilege, or their ironclad indentures ensure the same."

"Yes, I know," I said, thinking of the servants we had bribed just outside of Rothschan.

If my hunch was wrong and Baxley wasn't here, then we'd have to return to Orchwell for more money before setting out again. Or give up the commission entirely. Although Adallia wanted to find Baxley, from the things she mentioned, her funds would be limited. As well, Adallia and Delphine *couldn't* return to Orchwell, unless we could clear Delphine of any charges against her. But who knew what state of affairs they had left behind when they fled?

Well. I would just have to trust my Seeker instincts. And hope they wouldn't fail me. Although if Baxley wasn't a prisoner, then he must be hidden by strong magic. I had no other explanation for why he kept eluding me.

"Will you help us?" Adallia said to Jondan. "Can you release my daughter? If you're coming with us anyway ..."

But Jondan shook his head. "No, I can't. The cells are locked twice over. Once by physical means —" he indicated the key ring at his belt "— and then by magical means. I lack the magical ability to undo the spell on the cells." He nodded toward his snoring companion. "So does he, or anyone else except the Hauduare. It's done that way on purpose. These prisoners have fetched a high price for the Family, but they won't get full payment until the commission is complete. The Family wouldn't want anything to jeopardize that."

Adallia looked as if she might cry. "Then nothing can be done to save my daughter?"

"I wouldn't say that," Jondan said. "It will be tough, but it's possible we could free your daughter during the Ceremony."

Chapter Twenty-Six

ADALLIA AND I HURRIEDLY made our way back upstairs, whispering furiously.

"I don't know, it seems too risky," Adallia said.

"I agree, but it doesn't seem like we have any other options," I said. "Well, any other *good* options."

We had reached the top of the stairs and were about to head down the hallway, toward the kitchen, when someone exited a room just a few paces in front of us, his back to us. He was wearing an extremely gaudy outfit of green and gold, with a matching oversized green fedora atop his head. There was a gold feather sticking out from the ostentatious hat.

Beneath the hat the man sported long blond hair, tied back with a green ribbon.

I put my arm out, stopping Adallia from moving forward while I walked toward the newcomer. The man's stocky frame and somewhat familiar tied-back blond hair made me think of ...

"Lord Olivera?"

The man turned around at my exclamation. It was, indeed, Lord Olivera. *But I thought he was dead!*

Yet here he was, standing in front of me. Very much alive.

When Lord Olivera saw me, he snarled. "Kaernan Asthore! What are you doing here?"

"I could ask you the very same thing," I said in shock.

"You're looking for a lost love, aren't you?" He stepped toward me, brandishing a fist. "Well, you can't have her! This is one commission you will fail." His lips pulled back in an ugly grimace. "Or maybe I should say, this is the *second* commission you will fail."

"Her? Who are you talking about?"

"You think you can collect double, don't you?" Lord Olivera wasn't even registering my confusion. "Get your commission, and collect the reward money? Clear out of here, or I'll make sure there's trouble for you, both in Rothschan and back in Orchwell."

Reward money? He must think I was there for Delphine! He was right, but not for the reasons he presumed.

"Are you here for the reward money?"

Lord Olivera laughed nastily. "I don't need some stupid reward money, not when I hired the best bounty hunters in all of the Gifted Lands to get who I wanted. No, I'm here for the girl, and I will have her."

He stepped even closer to me, so close his hot breath washed over my face. "And no one will stand in my way."

Behind us there was a rustle of fabric and a whoosh of air as the bottom of a heavy wooden tray clipped the side of Lord Olivera's head. Dirty spoons and bowls went flying around the hall.

The nobleman's eyes widened comically before he slumped to the floor. I knelt down to examine him; he was still breathing, but definitely unconscious.

"Nice hit," I said to Adallia, who was standing above us, breathing heavily and staring daggers at the man she had just knocked out.

"Thank you," she said, getting her breathing back under control. "I've always wanted to do that. That was extremely satisfying."

I smiled. "I've had my own encounters with the man, and I'm rather jealous of you right now."

Adallia knelt down and started picking up the scattered dishes. "What are we going to do with him, though?"

I looked down at the green-and-gold heap on the floor that was Lord Olivera. "I have an idea. Help me take his clothes off."

Adallia wrinkled her nose in disgust. "Ew. No, thank you."

I laughed, even as my hands worked rapidly to undo the buttons on Lord Olivera's flashy coat. "I don't know what *you're* thinking, but *I'm* thinking this is a perfect opportunity to help Delphine. I'll pretend to be Lord Olivera and 'collect' Delphine after the Ceremony. You and the rest of the team can follow me afterward."

"Oh!" Adallia put the full tray of dirty dishes aside and started removing Lord Olivera's shoes. Soon the man was lying on the floor in just his undergarments, with his brightly colored clothes in a pile beside him.

I quickly donned the nobleman's clothes over my own. His much larger size meant that his clothes hung loosely on my slender frame, but the added bulk of my servant's garb helped fill out his ill-fitting outfit. Adallia eyed his gaudy shoes. "Do you want these as well?"

I looked at the shoes, two frothy bright green creations each boasting an ornate gold buckle. "No, his feet are bigger than mine; I couldn't wear those." The relief in my voice was evident.

Adallia picked up the belt Lord Olivera had been wearing and bound his hands. "It's not much, but hopefully it will hold him for a bit."

I briefly debated hauling Lord Olivera back into the room we had seen him leaving, but I also couldn't be sure that had been his private room. I didn't want to get into a bigger mess if I opened an unknown door and found several other people on the other side of it.

But that hall closet where we had stashed the brooms and buckets was nearby ....

"Here, Adallia, can you grab his legs?" She complied, while I lifted the loathsome man under his arms. Together we hauled Lord Olivera to the cleaning supply closet. I opened the door and we shoved him in. Even unconscious the man was annoying; he was heavy and unwieldy to lift, and his dead weight made it nearly impossible to put him inside the closet. As I pushed Lord Olivera in one final time, I heard a splash, and remembered belatedly how Farrah had stashed one bucket full of water in the closet.

Adallia grabbed Lord Olivera's shoes and threw them in after the man. We heard another splash before I hurriedly shut the door.

I turned away, grinning wickedly. Hauling those blasted buckets of water had been worth it after all.

RHYSS ITCHED THE BACK of his neck, shifting his weight uncomfortably. He tugged at his ill-fitting blue jacket, trying to tweak it into place.

"Stop fidgeting," Farrah hissed at him. She'd been able to find a jacket that fit her frame, along with Adallia. After our encounter with Lord Olivera, Adallia had returned to the kitchen while I changed into Lord Olivera's outfit. Adallia had given Cook some excuse about me being needed back at the great hall; Cook had barely cared as she directed Adallia and my other friends to a storage room just off the kitchen. I joined them in the storage room, which had several wardrobes filled with the formal dark blue coats I had seen other servants wearing. Seeing the stuffed wardrobes, I had tried not to think too hard about what may have happened to the servants before us who had been similarly outfitted.

As Rhyss, Farrah, and Adallia picked out coats to wear, Adallia and I had told Rhyss and Farrah about finding Delphine and meeting Jondan on the prison level, and about our chance meeting with Lord Olivera. We quickly outlined our plan to steal away with Delphine after the Ceremony transferred her bonds to me as Lord Olivera.

Both Rhyss and Farrah had been skeptical. "Too risky," were Farrah's thoughts on the plan. "But what about Baxley?" was Rhyss's objection.

They were both right. It *was* an incredibly risky plan, and we still had no idea where Baxley was. But at least we'd be able to recover two of the three people we'd come to find. I hoped.

I didn't even want to entertain the idea of what would happen if we failed. If we didn't make it out of here, I knew it was unlikely my family would ever know what happened to me. My father might not care, but my twin sister would definitely be bereft.

Or worse, if they knew who I was and learned of my family connections, they might try to ransom me for money or Seeker services ....

I had put the idea firmly out of my head. No sense in borrowing trouble.

"I can't help it," Rhyss now said in a low tone. He scratched his elbow, then reached around to scratch his back. Watching him made *me* feel itchy. "I hate waiting. I'd rather we'd just get things *going*, already. Besides, these jackets are uncomfortable."

"I told you to take the other one. The Ceremony will be starting soon enough, your fidgeting won't make the time go any faster."

"Feels like it's been going on for ages, with all the work we've had to —"

"Shh!" Adallia interrupted Rhyss. "Keep alert; they're coming in."

Sure enough, the door to the great hall was opening. We were about to get our first glimpse of the Hauster clan. Or, as those in their employ called them, the Family.

Rhyss and Farrah stopped their whispered argument and stood up a bit straighter, eyes watchful and wary. I stepped away from my friends, trying to appear like I had just wandered to the great hall early. Around the room, the other blue-jacketed servants who were in attendance also stopped their tasks and looked toward the doors, now fully open.

Entering first were a handful of guards, Jondan included. The prisoners from the floor below were in their midst, shackled and shuffling forward dispiritedly. Beside me, Adallia stiffened and bit her lip, trying not to cry out at the sight of her daughter.

As the guards brought their prisoners to the front of the room, I counted the people entering. Four prisoners, including Delphine — two men, two women. Five guards, not including Jondan. Even if we freed all of the prisoners and they were willing to help us fight our way out of here, none of them looked in any condition to actually fight. They were healthy, but their time spent languishing in prison would mean they weren't in peak physical form.

So that really left any fighting to Rhyss, Farrah, Jondan, and me. Possibly Adallia could help, but I wasn't sure if she had any training or how skilled she was. She could be more of a liability than a help. So that was four of us against five guards ... somewhat decent odds. But we also had to contend with —

The Family, now entering the room.

A young woman, perhaps in her twenties, assisted an elderly couple to some seats on the far side of the room and then stood beside their chairs. A handsome middle-aged woman strode in behind them. From their similarly lean figures and intense dark eyes, it was easy to see they were related.

Surreptitiously, I caught Jondan's eye. *Was this the infamous Hauster family?*

Jondan nodded back, ever-so-slightly. My brows furrowed as my eyes flicked toward the elderly couple. Surely one of those was the Hauduare. Jondan shook his head in barely imperceptible movement. My eyes flitted back and forth between the two standing women and Jondan. *Any of these, then?* But, no. None of them was the Hauduare.

I frowned, hastily smoothing my face into a neutral expression.

The young woman waved at me. "Lord Olivera, there you are! I'm glad you found your way here. We wondered where you were when we didn't find you in the guest antechamber with the others."

I nodded back at her, worried that if I responded, my voice would give me away. Luckily, my acknowledgement seemed to satisfy the young woman, as she turned away to talk to the other members of her family.

A few more people entered the great hall. Of different heights and coloring, their looks were so varied, I surmised they must be the "honored guests" Jondan had spoken of, the ones who had commissioned the Hausters directly instead of going through more direct, lawful means.

As the guests took seats around the room, blue-jacketed servants appeared instantly at their sides, offering them cups of wine to drink or small tidbits of food to nibble on. I slowly sank onto a bench, near where my friends-disguised-as-servants were arranging food on a table. Across the room, the young woman and the lady I presumed was her mother also sat. Their immediate duties completed, the servants returned to their original positions by the back wall, near the entry. The anticipation in the air was palpable.

I looked around, wondering what we were waiting for, when the faerie lights set in the walls of the great hall went out. The room was plunged into darkness, and several voices cried out in confusion.

And then the lights suddenly returned, concentrating on a single hooded figure standing at the front of the room in a dark blue robe, similar in shade to the formal coats the servants wore.

The hooded person chuckled. "Please forgive the theatrics, but it always gives me great pleasure to indulge in them."

In a more dignified manner, the decidedly masculine voice continued, "Welcome, honored guests, to the sanctuary of the Hauster family. I am the Haudaure, and it is my great honor and privilege to present to you those you have tasked us to hunt."

He waved a hand, and Jondan and another guard brought forth the four prisoners. Two of them looked completely confused or unaware of what was about to befall them. One of them, a man shackled next to Delphine, had a terrified expression on his face. Delphine squinted against the light, looking into the darkened room. A casual observer would have thought she was just resigning herself to her fate, but I knew she was trying to ascertain where her mother and her friends were in the room. Unfortunately, we hadn't had a way to let Delphine know the details of our plan to rescue her. I hoped she wouldn't fight me when it was time for 'Lord Olivera' to take her away.

"It is customary, and necessary, for us to magically bind our quarry to the Hauster estate for safekeeping," the Hauduare said. "As such, when our esteemed patrons have gathered here, we can then release that binding and turn them over to you. The magical binding will link a patron to their intended prisoner, allowing you to remove them from our stronghold, and will expire the moment you leave the hill and step aboveground. Dear honored guests, I hope you came prepared."

There was a slight chuckle from the seated Hauster patrons.

"Now then, we shall begin."

The hooded man turned to Delphine, the first prisoner in the line. "Delphine Pahame, commissioned by Lord Olivera for us to find. Lord Olivera, if you would approach, please?"

My breath caught as my heart pounded. But what else could I do? I had to get Delphine's binding transferred to me. I stood up, a bit shakily, and carefully made my way to where Delphine was standing with the mysterious hooded man in the pool of faerie light.

Meanwhile, Jondan unlocked the shackles that bound Delphine to the other prisoners. Delphine made a slight movement, as if she was going to run. Her eyes widened when she realized she couldn't move from the spot where she stood.

"You are Lord Olivera?" the Hauduare asked me when I reached them.

I nodded, that silly gold feather keeping time with my bobbing head. I briefly lifted my chin higher and looked squarely at Delphine.

Our eyes locked. Her mouth opened slightly as she recognized me under the ridiculous green hat.

Please don't say anything! Please don't give me away!

She composed herself quickly and looked down, but not before I saw a slight smirk creeping over the corners of her mouth.

"Lord Olivera, the final payment, please." An expectant hand reached out from the dark blue robe towards me, palm up.

"Mmmm ..." I started, not sure what to say or do.

The hand withdrew. "My goodness, I nearly forgot. You already paid us, last night. And with an extremely generous bonus. Thank you for that."

"Mmmm ..." I said again, putting a haughty confidence behind the sound. It seemed the safest thing I could say.

"Well, then," the Hauduare said. He took Delphine's hand in one of his, ignoring her shrinking away from him. Reaching out toward me again, he placed his other hand on my shoulder.

"Delphine Pahame," he intoned, "your binding to the Hauster family and our land is no longer. You will be bound to this man until the moment you both leave our holdings. Should you find a way to circumvent this magical binding, your life will immediately be forfeit. *Fiat*."

Where the Hauduare's hand enveloped Delphine's, a blue light pulsed. It traveled through the man's arm, into his body, and ran down his other arm to where his hand touched my shoulder. The blue light grew stronger and brighter, then suddenly winked out. When the man released my shoulder, I touched the area where his hand had been, feeling the slight tingle of magic in my muscle.

The Hauduare released Delphine's hand and turned to me. "Thank you, Lord Olivera. You may sit down. Our next person is —"

A commotion in the back of the room caught our attention. The door to the great hall slammed open, and an angry man's voice called out, "That's not Lord Olivera. I am."

Chapter Twenty-Seven

THE HAUDUARE CLAPPED his hands, and all the lights in the room came back on. As the rest of the onlookers squinted in the suddenly bright room, Lord Olivera stomped into the great hall, holding the remains of his gaudy green-and-gold belt. Or, more accurately, he squelched. One of his shoes and part of his breeches were completely soaked. Despite the seriousness of our situation, I had to suppress a smile at the thought of Lord Olivera waking up in the cleaners' closet after snoozing in a puddle of water.

He threw the belt down as he furiously walked toward the front of the room, pointing at Delphine. "That woman is mine. I paid for her. I even paid extra to ensure that your family would get to her first, before anyone could act upon those wanted posters! Her binding should have been transferred to me."

A guard stepped in front of Lord Olivera, preventing the nobleman from stepping right up to the Hauduare. Without a break in stride, Lord Olivera punched the guard square in the jaw. While the guard was disoriented, Lord Olivera grabbed the sword from the man's belt and lunged forward, skewering him with his own weapon. The guard crumpled to the floor.

The great hall erupted into chaos.

Lord Olivera, now armed, continued his advance. Someone — one of the honored guests, I think — screamed. Scared servants scattered out of the room. Another guest fainted.

Jondan and the other guard in charge of the prisoners both drew their swords, placing the Hauduare behind them. I grabbed Delphine's wrist and pulled her around the far side of the great hall, hoping to escape with her in the pandemonium.

At one end of the room, the elderly man started to stand, waving his arms. "Order! Order, I say!" His words were choked off as he fell back in his seat, clutching at his chest. Dismayed, the other members of the Family fluttered around him.

Lord Olivera was so intent on reaching the Hauduare that it took him several moments before he realized Delphine was no longer among the group standing at the front of the room.

"Where is she?" he roared, swinging his sword around wildly.

Jondan had been herding the Hauduare farther away from the commotion. The other guard, left to protect their retreat, raised his own sword to block Lord Olivera's swing. Lord Olivera turned toward him and almost casually cut off the guard's hand. The guard screamed and fell back, clutching his bloody wrist. The guard's now useless sword clanged to the stone floor.

Delphine and I were now halfway to the door of the great hall. Adallia, Rhyss, and Farrah fought their way to our side. Between the frightened servants and the screaming guests running around and getting in our way, we hadn't covered as much distance as quickly as I would have liked.

"Why didn't you kill him?" Rhyss panted as he reached us.

"I can't kill a nobleman," I said. I realized how incredibly inane the words were the moment they left my mouth.

"He was already dead!" Rhyss countered.

At the front of the room, Lord Olivera quickly knelt down and retrieved the injured guard's fallen sword. Now doubly armed, he spotted us trying to make our escape.

Delphine shrieked. I looked up, right into Lord Olivera's manic eyes. There was no one standing between him and me, but for the moment, I was hemmed in by my friends on one side and a crush of people on the other.

Time seemed to slow as Lord Olivera desperately wielded one of the swords like a spear and threw it at me.

Next to me, Dephine's eyes were wide in terror and she began shaking violently. The feeling of gathering magic was thick in the air, and I knew, with sickening certainty, that Delphine's untrained magic was about to be unleashed.

So I would either be killed by Delphine's wild magic, or by the point of the sharp sword that was even now hurling through the air toward me ....

Before the sword could reach me, and before Delphine lost control, the Hauduare stepped past Jondan and spoke. Even though he didn't raise his voice over the noise in the great hall, it somehow rang through the entire room loud enough for all to hear.

"That. Is. Enough."

As everyone's heads turned toward the Hauduare, the waiting magic gathered around Delphine flew from her side to his. He twisted his left hand in the air and everyone in the room froze in place, able to move our heads but not our bodies.

The sword stopped where it was mid-air, just a finger's length from my face.

My Seeker senses had come fully alive. A powerful force was drawing me to the man, made more painful by the fact that I couldn't move my body due to his magical freeze spell.

The Hauduare, unaffected by the spell, stepped toward Delphine and me. His hood fell back as he studied us with an inscrutable expression.

Adallia gasped in shock.

"Baxley?"

Chapter Twenty-Eight

THE HAUDUARE — OR, Baxley — turned to fully face Adallia when she called his name. Gray streaks ran through his dark brown hair, but his gaze was sharp as he turned his dark brown eyes in our direction.

For a long moment, he didn't say anything, just stared back at Adallia. Everyone in the room seemed to be collectively holding their breath, either confused or worried as to what was happening.

Then Baxley spoke, his sonorous voice now barely above a whisper.

"Adallia?"

Mutely, Adallia nodded once. A tear slipped down her cheek.

Baxley stepped toward Adallia.

With his attention divided, I could feel the stillness spell beginning to fray. The sword at my face clanged to the floor. Crisis averted, I tried to move my arms, my legs, anything.

But Lord Olivera overcame the spell first. Yelling incoherently, he charged at Adallia, his remaining sword raised to strike.

Still bound by magic, Adallia could only turn her head as she saw Lord Olivera running toward her.

And then Baxley reached out a hand toward Lord Olivera. The nobleman's sword clattered to the ground as his face and arm twisted in pain. The sword just missed Adallia, as Lord Olivera flew through the air, his back slamming against the wall. He seemed to be pinned against the wall by an invisible force.

Baxley made another motion with his hand, and several vines suddenly grew out of the immaculate stone walls, binding Lord Olivera securely.

Spell completed, Baxley dropped his hand, reaching out to Adallia, who had slumped to the floor when the original spell freezing us in place had lifted.

"Are you all right?" he asked, his voice gentle. Adallia took his proffered hand and allowed him to help her up.

"Yes, I am. Th- thank you." The normally self-possessed Lady Adallia Pahame seemed flustered and unsure of herself. Indeed, both she and Baxley seemed hesitant, as if they didn't know the proper way to greet each other after all these years. Which, given the circumstances, of course made sense.

A discreet cough from the direction of the Family recalled Baxley to himself. He released Adallia's hand. Reluctantly, perhaps?

Baxley looked around the great hall. His face darkened as he took in the two guards on the floor, one slain and one wounded. Around the room, everyone else was moving fingers and legs experimentally, shaking off the residual feeling of being frozen in place.

Baxley snapped his fingers at a servant who had recovered from the spell faster than the others. "Go fetch more guards. And servants." The servant nodded and scurried away.

To two nearby guards, Baxley said, "Before you can take care of your fallen comrades, I need you to take this one —" he flicked his chin at Lord Olivera, still pinned by vines to the wall "— and secure him in a cell. If he gets roughed up in the process, I don't really care."

The men moved toward the nobleman pinned to the wall, daggers in hand. Lord Olivera eyed them warily, noting the gleam in both guards' eyes.

Jondan, now completely free of Baxley's frozen spell, quickly moved to the side of the injured guard and took off his uniform jacket, wrapping it around the man's bleeding wrist.

On the opposite side of the room, the young woman spoke up. "Hauduare, what of the Ceremony?"

Baxley shook his head. His voice strident once more, he said, "We will have to postpone it. There's too many questions that need answers." He looked again at Adallia. "Starting with you. What are you doing here?"

Adallia faltered under his gaze. "I ... I —"

For the first time, Baxley noticed what Adallia was wearing. He took in Rhyss and Farrah, standing just behind Adallia. He frowned, not recognizing them.

Then he turned to me, dressed as Lord Olivera, and saw my hand still wrapped around Delphine's wrist. I could see him rapidly puzzle out what was going on.

"None of you are servants, are you." It was a statement, not a question.

"Baxley, I can explain," Adallia started. "These people are my friends, they're —"

There was a perfunctory knock at the door of the great hall, and four new guards entered.

Baxley pointed first at the group of prisoners at the front of the room, and then at Delphine. "Secure them back in their cells."

A pair of guards stepped forward to herd the prisoners out of the room while another guard knelt down to help Jondan with the injured man. The two guards marched the three shackled prisoners out of the room, collecting Delphine on the way. She threw me a desperate look as she was taken from the room.

The guards at the wall had finished cutting Lord Olivera down and had bound his hands none too gently with the remains of the magic vine. They escorted Lord Olivera out of the room.

Baxley turned to my group, grumbling. "Now, what to do with you? I should lock all of you up as well."

His resolve softened when his eyes glanced at Adallia again. He called out to Jondan. "You there!"

Jondan immediately stood to attention. "Sir."

"You and one of the other guards, take these people to the empty rooms in the east wing of the Family level. Then stand watch outside their rooms."

Baxley leveled that steel gaze on Rhyss, Farrah, Adallia, and me again. "For now, they are to be my guests. Until I decide otherwise."

Chapter Twenty-Nine

SENSING THAT IT WOULD be unwise to put up a fight, Farrah, Rhyss, Adallia, and I fell into step as Jondan and another guard corralled us out of the room.

The injured guard got to his feet with the help of his friend, and the two of them followed behind us.

As we marched away from the great hall, a flurry of servants passed us, ready to begin the thankless task of cleaning the Ceremony's aftermath. Patrice took up the rear, fuming. "Where are my cleaners?" As she caught sight of us and our escort, she stopped. "Oh. Never mind."

We continued down the hallway, with the injured man and his escort going up a level while we went down two flights of stairs, entering the floor where the Family's private rooms were. My mind raced furiously. Jondan was on our side; surely if my friends and I wanted to overpower the other guard and escape, he would help us. Even though we didn't have any weapons between us. But there was still the matter of Delphine, who was now locked away again on the prison level.

And if we left now, we'd never be able to retrieve Baxley, either.

No, it really would be unwise to try to fight our way out of this. Better to play along, for now, and be watchful for a better opportunity to escape.

We reached the end of the hallway. Jondan opened a wooden door and strode inside. My group shuffled in, looking around at our new, and hopefully temporary, surroundings.

The rock walls, emitting their strange magical light, grew brighter as we entered the room. The room was plain, but serviceable. There was a bed in the middle of the room, big enough for two people to sleep comfortably. A blue velvet divan was tucked into one corner of the room. There was also an overstuffed blue paisley armchair with a matching ottoman in the other corner.

"If they're to be guests, should we put them in separate rooms?" Jondan's companion asked him.

"There really aren't any extra rooms," Jondan said. "I suppose we could use Lord Olivera's room, since he's now staying in a prison cell, but one of the servants would have to clean it out, first. I'm sure Lord Olivera's things are still in his former room."

The other man nodded. "Then I suppose this will have to do, for now."

"And us guards will be stretched thin, what with Rennin gone and Trest losing his hand ... curse that Lord Olivera." Jondan frowned. "Rennin was a good man, from the short time I knew him. I hope Trest will be all right."

The guard sighed. "It's the perils of the job. Doesn't make it any easier. I can stand watch, if you like."

My heart sank. I had hoped Jondan would stay and be our guard, so perhaps we might be able to discuss a new escape plan once the other man had left.

"Thank you," Jondan said. "That would be most helpful. I need to get back to the great hall right away; I'm sure the Hauduare will want a full report of what occurred."

The other man walked out of the room, Jondan on his heels. At the door, he turned slightly, catching my eye and giving me a significant look. He then left, shutting the wooden door firmly behind him.

We heard a key turning in the lock. One set of footsteps receded into the distance. Then, silence.

Farrah sank down slowly onto the edge of the bed as Rhyss flopped dramatically into the overstuffed armchair. "So, now what?" He wiggled further into the armchair, getting settled. "Although as prisons go, this is actually quite comfortable."

I crossed the room, taking up residence on the velvet divan. "Well, the good news is: We found everyone we came here to find." Both Farrah and Adallia gave me a "you can't be serious" look. I shrugged. "Just thought I would lead with the positive."

"We found everyone," Farrah repeated flatly. "Great. Except Delphine's locked up again, Jondan just abandoned us, and Baxley turned out to be the leader of one of the most feared bounty hunter families in the kingdom of Rothschan. You'll have to excuse me, but I'm missing the 'positive' parts of all of this."

Adallia sat down next to Farrah, her face pale. Her hands were shaking. "I can't believe ... after all this time ..."

Farrah took the noblewoman's hands in her own. "Are you all right, Adallia?"

Adallia shook her head. "The Baxley I knew would never have aligned himself with a family like this. And to see Lord Olivera, alive and unharmed! If he hadn't died due to my daughter's magic, then why were there wanted posters of her everywhere? He could have stopped it ... but he didn't."

The rest of us stayed silent. None of us had any answers for her.

Finally, I spoke up. "Does anyone have any ideas for how we can get out of here? And take at least Delphine and Jondan with us?"

But although we talked for some length, we couldn't come up with a course of action that seemed like it would work. We just had to hope Jondan would return, and would still want to be our ally.

There was nothing to do but wait. Rhyss fell asleep quickly in the paisley chair, limbs awkwardly hanging askew over the ottoman and the armrests. The two women each claimed a spot on the bed, and I stretched out on the velvet divan. My legs were a touch too long for the low couch, but I arranged myself as comfortably as I could.

The excitement of the day caught up to me. As my eyelids grew heavy, I barely managed to send a prayer out into the universe, to whatever gods were listening, that we would somehow find a way out of this situation.

Chapter Thirty

THE SOUND OF THE KEY turning in the lock again instantly woke me out of a dreamless sleep. I sat up, squinting in the light radiating from the rock walls.

Farrah and Rhyss, already fully awake, held themselves in readiness. Adallia's eyes fluttered open and she sat up groggily as the door swung open.

A servant entered the room first, bearing a tray of food and a small ceramic pitcher with a few stacked glasses. He put the tray down on a nearby table and left the room.

Jondan entered next. I stood up to greet him, but he put his hand out and his finger to his lips. He jerked his head toward the door, indicating there were people out there who could be listening in. He stepped to the side as he announced, "The Hauduare."

Baxley appeared at the door.

Now even Adallia was fully awake, although I was the only one who had actually moved from their spot. We all just stared at Baxley as he entered the room. Baxley nodded at Jondan, who nodded back and then closed the door, leaving the leader of the Hauster family alone in the room with us.

Baxley regarded each of us in turn, studying Adallia the most. There was an incredibly long and uncomfortable moment of silence.

And then:

"It really is you," Baxley said, suddenly at Adallia's side in two quick strides. She hastily tried to smooth her hair and straighten her dress, but from the rapturous look on Baxley's face, it was obvious he didn't care about her disheveled appearance. He was seeing the Adallia he once knew, the girl he had loved and lost so many long years ago.

From the look on Adallia's face, she was seeing Baxley as he once was, too.

I looked away, suddenly feeling like I had intruded on a private moment, even though technically Baxley was the one barging in. I noticed Farrah and Rhyss studiously avoiding looking at Baxley and Adallia as well. Apparently I wasn't the only one feeling vaguely embarrassed.

I also felt a bit weightless, like I had been relieved of a huge burden that, up until this moment, I hadn't been aware I was carrying. Which was exactly how I felt after a commission was fulfilled. Except usually that relieved feeling was immediately replaced by one of dread, since my commissions rarely ended on a happy note. Often one or both parties were left the sadder for having found each other. If my "gift" of seeking had taught me anything, it was that it was best to leave the past alone.

I sneaked a peek over at the — happy? — couple. They were still lost in each others' eyes; nothing more untoward than that was happening. I coughed discreetly, hoping to get their attention.

It didn't work. I coughed again, a little louder. I inhaled a little too much air and started coughing in earnest.

That got their attention. Baxley stepped back, the moment between them broken.

He grabbed the pitcher and the glass on the top of the stack, pouring a half glass of water and then holding it out to me. I nodded at him gratefully as I took the glass from him, downing the water in one drink.

"Are you all right?" Adallia asked once I had finished drinking.

"Yes, yes, I'm fine," I said, waving off her concern. I looked at Baxley. "Thank you."

"You're welcome." Looking around at all of us, he sighed. "Well, I suppose we should start. Who are you, and why are you here?"

"We came to get my daughter back," Adallia said. "We were traveling west, with the intent to stop by Rothschan, when your people took her from our camp during the night."

"Your daughter?" Baxley looked thoughtful. "Ah, yes, Lord Olivera's commission."

"Why did you —?" Adallia started to ask, but Baxley held a hand out to interrupt.

"I will have my answers first. Then, if I deem you worthy … perhaps you shall have yours."

We settled down. Baxley said, "So you came here, disguised as servants, to try to steal your friend and daughter back. Fair enough. But, if I may ask, why were you traveling to Rothschan in the first place? Of all the kingdoms in the Gifted Lands, it's not known for its … hospitality."

Rhyss, Farrah, and I stayed silent, waiting for Adallia to mention the commission that brought us out this way in the first place. But she didn't say anything. Was she embarrassed to admit to wanting to find her lost love?

Or was she too scared and upset by what he had become?

When the silence stretched out uncomfortably, Baxley said, "All right, if you don't want to answer my questions, no matter. So then, I won't be answering any of yours." He turned to open the door.

"We came to find you," I blurted out.

Baxley slowly turned back around. "You came to find *me*? Why?" There was a slight undercurrent of menace in his voice, reminding me that he *was* the head of one of the most feared bounty hunter clans in the kingdom.

Adallia turned horror-stricken eyes on me, but I shrugged. What did we have to lose by telling him? If anything, maybe it would help us gain his trust.

"I am a Seeker," I said. "My specialty is finding lost loves. I am the only one in my family with this gift; my sister and my father are talented Seekers whose abilities work normally to seek out people's true loves. Lady Adallia Pahame commissioned me to find her lost love. We were following your vague trail when her daughter was captured. We didn't expect that, in trying to rescue her daughter, we would also find the person we were ultimately seeking."

I thought that Baxley would be flattered, or at least intrigued, to find out that Adallia had been wanting to reconnect with him. But I was surprised at what he latched onto from my little speech.

"You're a Seeker?" Baxley asked me. I nodded. "You mentioned a sister. What is her name? And your father? Both Seekers like you?"

"Not at all like me," I said. "Their gifts —"

"Yes, yes, you said that," Baxley said, a touch impatiently. "I mean, their seeking abilities — your whole family's — has to do with love?"

"Yes."

"Well, then, their names. Tell me their names."

"My sister's name is Kaela," I said slowly. "She's my twin. And my father is Julian, Lord —"

"Asthore." Baxley finished my sentence without any hesitation.

"Yes. How did you know that?"

Baxley's eyes were bright as he stared at me. "Because Julian Asthore is my brother."

Chapter Thirty-One

"YOU'RE MY UNCLE?" I asked incredulously.

"Yes," Baxley said.

"But ... I don't have an uncle." Or did I? Frantically, I racked my brain, trying to remember any family gatherings where he surely would have been present. Or any mention of him by my father or mother. But ... there was nothing.

Baxley smiled wryly. "Should I be hurt that my esteemed and loving family completely forgot to mention me to my nephew?" The sarcasm that dripped from his voice told me what he *really* thought of the Asthores.

"Why don't I remember you, though?" I wondered. "I'm trying to place you in my memory ... but I can't."

"Because I left Orchwell — and the Asthore family — when you and your sister were very small. I don't think you two were even a year old yet."

That made sense, then, why I didn't recall ever seeing him at any family functions. But ... "Father never talked about you, though. I sort of remember him saying something about a younger brother, but for some reason I thought you had died before Kaela and I were born."

Baxley snorted. "I'm sure he and the rest of the family wished that I had, but alas, that is yet another way I am a disappointment to them."

Small vague fragments of memory started to pop into my mind. One of my first conversations with Adallia, about the man she was seeking and what had happened between them. A man from a long and cultured line of Seekers. One that would disown him for marrying beneath his station. And obviously, my father had known who Adallia was.

And Adallia, knowing the full history between my family and hers, had chosen to keep some information from me.

Some crucial, important information.

I rounded on Adallia, who was still sitting on the bed. "Madam, you *knew*. You knew that we were were going to be looking for my *uncle*, and you didn't tell me."

Adallia shook her head, tears silently running down her cheeks. "If your father didn't see fit to tell you, I certainly couldn't. It wasn't my place. I've already hurt your family enough. And if we never found him ... then would it even matter if you knew that my lost love and your lost uncle were one and the same person?"

She had a point, albeit a weak one. My head was spinning from all the revelations that were coming to light. It was enough to make me long for one of my regular commissions — the kind that inevitably ended in misery and drama, but at least it was not drama that involved me and my family directly.

I turned back to Baxley. "Well then, uncle, it's nice to meet you. And, seeing as how we're *family* —" I grinned at Baxley, who grinned back "— then I hope you would ever-so-kindly answer some of *our* questions. Starting with, Why are *you* here?"

"That's simple," Baxley said. "I married into the Hauster family several years back. But to give you the full answer I know you want ... May I?" He indicated the ottoman at Rhyss's feet. Rhyss nodded, taking his feet from the ottoman and pushing the small seat toward Baxley.

"Thank you," Baxley said, as he pulled the ottoman away from Rhyss and toward the table by the door, where he could see all of us as he spoke. As he settled himself on the ottoman, I sank down at my original place on the low couch.

"Let's see, where should I begin," he mused. "Well, after I left Orchwell, I came to Rothschan with some vague idea of hiring myself out as a mercenary. Which was a very short-lived idea." He chuckled to himself. "When I left home, I hadn't really thought things through, other than wanting to run away from my pain as fast and as far away as possible. So I was living on the streets of Rothschan, broke and utterly emotionally devastated."

Adallia looked down at her hands, placed demurely in her lap. "I'm so sorry."

"Don't be," Baxley said gently. "You couldn't have known. And you were dealing with your own issues back in Orchwell."

"If I had gone with you ..."

"Then we *both* would have been struggling on the streets. It worked out the way it had to, my dear."

There was an uncomfortable moment of silence. Then, sighing, Baxley continued. "It was at my most desperate point that Eldan, the previous head of the Hauster clan, found me. I would have been happy enough to do even the most menial task for him, if it meant regular meals and a roof over my head. But when he learned that I came from a well-known line of Seekers, he decided that I could best serve by using my special abilities in service of the Family."

"How?" I interrupted. "You can't tell me the Hauster family suddenly needed to find several love matches for their children? Unless I was mistaken, I only saw one girl of marriageable age among your group."

"You are correct," Baxley said. "And Shelda is not married, or even betrothed. The others you saw with her are her great-grandparents, from her father's side, and her mother. Both couples had been quite happily matched and had no need for an Asthore Seeker's services."

"So, then, what did this Eldan want with your abilities?"

Now it was Baxley's turn to look down at his hands, fidgeting in his lap. I realized in the short time since I'd met him, the last thing I would have expected of this poised, authoritative man was *fidgeting*. He seemed almost ... ashamed.

"I'm sure you've noticed this fortress, and how magic is part of its makeup," Baxley said. "Eldan was a powerful magician, and used his magic to create this hidden house in the hillside for his family. While his family excels in what they do as bounty hunters, the magical ability doesn't always breed true. His parents — the elderly couple you saw in the great hall — don't have it. Neither did Eldan's son, who passed away years ago, nor his granddaughter, Shelda. She was the young woman you would have seen earlier. I wasn't born a magician either, but with the right, shall we say, *magical persuasion*, my inborn ability to find someone's true love could be adjusted to seek out things that assist the Family ... out of love."

Around the room, the horror I felt was reflected on the faces of my friends as we all stared at Baxley. It felt like no one dared breathe, let alone speak. Finally, outrage laced through my voice, I said, "Eldan perverted your Seeker ability to only work in service for the Hauster family?"

Baxley's mouth twisted into a bitter smile. "And imagine how much easier it was to fulfill commissions after that! Not to mention other, occasional odd jobs that somehow seemed to become more frequent. Indeed, the Family's fortunes practically tripled after I came. And as a reward for my ... *help* ... Eldan taught me some rudimentary magic. More importantly, he allowed me to marry his daughter and trained me to be the next Hauduare.

"We were happy enough, I suppose. She was a sweet woman, but she had the misfortune of being born into the wrong family. She didn't have the temperament for it. She died while on a commission with her father Eldan and her niece Shelda. Shelda was the only one to escape with her life that day; I understand Eldan died trying to defend my wife. I didn't have much love for the man, but I did admire his fierceness in protecting what he loved."

"If your wife and father-in-law are both gone, what's keeping you here?" Rhyss asked. And then, "Ow!" as a shoe flew through the air and hit him in the shoulder. He rubbed his shoulder and glared at Farrah, who had picked her shoe off the floor by the bed and launched it at him. "Why'd you do that?"

Farrah glared back unrepentantly. "I swear, Rhyss, someday your mouth's going to get you into some real trouble, and I won't be around to help you. You can't just ask such rude questions."

Baxley's laughter lightened the room's mood considerably. "I appreciate your concern, Miss, uh ...?"

"Farrah."

"Good to meet you, Farrah," Baxley said, a chuckle coloring his words. "It's all right, though, it's a fair question."

Rhyss shot Farrah a triumphant look. Farrah rolled her eyes back at him.

Baxley grew somber again. "The truth is, I can't leave. To tap into my ability completely, Eldan tethered my Seeker gift to this place. Which is why I never go on any commissions with the others. I haven't been more than a few feet beyond this hill since I first stepped foot inside. And, before you ask it, I will say again that Eldan was a powerful magician."

Ah, of course. That explained it, then. I didn't know much about magic, but from what I understood, most spells died with the caster. Only those with great power and ability were able to create spells that lasted beyond their lifetime, although even those spells would eventually decay and fade as well. The sheer scope of the Hauster fortress and all its inner workings told me that Eldan had been quite powerful.

Adallia spoke up, her voice unsure. "But Baxley ... do you ... do you *want* to leave?"

He regarded her thoughtfully for a few moments before answering. "I didn't come here under the best of circumstances, but I've come to care about the Family as if it were my own. In some ways they've been better to me than the Asthores were. I'm not even considered an Asthore anymore — my own family disowned me when I ran away, and I had to adopt the Hauster name when I married into the family. And, as they are my in-laws, they *are* my family.

"But I'm also so, so weary. Every time I use my ability to assist the Family, I feel another piece of my soul chip away. Using my Seeker ability, twisted beyond recognition, is ultimately killing me. Soon there will be nothing left of what Baxley Asthore once was, and I shudder to think of what will remain." He looked at each of us in turn, his gaze finally resting on Adallia. "Which is why I will help you free your daughter and leave this place. And when you go, I will go with you, even if it means my death."

Chapter Thirty-Two

RHYSS RELAXED BACK into his chair, the ottoman under his feet once more. "Well, that was a lot easier than I thought it would be."

Baxley had left our room, promising to return as soon as he could. Hopefully with Delphine, and without any problems. Jondan was still "keeping watch" outside the door, having been drawn in for a brief but intense round of planning with our group.

Baxley had gone to the prison level to retrieve Delphine. As the Hauduare, no one would question his motives if he wanted to interrogate a prisoner away from her cell. Once Baxley and Delphine returned, we would slip away from the compound under the cover of night. My friends and I had been in the Hauster fortress for the greater part of the day, with the aborted Ceremony taking place in the afternoon. If it wasn't dark already outside, it would be soon.

Rhyss sighed, leaning his head back and closing his eyes. He looked like he didn't have a care in the world. I was envious. And a little worried. He was right, it *had* been easy to convince Baxley to leave his life here behind and come with us. Perhaps it had been a little too easy?

Adallia frowned at me. "He's not going to betray us. Baxley does want to leave, and he's truly going to help us. I know it."

Oops. I must have spoken aloud.

In a placating tone, I said, "You know him better than any of us do. If you say he can be trusted, then we'll trust him." *Mostly because we don't have any other options, either.*

Adallia looked slightly mollified. "Anyway, Kaernan, he's your uncle. Now that you've found each other, he won't let go of that easily. He's family, and family is important to him."

Farrah, sitting next to Adallia in the bed, caught my eye. She wisely refrained from saying anything, but I could see my worries reflected in her eyes. *Yes, family was important to Baxley. But which one?*

Something in Farrah's gaze flickered ever so slightly, and I knew she, too, would be on her guard. We wouldn't be safe until we were in Orchwell again — and maybe not even then. Would it be possible for Baxley to safely extricate himself from the Hauster family, or would they forever be hunting him?

But I knew better than to voice *that* aloud. I didn't know if that thought had occurred to Adallia, or if the excitement of finding Baxley overshadowed any of the realities that would inevitably come their way. Then again, Adallia and Delphine were technically on the run, so perhaps they would be accepting of a life of constant pursuit. Although finding Lord Olivera alive meant they could return home without his supposed murder hanging over Delphine's head anymore. If they could prove that he was still alive to the Orchwell authorities, of course.

I forced myself to stop chasing the various threads of thought, lest I get sucked into the whirlpool of never-ending possibilities. Best to just focus on one thing at a time. And the thing we needed to focus on was getting out of here undetected with Delphine, Jondan, and Baxley.

"I know it's hard, but try to relax," Rhyss said, eyes still closed. "Lie down, take a nap. There's nothing else to do while we wait, anyway."

"Rhyss is right, Kaernan, conserve your energy," Farrah said. "We're going to need to be as sharp as possible later on."

I stretched out on the low couch again, my ankles and feet awkwardly dangling off the end. Settling in as best I could, I closed my eyes, all of my worries and unanswered questions chasing each other in my mind.

A SOFT TAPPING AT THE door roused me out of my sleep. This time it was harder for me to wake up; I felt like I was fighting through layers upon layers of fabric, trying to break free. I opened bleary eyes and sat up, still shaking off the feeling of grogginess.

Jondan entered, followed by Baxley and ...

"Delphine!" Adallia was instantly on her feet and embracing her daughter. Her voice was thick with the tears she was trying to hold back. "I was so worried for you, afraid we'd never be able to get you out of that cell. And when that hateful Lord Olivera tried to take you ..."

Delphine shuddered, even while she held her mother close. "It's all right, mama. I'm here now."

Delphine stepped back from her mother's embrace, greeting the rest of us in turn.

Once the greetings had died down, Baxley took charge. "Sunset approaches, and with it a guard change. Jondan has the first watch tonight."

"Convenient," I remarked, and Jondan grinned.

"Quite," he said. "It helps to have people in high places on your side."

"Once Jondan is in place, we'll wait until it's fully dark, and then leave the fortress. It shouldn't be too difficult; once we reach the forest we'll be fairly well concealed," Baxley said.

I snorted. "You make it sound easy, but I know better than to believe that." To Jondan, I asked, "Will you be returning back to your family in Rothschan? I'm sure your mother and sister are anxious to see you and know that you're safe."

Sadly, Jondan shook his head. "It's not a good idea; Rothschan is too close to this place, and I don't want to endanger them by returning home and making them a target. I'll head to Orchwell with you, and send a message back home once I'm there. If that's all right with you," he added, a note of uncertainty creeping into his voice.

"Of course it is," I said. "And you're welcome to be a guest at Asthore Manor for as long as you need to stay."

"Hopefully it's not as long as all that," Jondan said, but his original uncertainty was replaced with relief and gratitude.

Turning to Baxley, I said, "And if you need a place to stay, you're also welcome at Asthore Manor. If my father gets upset about it ... well, let's just say it won't be the worst thing he's been upset with me about."

"Thank you." Baxley smiled wryly. "I don't think my brother will exactly greet me with open arms, but I appreciate the invitation. But first, I have to make it as far as Orchwell to be able to take you up on that."

"You will," Adallia said encouragingly. Rhyss, Farrah, and I kept silent. Delphine looked confused.

"What should we do now, while we wait for it to get dark?" I asked. "How are we going to slip out without anyone seeing us?"

"Don't worry, it should be fairly easy for all of you to leave," Baxley said. "I have called a Family meeting, to be starting shortly. We have much to discuss since the Ceremony never happened, plus we need to decide what to do with Lord Olivera. I hope it won't take too long, but having this meeting will definitely pull attention away from the hallways — and your group. There are two ways in and out of the hill, but one of them is a secret entrance only for Family use. Everyone else must use the main entrance, the hillside's hidden door. Just take the back stairs all the way to the top level and exit out that door. Jondan will already be in place as guard. Wait in the forest until Jondan and I join you."

"But what about the servants? Or the guests? Won't they see us if everyone's leaving at the same time?"

Baxley shook his head. "The day servants have gone home, and the night staff has already arrived. Our contracts are magically binding; while the servants are allowed to leave, they are unable to disclose our location. Our guests meet us at our original estate in Rothschan to stable their horses or carriages, and are then blindfolded and escorted to the hill. Once they enter, they are magically unable to leave until after the Ceremony. We make exceptions, but in very rare cases. When a commission is completed and a guest leaves with their person, they step outside the hill and are magically transported back to the old estate. It's rather elaborate, but it's necessary to keep the Family safe."

I nodded, hoping our escape really would be as easy as Baxley made it sound. We all filed out of the room and into the hallway, where Baxley pointed out the servants' stairwell at the end of the hall.

"Hide there for a few moments, until Jondan has been relieved of his duty at your door. By that point, the Family meeting will be underway and no servants should be using the stairs, as they should be attending the needs of the Family and our guests, who will also be present at the meeting. After Jondan has left his post here and you reach the top level, he'll head straight to his new post at the front."

"Won't the other guard see us? The one Jondan is relieving?" Farrah asked.

"The guards usually don't bother with the servants' stairwell," Jondan said. "It's much faster for the guards to use the main stairs, as it's a more direct path."

Rhyss nodded. "We'll just wait for the other guard to clear the hallway, then. And if not ..." He reached down toward his boot, where his dagger was hidden, and waggled his eyebrows suggestively.

Farrah rolled her eyes, a common expression she used with her friend. "Let's try not to leave an obvious trail behind us as we sneak away, shall we?"

Jondan chimed in. "And many of those men are my friends. We're all just trying to earn a living ... or pay off a debt."

"No blood, then, sorry, got it," Rhyss said sheepishly. "Just unconscious?"

"How about not calling any attention to our group at all?" Farrah said.

Baxley coughed discreetly. Farrah and Rhyss immediately broke off their bickering. "I really shouldn't be late to the meeting I called," Baxley said pointedly. "If you would ...?" He pointed to the stairwell.

"Yes, my replacement should be here any minute," Jondan said, sounding worried.

Farrah, Rhyss, Adallia, Delphine, and I hurried to the end of the hall, climbing partway up the stone steps. As the last one up the stairs, I paused, straining to hear what was happening back at our former guest room.

We had just made it to our hiding spot. Footsteps echoed down the hallway, becoming louder until they stopped right around where our room was.

"Hey, Hahlrath," Jondan greeted the new guard.

"Hello yourself, Jondan. How's it been?"

"Boring. They just finished with dinner, and they're locked in again." I heard a door handle rattle slightly as Jondan demonstrated that fact. "It's not like anything's happening here. They're rather boring, as prisoners — guests? — go."

"Just my luck," Hahlrath said. "I'd much rather be in the Family meeting. There's sure to be good gossip to be had."

"Don't feel bad, I'm just as unlucky," Jondan said. "I'm on my way to do first watch up top."

The other guard laughed. "We'll have to grab some of the others for a pint later on to get caught up, then."

"Sounds good," Jondan said, laughing as well. "Have a good night, Hahlrath."

Hastily, I turned to the others and motioned that they should move up the stairs. Behind us, Jondan's footsteps retreated into the distance as he walked toward the other staircase. I hoped his departure would mask any noise our group was making.

Quickly and quietly, we headed up the stairwell to the second level. There, Farrah, who was in the lead, had us halt briefly while she made sure no one was around. But Baxley had been true to his word; the area was clear and silent.

We continued on, when Farrah stopped us again. She turned to us, her finger touching her lips as she cautioned us to stay quiet. Still at the rear, I strained to hear what was going on. Faintly, I could hear the heavy door open. I started counting mentally, trying to calm my anxious nerves.

... 30 ... 31 ... 32 ...

The fortress door shut. 38 ... 39 ...

Farrah waved her hand at us, indicating it was safe to move forward. Walking a little faster than the others, I reached the door to the outside first. Putting my hand on the door handle, I hesitated. Even though the other guard was at least one level down, it was so quiet in the fortress right now that I worried about any little noise.

Farrah caught up to me, eyebrows raised. Seemingly knowing what I was thinking, she shooed me away from the door. She touched the metal handle, concentrating as she muttered a spell under her breath.

The handle glowed a cool, icy purply-blue, a few shades lighter than Farrah's hair. As the color faded, she grasped the door handle and pulled.

The door opened effortlessly — and, to my surprise, completely silently. I couldn't help it; I gasped. On the other side of the door, a surprised Jondan peered inside at us. Farrah smirked at me before walking into the moonlight-bathed landscape outside.

The rest of us followed, awkwardly standing outside the hill fortress for a few moments as our eyes adjusted. Jondan shut the door behind us, asking quietly, "Nobody saw you?"

"No," I answered.

"Good. Are all of you ready, then?"

"Yes," I said, as the others in the group nodded their agreement. I looked around, realizing Jondan didn't have any sort of bag or knapsack with him. "How about you? Do you have everything you need before we go?"

Jondan held up his arm, where his sister Juneyen's bracelet was securely fastened in its proper place again. "I have everything I need right here."

He pointed toward the forest edging the meadow. "Hide in that stand of trees until Baxley and I join you. A Family meeting can sometimes last hours, but I know he'll rush them through things so he can get out here before the next watch. Our goal is to have at least a few hours' start from here before they discover anyone's missing."

"Wait!" I said as a horrible realization washed over me. "What are we going to do when the second watch guard comes to replace you? He'll realize you're gone and raise an alarm."

Jondan shrugged. "It's possible, but I doubt it. When I left him he was practically snoring in his cups ... and he'll have quite the headache when he wakes up tomorrow."

I frowned. "I didn't realize you had enough time to grab a drink with your comrades."

Jondan grinned. "Just one. But one is all you need when your boss gives you one of his sleeping potions to ... expedite things."

I shook my head, remembering how I felt the day after the Hausters had used their sleeping powder on us. "Poor man. He has my sympathies."

With that, we left Jondan and made our way to the forest, sticking to the shadows just in case, although I was fairly certain Jondan was the only guard on patrol. We made it to the forest's edge without incident and settled down, either on the ground or against the trees, to wait.

Chapter Thirty-Three

WAITING, EVEN WATCHFUL waiting, has a way of making it feel like time moves slowly. Slower, even, than waiting for my father to show approval. It hadn't been too long — maybe three-quarters of an hour, or a little more — when I saw movement in the shadows edging the clearing. Shortly thereafter, we were joined by the two final members of our group, Jondan and Baxley.

Jondan was holding up a surprisingly weak Baxley. Baxley was panting heavily, gulping in air so loudly that I was sure he could be heard inside the fortress. The moonlight streaming through the trees illuminated Baxley's pale, sweat-drenched face.

Horrified, I asked Jondan, "What happened?"

It was Baxley who answered me. "The ... spell. I ... can only ... go so ... far."

"It gets worse the farther we go," Jondan said worriedly. "And we're still in eyeshot of the fortress."

"There's no help for it," I said, hating at how callous I sounded but knowing we had little choice. "We need to get going. Let's find the horses; maybe riding will help ease the pain of the magical tether." *Or possibly make it worse.*

We slowly made our way to where we had left the horses earlier. Fortunately, they were still there, tied to the trees.

One of them nickered softly at our approach as Rhyss started to untie them. Farrah and Adallia began rummaging through the bushes, passing out our various belongings.

When Delphine reached for her pack, Jondan offered to carry it for her, but she shook her head. "I'm so happy to be carrying this again, because it means I'm free from that horrible ordeal," she whispered.

Our bags retrieved, we mounted our horses. While Adallia, Delphine, Farrah, Rhyss and I had our original mounts, we hadn't brought an extra horse for either Baxley or Jondan. Truth be told, Baxley looked too weak to be able to handle a horse on his own. We decided Baxley would ride with Adallia while Jondan rode with Delphine. It would slow us down, but maybe we could hire two more horses once we reached Meira.

ALTHOUGH WE MADE GOOD time riding — much better than if we had left our horses behind in Rothschan — our progress was still, to my mind, excruciatingly slow. It wasn't the horses; even carrying extra riders, they were fresh and excited to be out after several days' rest, first in the Rothschan stables and then while waiting for us to leave the fortress.

But Baxley's condition made it hard for us to go faster. No, that's not quite true. Once we cleared the forest and reached the road, we could have pushed the horses to a gallop to put as much distance as possible between us and the Hauster fortress. Indeed, we tried it. Baxley, who had already been moaning in intermittent pain as the horses picked their way through the forest, screamed in agony as soon as the horses increased their pace.

We immediately stopped the horses. I brought my horse alongside the mount Adallia and Baxley shared. Rhyss and Farrah kept a lookout, knowing that Baxley's scream would have attracted unwanted attention.

"What's wrong?" I asked urgently. "Baxley. Uncle ... are you okay?"

The poor man was shaking uncontrollably, shivering even as he sweated profusely. He could barely raise his voice above a hoarse whisper. "It hurts ... so much."

"What do we do?" Adallia's worried voice bordered on frantic. "We can't leave him ... nor can we take him back. But this ... this is killing him."

"Keep ... going ..." Baxley coughed out. "But not ... too fast. Hurts ... more ..."

"We should get going." Rhyss sounded apologetic, but his eyes were still darting everywhere. "Someone was bound to have heard his scream; we really shouldn't linger."

"Yes ..." Baxley said. "Let's ... go."

"Okay, then." I touched my uncle's shoulder briefly. "I'm sorry." To Adallia, "Let us know if it gets worse."

I spurred my horse forward, pushing it to a brisk trot. Behind me, Baxley moaned softly. Back stiff, I listened for any sounds of more intense pain, but he seemed to be holding steady.

Resolutely, I tuned out the sounds of my uncle's moaning and focused on the road ahead. The sooner we got home to Orchwell, the better. I hated to say it, but maybe my father would know what to do to help ease his brother's pain.

WE RODE THROUGH THE night, stopping for a few hours' sleep. I don't know about the others, but the short rest was anything but restful for me — between the worries racing through my mind and the intermittent yelps of pain from Uncle Baxley, I didn't get much sleep.

When the sun started to lighten overhead, I was the first one up and about, getting a cold, quick breakfast ready for everyone else. Carissa had been kind enough to give us some extra provisions, for which I was now extremely grateful. We ate quickly, deciding to press on until at least the late afternoon. We were all eager to get as far as we could.

We pressed on as the sun traveled its own path overhead. I stayed in the lead of our little group, my mind going over the various scenarios we might encounter on the road, in Meira, or back home in Orchwell. Behind me, Jondan and Delphine were talking in low voices.

"... And when he wouldn't stop, I yelled, 'No!'" Delphine said. "The next thing I knew I woke up and he was laid out flat."

"You did that?" Jondan's voice was a mix of disbelief and admiration.

"I guess so, I really don't remember. I was so worried I'd killed Olivera, I didn't really take the time to think about how it happened."

Their conversation was occasionally punctuated by quiet moans from Baxley. I briefly looked over my shoulder and caught Farrah's eye. She brought her horse forward, riding alongside me.

"What's on your mind, Kaernan?" she asked me.

"I'm worried about Baxley," I admitted. "He's doing his best to hold himself together. But he looks worse the farther we go, and I'm wondering ... what if there's a breaking point for his tether? What will happen?"

"I don't really know," Farrah said. "I may know magic, but this spell is beyond my knowledge or ability. Maybe my friend, Princess Jennica of Calia, would know what to do ... but she's not here."

"Can't you reach her using your magic?" Rhyss asked. "Beyan said there was some sort of communication spell Jennica used to use with her lady-in-waiting all the time."

She shook her head. "We tried it once, but there were some issues with the connection. It seems Fae magic, even from someone who's only half-Fae, is incompatible with the type of magic Jennica does."

Farrah surreptitiously glanced over her shoulder, trying to assess Baxley's condition. Turning back to me, she said, "When we make camp, I'll take a look at him. Healing is my specialty; I might be able to remove the pain, or at least dull it. But anything I can do for him right now will be temporary. We'll have to find a way to permanently break the spell if he's to have any sort of life away from the Hausters."

"My father has an extensive library, back at Asthore Manor," I said. "I know it includes a fairly good collection of Seeker history and lore. Perhaps you can find something that might help Baxley's condition there?"

"I hope so, but in the meantime, I'll do all I can. I promise."

I nodded as another low groan escaped my uncle's lips behind us. "Thank you, Farrah. It's all we can ask for."

BY LATE AFTERNOON, the events of the previous night — and the lack of a good night's sleep — had caught up to us. We set up camp in a small clearing set back from the road. Rhyss, looking exhausted, grabbed his bow and slunk off into the woods. Jondan helped Delphine set up camp while Adallia and I helped my uncle settle against a tree trunk, with Farrah following close behind.

Baxley's breathing was now coming in shallow gasps, and he could barely stand, let alone walk. Closing his eyes as he leaned against the tree, his skin seemed translucent with all the color drained from his face. Every so often a shuddering cough would interrupt his tortured breathing, and my heart ached at seeing how, in less than a day, the strong, confident man who was my newfound uncle had deteriorated so rapidly.

Farrah looked at Baxley, then back at me, distraught. She stood, motioning for me to join her a few feet away from my uncle. Adallia continued to fuss over Baxley.

In a low voice, Farrah said, "I'll have to work quickly, but I fear it might not be fast enough. If I can't help him ... I don't think he can make it another day."

I nodded. "I agree, he seems to be getting worse by the minute. Whatever you need, you let me know."

Farrah pursed her lips and headed back to her patient. Placing a hand on his shoulder, she concentrated briefly, then recoiled violently. "It's like there's a chain or a rope laced with poison holding him fast. I think I can remove the poison, and perhaps ease the pressure of the chain, but it will still be wrapped around him, and it will eventually leach its poison into his body again."

"Even a temporary solution is better than nothing. I have every faith in you, Farrah."

"Well, that's one of us then."

"Speaking of this magical chain ..."

"What? What's wrong?"

"Could the rest of the Family follow it, and find Baxley?"

"I don't ... think so," a weak Baxley said. Embarrassed, I looked over at him, realizing I must have spoken louder than I intended. He was struggling to sit up, while Adallia made noises of protest at him, trying ineffectively to keep him calm.

"No one ... in the Family ... can use magic ... besides me. They may ... track me down ... by ... traditional means ... though." He slumped back against the tree, those brief words taking way too much out of him.

"So we still don't have much of a head start," I mused, turning back to Farrah. She was looking around the campsite, searching for something, which was mostly completed by this point.

"What? What is it you need? I'll go get it," I told her.

Farrah pursed her lips. "What I need ... it's a bit complex. Normally, if I was going to draw poison from someone, I would just absorb it into my own body. There's usually not so much poison that my healing magic can't neutralize the poison right away. But with Baxley ... there's too much, and it's too ... thick. It would overwhelm me, and could potentially kill me. I need ..."

Adallia came to us, hands open. "Would it help to share the burden? I'll gladly take on some of the poison if it will help Baxley."

Farrah shook her head. "No. I can draw on my ability to heal almost by instinct, which is why my body would be able to handle a small amount of poison. But as none of the rest of you have that ability ..."

"You could end up having to heal multiple people, instead of just one," I finished her thought.

She nodded absentmindedly as she looked around again. "I need a vessel of some sort, something that could contain it. Or something that I could transfer it into."

She studied the majestic tree that my uncle was propped up against. Placing her hand on the trunk, she closed her eyes and bowed her head. What on earth was she doing? She was wasting time, precious moments that my uncle didn't have. I was about to speak up when Farrah opened her eyes and raised her head. She pushed an errant strand of hair back where it had fallen into her face. "It said yes."

"What?"

"The tree. I asked if it would be willing to help this man, and it said yes."

She talks to trees? But then I remembered Farrah telling me she had grown up with some Faerie traditions, as she was half-Fae herself. Suddenly the talking to trees thing — as well as her healing magic — made sense.

"Uh, thank you, then. Tree." I felt foolish saying the words aloud, but Farrah looked pleased.

"All right, let's get started. We don't have any more time to lose," she said. Suiting her actions to her words, she placed one palm on the tree, and the other on Baxley's shoulder.

"What can we do?" I asked, pointing to Adallia and myself.

"For now, just be there next to him. Hold his hand and be a source of comfort. As I pull the poison from his body, it will hurt. I need to maintain contact with both him and the tree the entire time, and if contact is broken with either before I am done, then the magic could backfire. Or worse. So if he starts to thrash about, hold him down and keep him as still as you can."

"All right, then, let's get started." I echoed Farrah's earlier statement.

I gripped my uncle's weak hand in mine, rubbing my thumb over the top of his hand and murmuring encouragement to him as Farrah closed her eyes and began concentrating on her healing spell. On my uncle's other side, Adallia did the same.

At first, Baxley couldn't even grip my hand back, his fingers limp in my grasp. As Farrah continued weaving her spell, Baxley started to get a little bit of strength back. His fingers closed around my hand; his eyes opened and, for the first time since we had left the Hauster fortress, they held a spark of life in them.

And then his grasp on my hand grew tighter. His eyes squeezed shut in pain, and I saw the tension crease his face as the viscous poison tried to hold onto his body.

"Uncle, you're all right. Just listen to my voice. You're fine, you'll be fine, don't focus on the pain, just focus on me and Adallia." I spoke rapidly, trying to distract him. Across the way, Adallia's eyes met mine, her fear for her love plainly written on her face.

Baxley's body went rigid, then limp. He began shaking, at first a slight vibration which quickly evolved into a full-blown thrashing. Clamping our hands on his arms, Adallia and I threw all our weight into pushing him down, but it was getting increasingly difficult to keep him still.

Farrah's voice faltered slightly as she reacted to Baxley's thrashing, but she determinedly continued on with her spell.

Should I sit on his legs? Throw my entire body over his? I didn't want to do anything that would throw Farrah's concentration off, and my uncle still seemed way too frail to support my extra weight without hurting him. But if I couldn't get him under control, and soon ...

On the other side of the campsite, Rhyss loped out of the woods, holding a brace of rabbits.

"Rhyss!" If he couldn't catch the wildness in my eyes, I'm sure he heard my frantic desperation.

Rhyss immediately started running toward us, barely breaking his stride as he tossed the rabbits toward Jondan and Delphine, who had just returned from gathering firewood. He shed his bow as well, unslinging it from his back and tossing it aside as he reached Farrah, Baxley, and me. He dropped to his feet and threw his hands down on Baxley's legs, helping me still the afflicted man.

And not a moment too soon. Farrah's voice, up until now just a low, steady murmur, grew louder and faster as she completed her spell, doing one last draw of the poison from Baxley's body. He cried out, shaking so furiously I thought his body would break apart at any moment. Rhyss and I both doubled down, holding Baxley down with every ounce of strength we both possessed.

After one final violent spasm, Baxley's body went limp. At the same moment, Farrah completed her spell, and the tree at Baxley's back turned black and wilted, crumpling in on itself with frightening speed. It no longer bore its vibrant, healthy tones of bright green and brown. Instead, it was now cracked and withered, looking as if it had been dead for several years.

Baxley drew in a shuddering breath and opened his eyes, his expression more lucid than it had been for the last day. He opened his mouth to say something, then started coughing.

"Oh! Here," said Rhyss, hastily handing Baxley a waterskin hanging from his belt.

Baxley took a long drink from the waterskin. "Thank you." He looked around at all of us, his gaze finally landing on Farrah. He twisted slightly to look at the decayed tree. "Thank you, all of you, for everything."

"How are you feeling?" Farrah asked him. Her voice sounded rough, even though her spell casting had been barely above a whisper, and her face was slick with sweat.

"Much, much better. I can still sense the tether around me, but it's not as restrictive as it usually is."

"That won't last, I'm afraid," she said. "The tether will eventually snake its way back around you, grabbing on tight and leaching its poison into you again. If we can't remove this magical tether for good, then we will have to repeat this process over and over." She leaned against the blackened trunk of the now-dead tree, trying to catch her breath. "But this took a lot of out of me, more than I expected. I don't know if I'd have the strength to keep repeating this spell.

"There's one more thing I need to do, and perhaps that will slow the poison and buy us more time to figure out a permanent solution."

She grabbed Baxley's hand, closing her eyes as she focused on another spell. After a few moments, she released his hand and opened her eyes, looking pleased with herself. "The poison is all gone — for now. I've created a shield between you and the tether. The shield should hold for a few days, I hope until we reach Orchwell, before the poison from the tether eats away at it and destroys it completely." Her smile faltered. "I wish I could just remove the tether completely, but it's beyond my ability."

Baxley patted her hand. "You've done more than enough for me this day."

Rhyss helped a shaky Farrah get to her feet, while Adallia and I assisted my uncle over to the campfire. Delphine and Jondan had built a fire and were busily skinning the rabbits Rhyss had brought back. I helped Delphine and Jondan with dinner while Rhyss fussed over Farrah and Adallia fussed over Baxley. When it was time to eat, Adallia sat next to Baxley during the meal, engaging him in a low-voiced but innocuous conversation.

The sun had started dipping below the horizon by the time we finished eating and cleaning up our camp, and by then we were all ready for a good night's rest. Jondan offered to take first watch, with Rhyss to relieve him, and we had barely settled into our bedrolls when, exhausted, I drifted off into sleep.

Chapter Thirty-Four

I DREAMED SOMEONE WAS watching me.

Someone lithe, and strong. Man? Woman? I wasn't sure. They were just beyond my sight, hidden in the shadows. But I could see their eyes glinting in the moonlight.

My unease at this unknown presence grew, the ominous feeling growing until I could no longer contain myself.

"Show yourself!" I started to say.

I came awake instantly, the words I had spoken in my dreams thick on my tongue.

The glint that I had dreamed were watching eyes was actually the glint of sharp metal. Against my neck.

"What's going on? Who are you?" I demanded.

The person holding the dagger eased off a bit, enough to let me talk, but not far enough that the weapon couldn't be plunged into my neck at a moment's notice.

"As you seem to be the group leader, I would like to make a bargain with you."

I recognized the voice as the young woman from the Hauster stronghold's great hall. Baxley's niece by marriage. What was her name again? Shelda.

"I can't bargain with anyone if I'm lying flat on my back, unable to see who I'm talking to," I said.

"You may sit up," Shelda said. "But don't try anything funny, or my dagger may find its way into your neck. And that would be most unfortunate, don't you think?"

I sat up slowly, using the time to survey the camp and ascertain if the others were all right. I dragged my hands against the ground, wiggling in my bedroll and scattering nearby pebbles in an effort to make enough noise to wake up the others. From what I could see, everyone else seemed to be fine, but no one was waking. On the other end of the campsite, Rhyss, who was supposed to be keeping watch, was slumped over on a log.

I made a mental note, through the haze clouding my brain, to make sure Rhyss never took a watch by himself again.

I nudged Farrah, who was sleeping the closest to me. She groaned lightly, but didn't open her eyes.

"What did you do to the others?" I asked Shelda.

"Sleeping powder," Shelda said. "They won't wake for quite some time, or unless I give them the antidote to counteract it."

I cursed mentally. We had been so exhausted, and Farrah so drained from healing Baxley, that we had forgotten to set up any wards. Not that it would have mattered, as Farrah had said the wards were really only effective against the use of magical attacks.

"All right, then, you want to bargain," I said. "For what? Why didn't you just put some sleeping powder on me, too? Why wake me up? You could have just stolen Baxley away, and no one would have known until the morning."

Shelda sank down on my pack, which was lying next to my bedroll. Her dagger still out, she tossed it from hand to hand, the blade catching the moonlight as it went from side to side.

"I've been shadowing your group for half a day," she said. "We discovered all of you — Lord Olivera, the group of false servants, and the girl who Lord Olivera commissioned us to find — were missing in the morning, but it wasn't until we realized my uncle was gone that I came after you. It wasn't hard, really, you weren't even a day's hard ride away."

Something Shelda said stuck out at me. "Wait a minute. You said Lord Olivera left the fortress? He's free? How?"

"When Uncle Baxley left the hill, the magic weakened enough that all the prisoners could escape." Shelda snorted. "That stupid man. He thinks he's so quiet and clever, but you can't outfox a true hunter. I've been shadowing him as I've been shadowing you."

"But he's —"

Shelda stopped tossing her dagger and pointed it straight at me. I swallowed the rest of what I was going to say. "If you don't mind, may I continue?"

I croaked out a yes.

"Good." Shelda lowered her dagger. "I've overheard some of your conversations, and I witnessed what your friend —" she motioned with her weapon at the sleeping Farrah "— did to help my uncle. It would be very easy to just take Uncle Baxley now and bring him back home, but I don't think it's what he wants. Truth be told, I've suspected for some time now that my uncle was unhappy."

It was a bit unsettling to hear this fierce bounty hunter refer to my newfound uncle as *her* uncle, even though it was accurate. It was even more unsettling to realize that I was actually related to this woman and her outlaw family by marriage.

Her eyes flickered over to Baxley, who was sleeping peacefully a few feet away. Her face softened. "I love my uncle dearly. He ... When my papa died, Uncle Baxley helped raise me like I was his own daughter. I wish he hadn't left, but I also want him to be happy. After all I've seen and heard today have confirmed my suspicions, I'm willing to let him go. And I know my mother and great-grandparents will support my decision.

"But it also creates a problem, because ... we need him. Or rather, we need his Seeker ability. Our family has diminished over time; I was very young when Eldan passed away, but I remember it was a devastating blow to us. We needed his magic more than we'd like to admit. Uncle Baxley's abilities were helping to restore our family to its original greatness. Even if we could let Uncle Baxley as a person go, we cannot afford to let Uncle Baxley the Seeker go."

Shelda started tossing her dagger back and forth again. As other people's nervous habits went, it was incredibly intimidating to me. "Uh ... if *you* don't mind, could you just put the dagger down? Besides, I don't know if you realized, but technically ... we're family. I know families don't always get along, but sticking me with a dagger is a rather permanent way to end an argument."

Shelda's eyes widened. "That's right, that part didn't quite register until you mentioned it just now." She stuck the dagger into the ground, making me flinch. "Nice to meet you, cousin."

"Ah ... yes. It's lovely to meet you as well. Cousin."

Awkwardly, we shook hands. I smiled at the absurdity of the situation, which turned into full-blown laughter. Shelda's laughter joined mine, a surprisingly lilting sound.

After our laughter died down, I said, "Thank you for not killing me. Now that you've told me your story, what do you want me to do about it? I'm not sure I *can* do anything about it."

Shelda shrugged uncertainly. "Honestly, I don't really know what can be done, if anything. I just know that once his magical tether is removed, he will no longer be obligated to assist the Family with his Seeker ability. I don't know ... is there some way to remove his ability and contain it somehow, and give it to us?"

I balked at the idea. "I ... I don't know if that can be done. From what I know, removing someone's Seeker ability is dangerous, if not outright deadly. My father — Uncle Baxley's brother — might know more, but we won't know for sure until we get back home to Orchwell."

Shelda thought for a moment, then nodded decisively. "Very well, then. I will also travel to Orchwell, instead of returning home. Once I know what the options are, I can decide what to do next."

"That sounds reasonable. Will you be joining our group on the road, then?" I waved around the campsite. "There's plenty of room if you'd like to settle in."

She scoffed. "Join a group that sounds like a herd of crashing elephants? No, thank you."

Ouch. I consoled myself with the thought that Shelda and I had very different professions.

"I travel better alone. I'll continue to shadow your group, and I'll meet you in Orchwell," Shelda said. She looked at Uncle Baxley again. "You can tell the others about my visit, but don't bother to seek me out. If you need me, I'll be there. The most important thing is to get him to Orchwell."

With that, she grabbed her dagger and stood up in one fluid motion, disappearing into the nighttime shadows. She had completely melted into the forest when I belatedly realized: I still had unanswered questions about Lord Olivera following us.

Chapter Thirty-Five

SINCE MY FRIENDS WERE under a heavy magically-induced sleep, I stayed up for the rest of the night, watching the changing shadows and thinking over my nighttime conversation with Shelda.

As the morning light began peeking through the trees, the rest of the group began to stir. Rhyss groggily sat up, a look of confusion on his face as he took in the log he had been sleeping on. Horrified, he saw me blearily keeping watch, and said guiltily, "I'm so sorry, Kaernan. I must have been more tired than I thought."

"It wasn't your fault," I said. Everyone else was sitting up in their bedrolls, yawning widely or trying to shake off their sleepiness. "We had a visitor in the night, one who's rather partial to sleeping powder."

Delphine made a choked sound. "Was it —?"

"Yes, it was one of the Hausters," I confirmed. "But she wasn't here for you, Delphine. She wanted to discuss Uncle Baxley. Let's pack up camp and get going, and I can tell everyone what happened on the road." I stood up, stretching my back and legs after a long night sitting on the hard ground. "We have a lot of ground to cover, and a lot to talk about."

THE NEXT FEW DAYS SETTLED into an easy rhythm as we traveled toward Meira. I often rode in the lead, occasionally joined by Rhyss or Farrah. Behind me I could hear the various conversations of Adallia and Baxley, or Jondan and Delphine. Adallia and Baxley, as reunited lovers, often had subdued but sweet murmurings as they caught up on the last decade or so of each other's lives. Meanwhile, Jondan and Delphine seemed to be sparking up a new romance. Their bright laughter and excited conversations were quite the contrast to the older couple's seasoned romance.

Occasionally, a dragon would fly overhead as we rode. Jondan, who had never traveled beyond Rothschan and had never seen a dragon before, remarked on the majestic creatures and their array of colors.

"That one's an earth dragon," Rhyss said. "They can fly, but not for long distances."

Wide-eyed, Jondan turned to face Rhyss from where he sat riding pillion on Delphine's horse. "You study dragons, then?"

"Not exactly," Rhyss said. "Farrah and I used to travel with a dragon Seeker on his commissions, for several years. You pick up a few things after a while."

"That's fascinating! How did you end up working for a Seeker?"

The two men began conversing about Rhyss's former employment, punctuated by random remarks from Farrah. The discussion continued at various times as we travelled or settled into our camp at night. I could practically see the thoughts forming in Jondan's mind, and I was glad he had something to look forward to once we reached Orchwell. As a former guard, he would make a great addition to any Seeker's team.

In Meira, we hired two additional horses for Baxley and Jondan. While it would make the last part of our journey go much faster, I sensed that the two couples were a bit disappointed to be separated.

We had just enough money left to buy a few days' worth of provisions. As we dragged our road-weary selves into the Dancing Cat, the innkeeper Ravon greeted me warmly. "Kaernan, it's good to see you again! And you've brought more friends this time, welcome!"

I grimaced. "Are we still welcome when I tell you tonight will have to be on credit?"

Ravon laughed. "Of course, I know you're always good for the money. Eventually. How many rooms, then?"

After we had stored our belongings in our two rented rooms — I wasn't willing to go *that* much into debt over our large group — we traipsed back downstairs and picked out a large communal table, settling in for one of Ravon's delicious and generously-portioned meals.

We had just started eating when Delphine gasped. "He's here!"

"Who's here, Delphine?" I asked.

"Lord Olivera! He's outside! I saw him through the inn's window."

We all looked toward the front of the inn, either craning our necks or turning around in our seats, trying to spot Lord

Olivera. A shadow passed by the inn's window, but it was difficult to make out the person's features.

"I'll go look," I said, jumping up and hurrying to the inn's door. Pushing it open, I looked both left and right, surveying the area around the Dancing Cat. There were a few people walking about in the twilight, but none of them were Lord Olivera.

I went back inside and rejoined my group at our table. At my friends' inquisitive faces, I shook my head. "I didn't see him."

"I could have sworn it was him," Delphine said, sounding frustrated.

"I'm not saying he's *not* here," I said. "But I didn't see him when I was outside. Maybe it was Shelda you saw. She *has* been trailing us this whole time."

"It wasn't Shelda," Delphine insisted. "I remember what she looked like, and this person was bigger and bulkier than she is."

"We'll have to be on our guard," Baxley said. "We know he's trailing us, but so far he's been extremely careful not to be seen. I think he's just biding his time, waiting for the right moment."

Delphine pursed her lips but didn't say anything more as we resumed eating dinner. She kept shooting furtive glances at the inn's window, and it was obvious her mind was preoccupied. We finished dinner quickly, thanking Ravon and heading to our rooms upstairs. With the town festival in full swing, we were lucky to get two rooms for the night; Ravon said that some merchants had never shown up. Now that there were two extra men in our group, our shared room was a little cramped, but Rhyss, Baxley, Jondan, and I somehow all found fairly comfortable places to sleep and settled in for the night.

WE RESUMED OUR JOURNEY the next day, this time everyone in our group on their own separate mount. Delphine looked around wildly as we set off, searching for Lord Olivera. He didn't appear, though, and she eventually calmed down and engaged in a lively discussion with Farrah and Jondan.

Our travels after leaving Meira were without incident, at least when it came to outside threats. There were no more nighttime visits from Shelda, nor did we see any hint of Lord Olivera. And now that the horses weren't overtaxed, we made good time.

But Baxley's health started to slip. The first night after we left Meira, Baxley offered to help set up camp but stopped partway through, gasping for breath. When asked, he waved away any concern, saying the constant riding was just taking its toll on him. The next morning, he looked completely worn out, even though he had gotten a full night's sleep. Concerned, I kept an eye on Baxley as we broke camp and mounted our horses.

Farrah coaxed her horse forward, riding at my side. In a low voice, she said, "The shield is starting to crack, sooner than I thought it would."

I nodded. "That's what I thought might be happening. When we stop and make camp tonight, should you redo the spell you did before?"

She shook her head. "No. I would have to dismantle the shield first before putting up a new one, and I'm afraid if I do that, all the poison would rush his body and overwhelm him too fast for me to handle. It's better to leave things as they are. But the faster we get back to Orchwell, the better."

"Then let's do so," I said, spurring my horse to move faster. The others behind me followed suit. We were close enough to home that, if we pushed the horses to their limit, it wouldn't be too damaging. Farrah was right; we were running out of time.

And after a day and a half of hard riding, we were riding through the gates of Orchwell.

Finally, we were home.

Chapter Thirty-Six

WE RODE STRAIGHT TO my family's home. Asthore Manor loomed large and imposing as ever, but this time, instead of feeling defeated and small upon returning home, I felt ... alive. With a sense of purpose.

I looked at my uncle, whose face was tinged with regret and sadness as he stared at Asthore Manor. His childhood home. I reached over and touched his shoulder.

"Are you ready?" I asked him softly.

The thin layer of sweat on his forehead and his shaking hands were the only signs that betrayed his illness; with an effort, he sat up straighter on his horse and steeled his expression. "I never thought I'd see the day when I'd be back here. But if facing my past is the only way to reach my future ... then yes. I'm ready. Let's go."

We left the horses with a stablehand and paraded through the front door, just as the butler opened it. His mouth gaped open like a fish struggling for air.

"Where's my father?" I asked.

"In the study, sir," the butler responded, trying to regain his composure.

"Perfect," I said, leading the way.

"But ... sir! He's ... He won't like to be interrupted ..."

The butler's protests faded as we continued down the hall toward my father's study. Thinking about how shocked the poor man had looked, I nearly laughed aloud. What a group of outcasts we were! The unwanted son of the manor, bringing home his disgraced uncle. An accused murderess and her commoner mother, just barely made acceptable in society by her unwanted noble marriage. Two career adventurers, and a guard-turned-deserter.

And yet, somehow, this group of misfits had become like family to me.

I burst through the doors of the study. As the butler had said, my father was there, sitting in an overstuffed chair that faced the door. To one side, on the couch, sat my twin sister, listening intently to whatever it was Father had been saying before we interrupted their conversation.

A second overstuffed chair held another person, but as the chair's back was facing the study doors, I couldn't tell who was sitting there. Most likely it was Mother, and they were having some sort of family meeting. *Without me*, I thought with that familiar twinge of bitterness. *Of course.*

Father looked up, irritated. "What the —?"

He stopped as he got a good look at who was entering. "Ah, Kaernan. I'm surprised you made it back so soon."

Kaela squealed and jumped up, running over to throw her arms around me in an exuberant hug. "Kaernan! You're back! I've missed you — *we've* missed you, I mean —"

I hugged my sister tightly, giving her an extra squeeze before letting her go. "It's fine, Kaela. You don't have to try and sugar coat things. I missed you, too."

"Oh, but ... Well, I ... oh, dear ..." Kaela said, flustered. She stopped and composed herself. Taking a step back, she took in the group behind me. "Who are all these people you've brought back with you?"

I gestured at each person in turn. "You remember Lady Adallia Pahame, the one who hired me recently for a commission? This is her daughter, Lady Delphine. Rhyss, Farrah, and Jondan. And this —" I put my hand on his shoulder "— is Baxley. Or, perhaps I should say, our uncle, Lord Baxley Asthore."

At the far end of the room, my father's face grew still as he slowly stood up, even as my sister breathed, "Uncle? We have an uncle?"

Baxley regarded her fondly. "Oh, my dear Kaela. When I last saw you, you were a baby, barely learning to speak. But what a beauty you've become! You definitely have the Asthore eyes."

Kaela stood before Baxley awkwardly. "I ... I'm afraid I don't know how to greet you. Uncle. Baxley? Kaernan, should I ...?" She looked to me for an answer. I shrugged as if to say, *Do whatever you're comfortable with*. She paused, then held out her hand to shake his. As he warmly took her hand, her answering smile mirrored his. "Welcome home, uncle."

Baxley released Kaela's hand and looked to his brother, still standing and staring at him in shock. "Well, brother, aren't you going to come and greet me? It's been quite a long time."

Father moved toward us slowly, as if in a trance. He stopped before his brother, but didn't speak, only stared. Looking between the two men, I noticed they both had the same striking eyes — the Asthore eyes, Baxley had called them — and strong chin. Father was a few inches taller, and his features were a little more angular, but seeing them next to each other, it was easy to see they were brothers.

As the two men regarded each other, no one else in the room dared breathe.

Then finally, Father blurted out: "I can't believe it, you're really back. I ... I've missed you."

"I've missed you too, Julian." Baxley's voice was choked with emotion.

Father embraced Baxley, a tear or two escaping his eyes to stream down his cheeks. Kaela and I exchanged stunned looks. This was the most emotion we had ever seen out of our stoic father.

The two men stepped back, regarding each other with more warmth than when we had first walked into the room.

"Where have you been all these years?" Father asked. "Why didn't you send word, or —"

"It's a long story, one I'll be happy to tell you," Baxley said. The happiness in his voice couldn't mask his labored breathing. "But first, I need your help. You see, I —"

"This reunion is all quite touching," a deep voice interrupted. "But it's getting rather boring, sitting here forgotten."

Father gasped, looking embarrassed. "I'm so sorry, of course. We didn't mean to ignore you, my good sir. We just got a bit carried away with the moment."

"Yes, yes, I heard it all, as I said already, it's quite touching. But I really don't have all day. You can finish your reunion after I leave. If I let you." The speaker, who had been sitting in the second overstuffed chair, stood up.

As the speaker slowly turned, a hand shot out. A magical blast of air threw everyone back.

Lord Olivera smiled triumphantly.

Chapter Thirty-Seven

I SNARLED, "WHAT ARE you doing here?"

"Why, I'm hiring the services of a Seeker, of course," Olivera said. "Your father was surprised to see me, as I am apparently still considered dead, but I explained to him that it was a gross misunderstanding between my intended and myself, and would soon be straightened out with the Council and the Crown."

For once, Lord Olivera wasn't wearing one of his signature colorful outfits. Instead, he was in a muted blue-and-gray jacket and trousers. Almost as if he was trying to blend in.

"I nearly didn't recognize you without your usual gaudy hat. Is there a feather shortage in Orchwell?" I spat out.

Olivera frowned. "I did regret leaving that green hat behind in the hill. Leaving quickly was, unfortunately, more important than searching for it. But it's no matter. I'll make sure to buy a new one, a better one, for the wedding."

Behind me, Delphine gasped. "If you think —"

Lord Olivera raised his arm in a half circle, flinging a spell at everyone in the room.

My back hit the wall. I tried to move, but I was held fast like a pinned butterfly. Similar scuffling sounds around me told me my friends and family were in the same position as I was.

Lord Olivera regarded us, fingers still splayed as he continued to blast air at everyone. He muttered something and completed his spell, flexing his hand as he finished. His evil smile grew wider as he saw Delphine, helplessly immobilized against the wall.

He turned to Father and Kaela, giving them an ironic bow. In a voice dripping with sarcasm, he said, "Lord Asthore, it was a pleasure doing business with you. And Kaela ... your abilities are even more extraordinary than I had heard! But as you can see, your assistance is no longer needed. I thank you for your service."

Lord Olivera sauntered over to us, reaching out and almost casually plucking Delphine from the wall. She gasped at the sudden freedom of movement, but the magic still had a residual hold on her, and by the time she had recovered enough to try to run, Lord Olivera had a firm hold on her upper arm. She began struggling against his grasp.

A dagger suddenly appeared in Lord Olivera's hand. He pressed it against her side, and she instantly stilled. "Now, now, my dear, let's have none of that. Come quietly, now there's a good girl."

He gently prodded his captive forward. Even though I was unable to free myself from the wall, I couldn't let him leave with Delphine. So I ground out, fighting against the air that roared all around me, "You were supposed to be dead. Why didn't you stay that way?"

Lord Olivera laughed. "In the eyes of Orchwell, I'm still dead."

It hurt to fight against the magic holding me. It felt like Olivera's magical wind was stealing every word my mouth was able to form. Into the wind, I said, "But why? Why pretend you were dead?"

The nobleman preened a bit. "When people think you're dead, you can do pretty much whatever you want. Whatever is ... necessary. With no awkward questions, no inconvenient laws."

He frowned, remembering. "Although it would have been much easier if my stupid servants hadn't gossiped so much. Those wanted posters nearly undid my plans. I shouldn't have left them alive."

Then he smiled again, nastily. "I won't make the same mistake twice. I'm thinking that, after Delphine and I leave here, it would be a shame if Asthore Manor went up in flames. But I'm afraid it will. And unfortunately, leaving no survivors inside. A man must get his revenge, you know. In whatever form he desires."

He ran a lascivious hand down Delphine's arm. She shuddered, but with his dagger pressed into her side she didn't dare try to get away.

Grabbing her arm more firmly, he turned her toward the door. "But come, my dear Delphine. We've wasted enough time here."

Suddenly, the study's window exploded in a bright sound of tinkling glass.

Shelda burst into the room like an avenging angel, her sword at the ready.

Glass sprayed everywhere, but thankfully didn't reach the wall where we were all pinned, only able to watch the events unfolding. Errant thoughts ran through my mind. *Father's going to be displeased. It will take weeks for the glassmaker to create a window that big. And the servants are not going to be happy about cleaning that up ....*

Startled, Lord Olivera brandished his dagger at Shelda, who was coming at him fast, sword drawn. He dragged his captive in front of him, using her as a shield.

"Stop or I'll kill her."

Shelda stopped short. She could reach Lord Olivera in a few more paces, but she was far enough away that if she tried, Delphine would be dead within moments.

"Drop your weapon."

Shelda lowered her sword, but didn't drop it.

"Drop it, I say! Or her blood will be on your hands."

Shelda dropped her sword. For good measure, she kicked it away. The weapon skittered across the smooth wooden floor.

"Good." Still holding Delphine as a shield, Lord Olivera began backing toward the study door. "Now, stay where you are. Any moves toward us and I'll —"

"Pardon me for interrupting, but I saw the door open and thought negotiations were done. Would your guest like to stay for dinner?" My soft-spoken mother entered the study, stopping in her tracks with a confused look as she took in what was happening.

Lord Olivera growled. He threw his dagger at Mother, the weapon arcing in the air. Straight at her heart.

Delphine screamed.

Just before the weapon would have pierced her flesh, a silver flash sliced across the room, intercepting it and knocking it off its trajectory. Lord Olivera's dagger clattered to the side, falling to the floor where it could harm no one. A second silver dagger lay atop it — thrown by Shelda, it was the silver flash I had seen that had deflected Lord Olivera's weapon.

"Aarrgghh ..." Lord Olivera made a strangled sound. Protruding from his neck was another silver dagger.

Shelda straightened up from the throwing stance she had adopted when she threw both weapons, staring impassively at Lord Olivera.

The man released his hold on Delphine as his hands flew to his neck. Blood seeped from his wound as the life rapidly drained from his eyes. He made one last lunge at Delphine, but she easily stepped away as his body slumped to the floor.

The spell holding all of us to the wall disappeared, and everyone fell to the ground, trying to regain feeling in our limbs. Adallia crawled over to her daughter and slowly stood with Delphine's assistance.

"Are you all right, Delphine?" She looked her daughter over, brushing back a strand of hair from Delphine's face.

"I'm fine, mama. I'm just glad everyone else is fine, too."

Now that I was able to move easily again, I walked over to Shelda, who was retrieving her sword from across the room. "Thank you, Cousin. You really were there when we needed you. And then some."

She smiled. "Of course. That's what family is for, is it not?"

I smiled back. "Yes. Definitely."

I surveyed the room. Besides the broken window and the shards of glass littering the ground, the wooden floor bore scuff marks from where the various weapons had fallen. The wall now had a subtle dent from where our bodies had slammed against it, and the onslaught of air had noticeably rippled the wallpaper. Oh, and also, there was now a dead noble lying in the middle of the room. We'd have an interesting time trying to explain this to the authorities.

I crossed the room again and hugged a bewildered Lady Asthore. "It's good to see you, Mother. As you can see, I came home earlier than expected."

"I can see ... something," she said, her eyes darting back and forth as she took in the chaos. "Kaernan, must trouble always follow you?"

I hugged her again. She blinked, unused to such affection from me. "It's the nature of the job, Mother. Now, I think you said that dinner was ready?"

Chapter Thirty-Eight

UNFORTUNATELY, THOUGH, dinner would have to wait until a few things were taken care of. Such as the broken glass strewn throughout the study, the gaping window, and the dead noble lying on the plush carpet.

Staring at Lord Olivera and the blood pooling beneath his body, I felt a twinge of dismay for our servants. *That will be a pain to clean up. Although I've never liked that rug anyway ....*

Father called a servant, and sent them off with instructions to bring the constable. While we waited for the man to arrive, we retired to the dining hall.

Soon the constable arrived with several other men. They removed the now deceased Lord Olivera from the study, for which we were grateful, but they also took Delphine into custody, for which we were not.

"Why are you arresting her? She's obviously innocent," I argued with the constable.

"That's not for me to decide," he said. "She's still wanted by the Crown and the Council; I just follow my orders." He leaned toward me conspiratorially. "I'm sure it will all right, milord. The Council will probably bind her to the court immediately to ensure she stays in Orchwell, and then they'll send her home."

The constable and his men left with Delphine. A worried Adallia followed behind.

Dinner was subdued after the earlier events of the day, and especially as we worried over the fate of our friend. Shelda, our ever-present shadow while we had been traveling, stayed to eat with us.

But despite worrying over Delphine's upcoming trial, we had much to celebrate — Uncle Baxley's return, Lord Olivera's defeat, and successfully completed commissions for both Kaela and me. Although, as Kaela pointed out, you could hardly call her commission "completed" or "successful" since it was just sheer luck — or, maybe not luck, but *something* — that brought Delphine to Asthore Manor at the exact moment that Lord Olivera was hiring my sister to find her.

"If I had known what that horrid man *really* wanted with her, I would never have even entertained the idea of working for him," Kaela said disgustedly. "Although I don't think I would have been successful anyway, since technically he 'lost' Delphine. So, dear brother, he should have hired you, not me."

"No, thank you," I said, picking up my cup and draining it dry. A waiting servant immediately stepped in to refill it.

Across the table, Farrah closed her book, holding her place with her finger. She had been a bit antisocial during our dinner, absorbed in reading some book on Seeker history that Father had located for her in his library, at her request. I vaguely recognized the worn brown leather cover, remembering that I had found the history book rather dull and entirely forgettable.

"This is absolutely fascinating," she said, opening the book to the page she had been reading. "Some of this stuff I had heard before, but this ... Remember when you interviewed Rhyss and me? We talked about if someone from a non-Seeker family could become a Seeker, or if a Seeker could get rid of their ability? Here, listen to this."

She read a passage aloud. "'... to instill a Seeker's gift is a dangerous process. If the person receiving the gift does not have the correct constitution, then trying to imbue them with Seeker ability may very well result in their demise. Therefore, it is imperative to determine if the receiver has the correct constitution or not.'"

"'Correct constitution'?" I echoed, confused. "What does that mean?"

"I'm not entirely sure," Farrah admitted. "I understand that the writer meant, if you're going to try to 'create' a Seeker, then you need to make sure that person has the proper ... traits, I suppose? But the book doesn't define what those traits are. Does that mean they're physically strong? Magically gifted? Just a really good person? 'Correct' could mean all manner of things."

Rich laughter rang out across the room. At the head of the table, Father and Mother were engaged in a lively conversation with Uncle Baxley. Was Father actually ... smiling? And laughing? I shook my head in wonder. Maybe, finally, our family could act like ... a family.

An odd choking sound caught my attention. My uncle's laughter had suddenly changed into a slight wheeze, which steadily increased until it was uncontrollable.

"Baxley? Baxley! Here, drink this," Father said, pushing Baxley's water glass toward him. He made no move to pick it up, just kept wheezing and shaking.

Farrah sprang to her feet, rushing to his side. Touching my uncle, she recoiled immediately. "It's as I suspected," she said. "The protective shield has broken, and the poison is rushing through him."

"What should we do?" Father asked. Jondan and Rhyss were already standing, moving toward Farrah and Baxley's side of the table. They stood nearby, ready to assist Farrah if she needed them.

"Should we move him? Take him somewhere outside?" Rhyss asked. As we were indoors, there was nothing alive — besides people — that could take on the poison in Baxley's place.

Farrah shook her head. "No, he's beyond that. The poison is spreading too rapidly for him to even make it out the front door. And there's too much poison in him, anyway. No, what would be best is if we could completely strip him of his Seeker ability. The tether spell is tied to that, not to Baxley himself."

"But that would kill him!" I said.

"And this won't?" Farrah countered.

"Can you do that? Destroy Baxley's Seeker ability?"

"No. But I think I can move it. Just like I did with the poison, a few days ago."

Frantically, I turned to Baxley, who was now turning purple as he tried desperately to take in air. "Uncle! Uncle, is this what you want?"

He stopped coughing just long enough to croak out, "Y-yes."

My heart sank even as I nodded in acknowledgement. There had been plenty of times I had daydreamed about not being a Seeker, but it was more about not having my specific ability of finding lost loves, as opposed to not being a Seeker entirely. Even when I had faced the possibility of having my gift taken away by the Council, I hadn't wanted to lose that part of me that made me unique. That made me truly an Asthore.

I turned to Farrah. "What do you need? A container of some sort to hold his Seeker essence?" I scanned the table quickly. Plates? Cups? I mentally discarded pretty much everything I saw.

"No, no, it has to be … a person." She bit her lip, frowning. "But I don't want to experiment with anyone's life like that. Maybe we *should* try taking him out —"

"I will do it." Shelda stood up. "Transfer his ability, and the tether, to me."

"Are you sure?" I asked. "Shelda, if this doesn't work … either the gift or the tethering spell could kill you."

"It is for family," she said simply. "For some reason, I know this will work. I know I can do this."

"Come over here, then," Farrah pointed to where Father and Mother were sitting by Baxley. Both of my parents vacated their seats, backing up to stand against the wall. Shelda came forward and sank into the chair.

"Take both of his hands, and clear your mind of anything but him," Farrah instructed. To the violently shaking Baxley, Farrah said, "Baxley? I know you're in a lot of pain right now, and this might be difficult, but try your best to think only of ... Shelda, is it?"

"Yes."

"Focus on Shelda, as much as you are able. Shelda, perhaps it would help if you talk to him. That will draw his attention while I work on this spell."

Shelda nodded as she leaned forward and gently took both of Baxley's hands in hers. Farrah placed one hand on Baxley's head, and one hand on Shelda's, closed her eyes, and started concentrating on her spell.

Shelda began speaking. "Uncle, remember the first time we went to Rothschan together? For the big summer fair? I was so little, not even three years old if I remember correctly. And we got separated, I was so scared and ran around everywhere trying to find you. I kept asking the adults where my Uncle Baxley was, but since I couldn't say your name right they all thought your name was 'Batty', not Baxley ..."

Her calm, steady voice kept up a constant flow of chatter while Farrah continued her magic. Ignoring Baxley's rattling coughs, his constant shaking, and the alternate moans or shouts of pain, Shelda recounted memory after shared memory. As the excruciating moments passed by, Baxley started to calm down and breathe a little easier. Perhaps Farrah's spell was going to work after all.

Farrah's eyes flew open. "I've managed to seal off most of the poison and isolate his Seeker gift, readying it for removal. Shelda, I need your help for this."

Without taking her eyes off our uncle, Shelda replied, "Anything."

"Good. Imagine his Seeker ability as I see it right now, a gold heart about the size of your hand. When I tell you, I want you to imagine yourself pulling it, with all your might, toward you and inside of you. Can you do that?"

"Yes."

"If ... if the worst should happen, I'll do what I can to hold your life in place. But ... things might go too fast for me to stop anything."

"I understand."

"All right. Hold on." Farrah closed her eyes again.

To Baxley, Shelda said, "You've been a second father to me, and I would do anything to keep you alive and safe. If this doesn't work ... I love you."

"Now!" Farrah said.

Shelda took a deep breath and squeezed Baxley's hands a little harder. Her gaze grew unfocused as she followed Farrah's orders.

Baxley turned a stricken, wide-eyed look on his niece. "No!" His cry of protest turned into a long, agonizing scream of pain as essence, spell, and tether were ripped from his body.

A glowing golden ball of light, the size of Shelda's fist, rose out of Baxley.

"Grab it!" Farrah cried.

Shelda instinctively reached out, quickly cupping her hand around the golden orb. As her hand closed around it, the golden light seeped into her hand, and then traveled up her arm, permeating the rest of her body. She glowed as gold as the object she had just absorbed.

With one final, fierce body shake, Baxley slumped over.

Wonderingly, Shelda examined her hands and arms, which were still giving off an unnatural yellow light. She turned questioning eyes on Farrah ... and then the golden light grew blindingly bright. As it was unexpected, none of us had thought to shield our eyes or turn away. There was one great pulse, and then the light blinked out.

I blinked rapidly, trying to regain my sight after that intense flash of light. When my eyes readjusted, they were met with a sorry sight.

On the floor, sprawled in a motionless heap, was Shelda.

Chapter Thirty-Nine

THE ROOM ERUPTED IN a multitude of directions.

Father leaned across the table, reaching for his brother. "Baxley. Baxley, can you hear me? Are you all right?"

Baxley groaned, holding his head as he slowly blinked his eyes open. "I ... I think so? I feel funny."

"What do you mean?"

"I'm not sure. Lighter, maybe? Weak ... but I can tell ... the poison is gone."

"Thank goodness," my father said. He and Mother continued to fuss over Baxley.

Farrah knelt down by the unconscious Shelda, feeling for a pulse. "She's still alive," Farrah announced, the relief evident in her voice.

Kaela hovered nearby, waving a bottle of smelling salts. "Would this help?"

Farrah didn't bother to take the bottle. "No, unfortunately. This is magically induced. There's nothing to do but hope Shelda eventually wakes up from it." She sighed. "The bigger questions are *if* she wakes up, and in what condition."

"She'll need to be somewhere more comfortable than the floor, then," Kaela said. She motioned at Rhyss and Jondan. "Can one of you carry her upstairs? I'll show you where to bring her. And if whoever stays back could find one of the servants, please let them know we'll need some refreshments for Shelda should she wake up."

I looked around the room and realized that there were no servants present. They must have made themselves scarce during the spell casting. Not that I blamed them; we paid our servants well, but not so well that they'd want to risk themselves if a spell went wrong. I'd have done the same thing if I were in their place.

Jondan scooped up Shelda from the floor, following Kaela out of the dining room. Rhyss left as well, heading in the direction that Kaela indicated before she and Jondan went up the stairs.

"You should rest, too," Father said to Baxley.

Baxley grimaced. "I feel like I could sleep for a week. And my head hurts something fierce."

"It will probably be like that for a few days," Farrah said. "But Lord Asthore is right, resting is a good idea."

Baxley shakily got to his feet. Mother and Father stood as well, supporting either side of him.

"I hope another room is ready," Father remarked as they made their slow way to the dining room entrance.

"Don't worry, Julian, I'm so tired, I won't even notice," Baxley quipped. Before they left the room, he turned back. To Farrah, he said, "Will my niece be all right?"

"I hope so," Farrah said. "I'll do what I can to speed her healing, but the best we really can do is watch and wait."

He nodded somberly. Father and Mother escorted him out of the room.

I went to Farrah's side and helped her slowly get to her feet. "Farrah, are you all right?"

Panting slightly, she said, "I will be, in a little while. And now, Baxley will be all right as well. I just hope Shelda will be, too."

Chapter Forty

I WAS KEPT QUITE BUSY over the next week. Asthore Manor did have two guests, Baxley and Shelda, to watch over. While they were relatively easy to take care of — Shelda was still unconscious and Baxley slept most of the time — we still needed to see to their comfort.

Farrah and Rhyss had gone back to their respective homes in Orchwell, but both came by often. Farrah to check on her patients, and Rhyss to help out with the various house repairs that were now needed at Asthore Manor. Both the study and the dining room looked a little worse for wear after magical imprisonment, weapons being thrown around the room, and major spell casting before the dinner dishes had been cleared away.

Jondan had declined an offer to stay at Asthore Manor, and was instead staying at Adallia and Delphine's home, mostly to serve as protection for the two women. The ladies' home was in surprisingly good shape, with the house and their belongings still intact. Some of their servants had stayed loyal, keeping up the place while their mistresses were away, but a disgruntled few had left to spread rumors while looking for new positions.

It was the rumors that Lady Pahame and her daughter feared the most. Jondan could defend them against physical attacks, but he couldn't protect them against public opinion. And, now that Delphine had returned to Orchwell, she would either have to pay for her supposed crimes or prove her innocence.

And the cost of killing a noble would be steep. Anywhere from Delphine being stripped of her magic — which, if done improperly, could damage her mind — to being put to death.

"We've asked for the hearing to be delayed, hopefully for a few more weeks," Delphine said as she poured me a cup of tea. She handed it to me, then sat back down cradling her own delicate cup.

I was in the Pahames' parlor for a visit with Adallia and Delphine. I took a small sip of tea. "Did they grant the delay?"

"Quite reluctantly," Adallia said. "And we were told it would only happen once. If Shelda doesn't wake up by the time the new trial date comes around, we can only go forth with the evidence we have."

"Which will be enough," Delphine said. The slightest shade of doubt crept into her voice. "I hope."

"I'm sure it will be," I said. "Father is willing to speak on your behalf, and the word of a nobleman, plus all the others, should hold enough weight for the Council."

"But Lord Olivera is dead, and I have no proof of anything. It puts me right back in the same spot as before."

"Not necessarily. You have close to a dozen witnesses who can attest that Olivera was alive when he was supposedly murdered. And who can attest to what his goals were, or may have been, concerning you."

"Oh, I hope so. I don't want to be known as a criminal. And I hope Shelda does wake up, and soon. She ... she saved me. I owe her my life."

We all fell silent.

"Let's talk of other things." Delphine abruptly changed the subject. "I worry about this day and night; I'd like to have a brief break from thinking about it all the time. How is your uncle?"

"Uncle Baxley is doing well," I reported. "He pretty much slept away the first two days, but around day three he started getting back to normal. Walking around a bit, his appetite has returned. The poison is completely gone, as is the tethering spell. He says he doesn't feel that pull back to the hill that he used to."

"And his Seeker gift?"

"Gone as well." I paused, toying with my tea cup. "I'm not sure how he feels about it. One minute he seems elated, free of any burdens. The next, I'll find him weeping over this lost part of his identity. I don't know what to say or do to make him feel better."

Adallia leaned forward, her eyes sympathetic. "I don't think there's anything you *can* do, Kaernan. He'll eventually come to terms with it, but it is quite a loss for him. Even if it was one he willingly gave up."

I nodded, looking around. "Where's Jondan?"

"He went out with Rhyss," Delphine said. "He's obsessed with learning more about Orchwell and Seekers. Well, more like what it would take to join a Seeker's team as support. After we left the Hauster fortress, I worried that he would become depressed and aimless. I'm so glad he's interested in this."

"It's not the only thing he's interested in," I said dryly. Delphine turned a bright shade of pink while her mother laughed.

"Well, it sounds like he wants to stay in Orchwell. It will be good to have him around. But what about his mother and sister?" I asked.

"He sent word the day after we returned, telling them what happened and letting them know he was staying with us," Adallia said. "His family should be getting his letter soon."

"Oh, good. That should ease their worries somewhat."

"I hope so. And who knows? Perhaps they'll want to move to Orchwell to be with Jondan. From what we saw, and the stories Jondan tells us, I can't imagine there's much in Rothschan his family will want to stay for."

Remembering exactly how Adallia and I had met Jondan's little sister Juneyen, and the money troubles their mother Carissa had mentioned, I privately agreed.

When I returned home, I found Kaela in the foyer, running around in a frenzy. "She's awake! Well, she *was*. She fell back asleep. But at least she woke up!"

"What?" I grabbed my sister by the shoulders and made her stand still. "What are you talking about?"

"Shelda! I was in her room, I had just brought her some cold soup." Kaela looked ready to jump out of her skin. "You know the servants are all scared of her, even asleep. So a few days ago I took over making sure she was fed while unconscious. Anyway, I put the tray down on the nightstand

and sat down next to her on the bed, about to grab the bowl and spoon. And Shelda opened her eyes!"

"That's amazing!" I said. "But you said she didn't stay awake?"

"No ... right after her eyes opened, they rolled right back in her head and I couldn't wake her up again! I didn't know what to do!"

"Have you sent for Farrah?"

"Yes! Just a little bit ago. Oh, I hope she hurries!"

Luckily, we didn't have to wait long. A knock sounded at the door. Our butler started toward the door, but Kaela practically pushed him out of the way and flung open the door herself. I had to stop myself from laughing aloud, especially at our butler's affronted expression.

"Sorry," I mouthed at him. He sniffed disapprovingly, taking his place at the door and placing his hand on the door handle.

Farrah, standing on the front porch, opened her mouth to greet Kaela. Whatever she was about to say was whipped away as Kaela grabbed her hand and dragged her inside.

"Good, you're here!" Kaela said. "Hurry, hurry! She woke up!"

Farrah's eyes widened. "She did?"

"Yes! Come on!"

The two women bolted up the stairs. I followed at a more normal pace behind.

When I reached Shelda's room, Farrah was sitting on the edge of the bed beside Shelda, and Kaela was standing by the doorway. Shelda was sitting up, miraculously wide awake and smiling. She was in mid-conversation with Farrah, but broke off at my entrance.

"I'm glad you made it, cousin," Shelda said.

"*I'm* glad *you* made it," I said, moving to stand next to my sister. "You've been out for a week. We were so worried about you."

"You didn't need to worry. Didn't I tell you I'd be there if you needed me? Sometimes it might take me longer to bounce back than usual, but I never let my family down."

"That much is obvious." I smiled. "But you definitely went above and beyond this last time. What happened, when you took Baxley's Seeker ability from him? Or do you even know?"

Shelda nodded slowly. "I think I do know, although the details are a bit fuzzy. Farrah was successful in transferring the Asthore Seeker gift to me." She smiled at Farrah. "You're quite talented with magic, Farrah. Had he lived, my grandfather Eldan would have had much to learn from you."

"Thank you. From what I've heard of him, that's quite a compliment," Farrah said.

"Of course." Shelda reached for a glass of water that sat on the untouched tray that Kaela had brought up earlier. She took a small sip. "When I ... pulled Baxley's Seeker essence from him, it didn't resist. It came right to me, I could feel it settling in to every part of my body. But that tether came along with it. It felt like a thorny vine snaking itself around me. I could feel its sharp edges poking at me, trying to find ... I'm not sure? I think it was looking for something within me that it could latch onto.

"But ... it couldn't. Every time it started to gain ground, something would stop it. Block it from sinking its hooks into me. If a spell can get angry, then this one definitely did. I could feel its frustration when it couldn't do what it intended, growing stronger when the poison inside it built in intensity. And then ... it exploded. The magic doubled back on me and ... well, when I woke up, it was apparently a week later."

Farrah looked thoughtful. "As I am not the original spell caster, I can't be sure ... but from what Baxley told us before, and from what I was able to observe from my interactions with the spell ... I think a condition of the spell was that it was supposed to force a strong loyalty or connection to the Hauster family upon whoever was being enchanted, where originally there was none. But as you, Shelda, already have a strong loyalty due to being a blood relation and having an emotional connection, the tether wouldn't have worked on you. I think your incompatibility with the spell's limitations caused it to break apart. Permanently."

Shelda smiled, leaning back against her pillows. "Uncle Baxley always said I was a stubborn one."

"Yes, you are," said his voice from the doorway. "And I've never been so proud."

Baxley crossed the room to the bed, where Shelda was trying to rise and greet him. Farrah fussed at her to stay in bed, and Baxley gently pushed her back down, giving her a huge hug.

"My dear, I owe you a debt I can never repay." His voice was rough with held back emotion. "Because of you, I am finally free."

Shelda smiled at his words, but her eyes held a tinge of sadness. "I'm glad, Uncle. But ... does this mean you'll never return? Not even for a visit?"

"Well, that depends."

"On what?"

"On whether or not the Hauduare would permit me to return, with no threat of punishment for abandoning the Family."

Shelda bit her lip, frowning. "But we don't have a new Hauduare. Traditionally that role has been bestowed from the outgoing leader to whomever they deem worthy to succeed them."

Baxley's eyes twinkled. "I would have thought that my approval was obvious, but if you need me to make it more formal than directly giving you my powers ..."

"Oh!" Shelda sat up suddenly, causing Farrah to fuss at her again to stay calm and rest. "Oh my goodness! Uncle, do you mean to say ... *I* am the next Hauduare?"

"When the time came, you would have been my first choice, regardless," Baxley assured her. "But circumstances, ah, accelerated your taking over sooner than I would have thought." He looked at her anxiously. "I hope that's all right with you, Shelda?"

Shelda grinned. "It's a big responsibility, but there's nothing else I would rather do than spend my life in service to the Family. And now to be a Seeker as well ..."

Baxley answered Shelda's grin with a smile of his own. "Perhaps, with your newfound ability, you can lead the Family into a new direction. One that deals more with true justice, and not just justice for the right price."

Shelda lowered her eyes. "It doesn't always sit well with me, the things we do ... but who are we if we aren't ... you know ... the Hausters?"

"You'll always be a Hauster," Baxley said. "Now's your chance to find out what else that might mean."

When Shelda raised her eyes again to look at our uncle, there were tears in her eyes. She nodded, slightly sniffling.

Farrah said, "I think that's enough excitement for you for today, Shelda. You and Baxley will have plenty of time to discuss Family business after you're better. But for now, you should rest again." She gave us all a pointed look.

We took Farrah's hint and said our goodbyes. Baxley, Farrah, and my sister Kaela shuffled out of the room ahead of me. I was just about to follow them when Shelda called out to me. "Kaernan?"

I turned around. "Yes, Shelda?"

"Maybe ... in a few days ... could you show me how to use my new Seeker ability? It's a bit unsettling, to have this powerful gift that I know is a part of me, like my voice or my fighting skills, and yet I don't know how to properly use it. It feels inconsiderate to ask Uncle Baxley to teach me, and I don't know your sister very well ..."

"It's all right," I said. "I'm flattered you asked me. I'd be happy to. But it will definitely have to wait until you're stronger."

An impatient cough sounded from the hallway. Now that she had my attention, Farrah motioned for me to leave her patient alone, already.

Looking back at Shelda, I laughed. "And, of course, it'll have to wait until Farrah says I can."

Shelda's hearty laughter rang out behind me as I closed her door and followed Farrah down the hallway.

Chapter Forty-One

SHELDA RECOVERED QUICKLY. Within a few days she was walking around the grounds of Asthore Manor, growing physically stronger every day. Farrah examined her magically and declared her in perfect health; our uncle's Seeker ability had successfully transferred to Shelda, and the tether spell was truly destroyed, leaving no residual poison or other nasty effects.

With Farrah's blessing, I started training Shelda in how to use her new Seeker gift. Shelda was a fast learner and had mastered a solid understanding of the basics by the end of the week.

Training Shelda taught me a few things, too. Our abilities were strikingly similar — both of us could seek out people that were lost. In my case, this meant following a trail of sorrow and heartbreak.

For Shelda, her ability now made her a formidable bounty hunter. With her already honed skills now coupled with magical talent, no one would be able to hide from her.

"Remind me to never play hide and seek with you," I told her at the end of one our training sessions. We were in the study, now clean but a little worse for wear from the magical battle with Lord Olivera a few weeks past.

Laughing, Shelda flopped into an overstuffed chair and said, "No need to worry, dear cousin. I'll always play fair with you. I owe you too much."

"I would argue that it is *I* who owe *you*." I pointedly looked at the window Shelda had broken through, now boarded over with several planks of wood.

Following my gaze, Shelda laughed again. "Call it even?"

Now it was my turn to laugh. "Deal."

We lapsed into a companionable silence while Shelda took a brief rest. Her control and focus were rapidly improving, and using her new Seeker ability hardly left her winded now. I was impressed at how quickly she had mastered so much in such a short time, when it would usually take someone years to learn.

"It must be nice, growing up in a family like yours," Shelda commented.

"It had its advantages, I suppose, although it didn't always feel that way," I admitted.

"Having spent some time with your family, I can understand why you'd say that." She smiled. "But everyone's family has its quirks. I meant, it must have been nice to grow up in a family where you were able to openly use your skills. Where you weren't in hiding, and people didn't fear you."

"There's hiding, and then there's hiding," I said.

"Very truly spoken." Shelda gave me a measured look. "Will you continue to hide, cousin?"

I laughed in a weak attempt to hide my discomfort at her astuteness. "I'm not sure what you mean by that, Shelda?"

Shelda snorted. "Don't pretend you don't know what I mean, Kaernan. We're too much alike, you and I."

I leaned against Father's large wooden desk, studying Shelda. "I honestly don't know. I've always hated my gift ... if you could even call it that. And if my Seeker ability wasn't enough of a curse, you *have* to use your gift, or go mad. I've always felt trapped into doing a job I hate."

"Why do you hate it so much?"

"Who wouldn't hate it? Who wouldn't hate that every commission ends in tears and heartbreak?" I sighed. "But no one else understands that feeling."

"Except me."

I looked at Shelda sharply.

She smiled wryly. "You think the people we capture are thrilled to be there?"

"Good point." After our laughter died down, I asked Shelda, "So if you aren't going to use your newfound abilities to make the Hausters even more of a formidable bounty hunting team, then what are you going to do? Especially since you must exercise your talent."

"We'll always be bounty hunters, at heart. We can't just change our ways overnight. But I think ... instead of just accepting any job that comes along, we can probably afford to be more ... choosy."

"Choosy? How?"

Shelda looked thoughtful. "We usually don't question those who seek to employ us. We just take the commission, find the person, and deliver them. But in cases like Delphine's ... perhaps we can enable the hunted to become the hunter. Or at least, protect them in some small measure until justice can be served."

I smiled. "Shelda, you really are an avenging angel."

She shrugged modestly, but I could tell she was pleased at the compliment. "It would be nice if our family name was built on something positive, rather than fear. And ... perhaps you could join us on a job or two?"

Now it was my turn to be thoughtful. "I wonder ... perhaps that's one way of using my ability without having to deal with the other ... things ... that go along with it. A way of getting around it, as it were. And it would feel like a much more fulfilling use of my Seeker ability."

"Think about it," Shelda said. "If it truly interests you, we can ask Uncle Baxley how it can be done."

I nodded. "I will think about it. And speaking of avenging angels ... if you're summoned, are you ready for Delphine's trial?"

Shelda's face grew somber. "I had hoped — rather naively, I suppose — that it would have been called off. That they would just dismiss the charges against Delphine without any public fanfare. I underestimated how much sway Lord Olivera had, even in death."

"Well, he *was* related to the King of Orchwell. I believe Lord Olivera was the queen's first cousin, or something like that. So they were related by marriage. But from what I understand, he was also a blot on the family name. So perhaps that will weigh in Delphine's favor during her trial."

"Ah. Family can be either a blessing or a curse, as we both well know." Shelda and I smiled at each other.

A knock at the study door caught our attention. We both looked over to the heavy wooden door, which was being pushed open by one of the maids. As she approached, she nodded respectfully at each of us, then held out a creamy linen envelope toward Shelda. "Pardon the interruption, but this just arrived for Miss Shelda."

Shelda took the envelope from the maid, studying the elegant golden wax seal on the back of the letter. She smiled grimly and stood, moving briskly toward the door.

"Aren't you going to open your letter?" I asked her.

Shelda turned back to me, holding up the still-sealed letter. "I don't need to, I already know what it says."

"Then where are you going?"

Shelda walked through the open study door, tossing back over her shoulder, "To make sure our friend Delphine stays a free woman."

Chapter Forty-Two

SHELDA'S UNOPENED LETTER was the court summons that we had been anticipating. Uncle Baxley had already received a similar summons. We hadn't been entirely sure she would be asked to testify on Delphine's behalf; Shelda's unorthodox background meant it was quite possible the Council of Seekers — not known for their open-mindedness — would overlook her or dismiss her completely.

But for such a prominent trial, it seemed the Council wasn't going to discount any testimony. Which was good. Delphine would get a fair hearing.

We all hoped.

Delphine's trial caused a flurry of changes for all of us, even if we weren't directly involved with it. On the first day of the trial, Jondan came to stay at Asthore Manor, where he would remain for the duration of the trial. Delphine and her mother were being sequestered and not allowed to see or speak to anyone. Shelda and Baxley were allowed to return to Asthore Manor after each day's hearing, but as witnesses, they were under a magical geas to not speak of the trial's proceedings until after a verdict had been reached. It was maddening to know they knew what was happening, and being unable to talk with either of them about any of it. The rest of my family, Jondan, Farrah, Rhyss, and I were left to listen to the Orchwell rumor mill and speculate.

And speculate we did.

The rumors were wild, ranging from the truth — that Delphine was an innocent who accidentally killed Lord Olivera in self-defense — to crazier ideas, such as Delphine was part of a bigger conspiracy to overthrow the royal family of Orchwell, and Lord Olivera's death had been a test run of her powers. One of my particular favorites stated that Delphine was a shapeshifter from another part of the Gifted Lands who killed Lord Olivera when he discovered her changing from her animal form to her human self. I'm afraid I was outright rude to the person who posed *that* theory. I laughed right in his face. Just because the Crown Princess of Calia and her birth father were able to shapeshift, it didn't mean everyone could do that. I'm sure they were the only one in the Gifted Lands with that rare ability.

And then I received a summons from the Council to appear at Delphine's trial the following day.

That night was a restless one for me. For some reason, I was more nervous for this trial than I had been for my own hearing. Then, I had only felt a bleak numbness, wanting only to get through the day. Now, knowing that a friend's life hung in the balance — and, quite possibly, on my very words — made me fearful.

As the sun finally began to lighten the sky, I rose from my rumpled bedsheets and got ready for the day. I opened my bedroom door and stepped into the hallway, still tying my cravat, and nearly bumped into Uncle Baxley.

"Welcome to our little club." Baxley was dressed just as formally as I was, but I could hear the exhaustion in his voice. "Glad you could join us."

"I wouldn't want to miss out on all the fun you two are having," I said.

He laughed. "I'm not sure 'fun' is the word I would use for what we've been going through during this trial, but it will be nice to have you along."

Outside the manor, Shelda was waiting for us, with some bread rolls she absconded from the kitchen in her hands. She handed us each a day-old roll and a waterskin. The first part of our walk to the Council chambers was mostly silent, punctuated only by the occasional sound of chewing or swallowing.

When we had finished our hasty on-the-go breakfast, I said, "I know you're both under a geas to not speak of the trial. But is there *anything* you can tell me to help me prepare?"

My uncle and Shelda exchanged looks as they each opened their mouths to speak. No sound came from either of them. If the situation wasn't so serious, I would have laughed to see them, their mouths flapping open and shut like fish. I could tell they were mentally running through the events of the last few days, testing the limits of the spell to see what they could say.

Finally, from Baxley: "While it seems the geas is stopping us from giving you the facts of the trial, it is not stopping us from giving our opinions. So, in my opinion, I think the Council is sympathetic to Delphine, but because of Lord Olivera's close connection to the royal family, they are being very cautious. They cannot afford to let her go without making some sort of example of her, if there is even a hint of guilt about her. Otherwise everyone in the Orchwell monarchy could become a potential target."

"I'm not sure what I could say that would help Delphine's case," I said. "You and Shelda have already provided the most damning testimony against Lord Olivera, that he hired you to bring Delphine back after his supposed death."

Shelda shrugged. "Don't discount the value of anything you have to say. Even the smallest, most insignificant detail may help Delphine. And it will give her and her mother some hope, to see one more friendly face in the crowd."

I nodded, feeling a little less nervous than I had when I woke up that morning. But as we approached the building that housed the Council of Seekers, my feeling of calm immediately evaporated.

The imposing structure gleamed in the sunlight. White and black marble columns flanked either side of the huge gray wooden doors. The entire building had been constructed in shades of black, white and gray — a visual reminder to the people of Orchwell that, while there were two sides to each tale, the truth of the matter often lay somewhere in between.

As we approached, the two men standing guard opened the doors for us, allowing us to pass through unchallenged. I was surprised until I realized the geas on my two companions would be visible to the magically trained guards, letting them know Baxley and Shelda should have automatic entry.

But still, shouldn't they have stopped *me* for questioning?

The heavy gray doors closed behind us with a loud finality.

A severe-looking woman approached us. I recognized her as Chenne, the Council's public liaison, from my previous visit to the Council.

"Good morning, Chenne," Shelda and Baxley said.

Chenne nodded back in greeting. "Good morning to you both, as well. You know where to go."

They both nodded, each of them giving me a look of encouragement before turning and walking down the black-and-white marble hallway to our right. Their footsteps echoed against the marble as I watched them go, the uneasy feeling returning full force as their steps faded away.

Chenne cleared her throat, drawing my attention back to her. "Lord Asthore, if you will come with me." She turned on her heel and started down the same hallway I had watched Shelda and Baxley disappear in. It took me a brief second to realize that when she had said "Lord Asthore," she had been referring to me. I blinked away my confusion and hurried after her.

Even though we were following in my companions' footsteps, I saw no sign of them as Chenne and I made our way down the hall. We hadn't gone very far when Chenne stopped before an unassuming door, the same shade of gray as the one the guards had let us through, but much plainer and not imposing at all. Chenne pulled the door open and indicated I should step through.

I swallowed hard, remembering the last time I had entered a similar room. It had been several months prior, for my own hearing regarding my failed commission for the lady Rosemary and her subsequent madness and death. I had had a geas placed on me then, the same that Shelda and Baxley were now under. But knowing what was about to happen didn't make what was about to transpire any more pleasant.

In the center of the all-white room was a simple black chair, made of the same elegant marble that featured throughout the Council building. Chenne motioned toward the chair. "Please. Sit."

I slowly lowered myself into the chair, my eyes never leaving Chenne's impassive gaze. As I settled in, I felt the magic of the chair envelop me, binding me to it more securely than any ropes or chains ever could.

"Lord Kaernan Asthore, to ensure your true and accurate testimony in the trial of Lady Delphine Pahame, you will hereby be bound to the Council courts for the duration of said hearing. You will be unable to communicate to other parties, by speech, writing, or any magical means, until such time when the courts see fit to lift this geas. If you do find a way to circumvent this magical binding, depending on the severity of your breach, you will be subject to fines, punishment, or even death. Do you agree to be bound by this?"

I briefly toyed with the idea of saying no, but much like the last time, I knew I didn't really have an option. And, most importantly, Delphine's fate hung in the balance. When I had been here before, for my own trial, I had listlessly gone through the motions, so emotionally wiped that I could have cared less what happened to me. Knowing that someone else's life was at stake meant more to me than saving my own.

"Yes," I said.

Instantly my chest, my head, and my face bloomed with heat, which grew rapidly in intensity. "Fire to purify your words, so only the truth remains," Chenne intoned.

The magical fire became hotter and hotter, so much that I feared being consumed by it despite knowing, logically, that that would would not happen.

Just as the heat reached a point where I was sure I would pass out, it disappeared. I gasped for air, trying to catch my breath after the cloying heat, but only had a brief respite before the next part of the court binding came upon me.

"Earth to hold you to the Court, for the duration of this trial and no longer."

From the base and back of my chair, vines appeared and snaked up my legs, my arms, and around my forehead. Thoroughly restrained, the vines gave me just the slightest leeway to breathe. Barely. But the more terrifying part was yet to come.

I gulped in as much air as I could, as the vines spread and transformed into a brownish-gray clay, solidifying and enclosing the entirety of my seated self. First the legs, then my arms, spreading to my torso, up my neck, until even my face and head were under the hateful clay, giving me the horrifying feeling of being buried alive. I held my breath and counted slowly to distract my mind. The last time, I hadn't been prepared for this and had panicked, with no way to break free. At least this time I could mentally steel myself — even if I still hated this process.

My count had reached thirty — and my mind was now beginning to panic, despite my best efforts — when the hardened clay around my body cracked slightly, then burst open. As I was still magically bound to the chair, I couldn't move to brush away the flakes of clay, but fortunately the next sequence of the magical binding came quickly.

My eyes were closed to keep the clay from falling into them, so from somewhere nearby, I heard Chenne say, "Air to keep you insulated from outside influences."

The wind in the room picked up, although there were no windows and the door was firmly closed. It swirled around me, whirling faster and faster as it plucked at my clothes and my hair. I couldn't hear anything around me except the incessant wind. Chenne stood emotionlessly in front of me, her eyes impassive, completely untouched and affected by the windstorm.

Although I knew it was impossible, that it was just a magical spell, I began to feel my body being whipped around by the wind, lifting from the chair, being swept up into the swirling air —

— As it abruptly stopped, leaving me with my head lolling to the side, panting, as I tried to get my racing heartbeat back under control.

One more magical binding left. I mentally shuddered. This final binding was the one that had marred my memory the most.

"Water to cleanse your mind of any thoughts of deceiving the court."

I didn't even bother trying to hold my breath this time. From what I recalled, it wouldn't have made a difference, anyway.

At first the sensation was pleasant, like I was sitting in a lukewarm bath, or wading ankle-deep in a relatively calm stream.

And then the water engulfed me, rising over my head, catching me in its current. I was an insignificant pebble helplessly tossed by this now raging river, unsure when my impromptu journey would end. Or, indeed, if it ever would.

Eyes wide, I stared at my torturer through a blurry, watery film. A completely dry Chenne regarded me back. My dark hair floated in a halo around my head as water rapidly filled my lungs, but somehow this magical river touched only me.

I'd never been a strong swimmer, and this sensation of drowning touched on one of my deepest fears.

As the last bit of air in my body was replaced with water, the river receded. I coughed uncontrollably, my clothes thoroughly soaked, teeth chattering as I shivered, chilled to the bone. Chenne lifted her arm, almost casually waving her hand at me. Instantly my clothes and my hair dried up, and the chill left my body. The only thing I was left with was a slight sniffle to hint at the ordeal I had just gone through.

The magical force holding me to my chair disappeared. I nearly fell out of my seat.

"You are ready," Chenne said. "Come."

Without waiting to see if I would follow — or if I was even physically capable of standing — Chenne opened the door to the windowless room and left. I scrambled to my feet and hurried after her, following the sound of her heels clacking against the black-and-white marble floor.

I was still a little winded from the magical geas being placed upon me, but fortunately Chenne hadn't gone too far. She was just a few feet away, entering the same room that Baxley and Shelda had disappeared into earlier.

I caught up to Chenne just as the door to the new room nearly shut. I pushed it open to see yet another spartan black-and-white hallway stretching out before me.

Chenne stalked to the end of the hall, stopping in front of a set of gray wooden doors, similar in style to those that graced the front of the Council hall, but smaller to fit inside the building. As I approached the wooden doors, Chenne put her hand on the door handle. Pausing, she gave me a measured look. "Are you ready?"

I nodded, not trusting my voice to hide my nervousness.

"All right, then." Chenne pushed open both gray doors.

"Lord Kaernan Asthore, here to give his testimony in regards to the matter of Lady Delphine Pahame."

I swallowed hard, and stepped through the doorway and into the courtroom.

Chapter Forty-Three

ALL EYES FOCUSED ON me as I entered the courtroom. Panic rose within my chest as I tried desperately to stop the flow of memories from the last time I had been in this room. Even though I wasn't the one on trial, it still certainly felt that way.

I saw Delphine's face, pale and scared. A wary expression of hope slowly lit her face as she saw me. Uncle Baxley and Shelda were seated a few feet away from her, both of them giving me varying looks of encouragement.

I turned around just in time to see Chenne give me the smallest of nods as she pulled the grey wooden doors shut behind me. The sound of the closing doors echoed throughout the courtroom.

A deep, gravelly voice spoke from the front of the courtroom. "Lord Kaernan Asthore. Please approach."

Even though it had been many months since I had been in this place, I still remembered that voice. How could I forget it? It was Pellham Ravenwood, head of the Council of Seekers.

The sound of my footsteps against the cool black-and-white marble sounded incredibly loud in my ears. Could one's very stride sound nervous? If that was true, then I was sure the entire Council could sense my skittishness.

All too soon, my steps brought me to the stand in the front of the courtroom, where I stopped before the six seated members of the Council of Seekers. One seat was noticeably empty — the one formerly occupied by Lord Olivera.

Carefully, I bowed first to the council members on my left, then to those on my right, and lastly to the man in the center, reserving my deepest bow of respect for Pellham Ravenwood.

"The Council recognizes you, Kaernan Asthore," Pellham said.

"Thank you," I responded automatically.

"I'm sure you're wondering why you were summoned to appear before the Council in the matter regarding Lady Delphine Pahame and the death of Lord Olivera."

I stayed silent, although part of me wondered how the Council would react if I actually responded to Pellham's redundant statement.

Pellham continued on, unaware of my inner musings. "The Council has just a few questions for you, Kaenan Asthore. Other testimonies seem to suggest you play a part in this tale as well. The Council hopes that your testimony will perhaps provide further illumination in this hearing."

"I hope that as well, Your Grace," I said dutifully, still unsure how anything I could recall would aid the Council, or Delphine.

"Good. If you would, describe for the Council your exact commission for Lady Adallia Pahame, and what transpired after."

I blinked. This was unexpected. Haltingly, I described my initial meeting with Adallia, and who she had hired me to seek.

"Were you aware that Lady Pahame's daughter would be joining your team?" Pellham asked.

"No," I replied honestly. "It caught me — and the rest of my team — by complete surprise."

"And were you aware, at any time, of the bounty on Delphine, or the charges against her?"

"Not at first," I said. "We were in the town of Meira when I first learned that Delphine was potentially in trouble with the law."

"So you were not trying to deliver Delphine to the Hauster family, or to Lord Olivera?"

"No. I did not even know who the Hausters were until they, um, took Delphine to their stronghold."

"And you were not aware of the bond between your family and the Hauster family?" Madame Kenestra's white hair was piled high on her head in a perfectly arranged, severe bun. Her brown eyes regarded me just as severely.

"No, Your Grace," I said, turning slightly to address the woman.

Madame Kenestra sniffed and sat back in her seat. "As it apparently led you to a reunion with your long-lost relative, as well as the discovery of a whole heretofore unknown side of your family, I find such a coincidence hard to believe."

So Shelda and Baxley had told the Council of our familial connection. I fidgeted under the collective stares of the Council of Seekers and those in the courtroom.

"Coincidence or not," I said, trying to keep my voice even, "that is what occurred."

Sir Lantley waved a languid hand at Madame Kenestra, his salt-and-pepper hair falling into his eyes. "I do agree with Madame Kenestra that there are rarely coincidences in the life of a Seeker, especially when a Seeker is actively using their ability. A Seeker's particular gifts do not lend themselves to 'coincidences,' as I'm sure you well know."

I did, but I had no idea where Sir Lantley was headed with this reasoning.

And why did it feel like *I* was the one on trial, when I was only here to testify on Delphine's behalf?

Pellham leaned forward, his eyes boring into mine. "Once you learned the, ah, *nuances* of Lady Delphine's situation, did you feel compelled at any time to cancel your commission and return to Orchwell?"

Frowning, I thought back over recent events, from the time I first met Adallia to the showdown between Shelda and the obviously-not-deceased Lord Olivera in my father's study. Even when Delphine's innocence and character had been called into question, I had never, at any point, felt I should quit the commission.

Pellham nodded as if he could read my thoughts. "I thought so. But you *have* felt compelled before to cancel a commission, even if you did not act upon that compulsion. Is that not true?"

Suddenly, with illuminating clarity, I knew what Pellham was about. "Yes, Your Grace, that is correct."

Being a Seeker meant that, along with one's gift, a Seeker also carried a heavy burden of responsibility. Bringing two things together— whether it was a person with another person, a creature, or an object — meant that Seekers had to trust that person hiring them had altruistic motives. A Seeker's first obligation was to do no harm to that which was being sought. We weren't hunters, in the basest meaning of the word. To act as such would be a perversion of our abilities. It could destroy our minds and even end our lives.

Because of this, many Seekers learned to develop a strong instinct — about who was hiring them, about the task they were being hired to do. Some of it was innate, and some of it was learned from experience, but the best Seekers often could spot a bogus commission and turn it down before anything untoward happened.

Of course, from time to time there were cases where Seekers, against their better judgement, ignored that instinct, took a commission, and then found themselves in a bad situation. Such had been the case for me, when I had taken that foolhardy commission for the lady Rosemary all those months ago.

"Why is that?" Madame Kenestra asked me. "From what the Council has heard, the whole situation was ... unsettling at best. Certainly there were many moments during your travels that you might have felt it wiser to stop your search and return home. Or, once Lady Delphine was captured, you could have just left her to her fate. Why didn't you?"

I studied the six faces seated before me. Their faces were carefully schooled to reveal no emotion, with no hint as to what any of them were thinking.

I knew that several of those on the Council — Madame Kenestra, for one — were sticklers for tradition. Instead of viewing the Council of Seekers as a compliment to the Crown, they instead felt the Council was there to protect the Crown's interests, whether or not those interests were outdated.

But others, including Sir Lantley, tried to push the more progressive ideals of the Council. Change, they felt, was not only inevitable but necessary if Orchwell was going to remain one of the strongest and most respected kingdoms in the Gifted Lands.

And then, of course, there was Pellham Ravenwood, the most inscrutable of them all. Often the tiebreaker vote, he was extremely guarded as to his actual political views, unlike his peers on the Council.

Choosing my words carefully, I said, "Even after Delphine's ... situation regarding Lord Olivera was brought to light, I never got the sense that I should end her mother's commission. If anything, I felt more compelled to finish it, as if somehow completing the task would answer the question of Delphine's innocence. I know that makes no sense, but ... it did to me."

Sir Lantley nodded broadly, a slight smile playing on his lips, as if pleased by my answer. Madame Kenestra frowned, regarding me through narrowed eyes as she folded her arms across her chest and leaned back in her seat.

Pellham's expression was, as always, unreadable.

The silence stretched out. I fought the urge to fidget, uncomfortable under the collective weight of the stares of the entire Council of Seekers.

Finally, Pellham spoke.

"The Council thanks you for your testimony today, Kaernan Asthore. Please be seated with the other witnesses." He pointed to where Baxley and Shelda sat, with a few other faces I didn't recognize.

In a daze, I walked over to where my friends were and sat.

"I believe the Council has now heard enough testimony that we will be able to come to a decision. We will now retire to our private chamber to deliberate. The Council appreciates your patience as we do so."

As one, the six members of the Council of Seekers stood up and walked single file through a hidden door at the back of the courtroom. As soon as the door closed, Delphine stood and rushed over to us.

"Kaernan, I'm so glad you're here," she said, giving me a fierce hug.

"I only hope what I had to say was helpful," I said. "It's hard to know what anyone on the Council is thinking."

"What do you think will happen?" Delphine asked, wringing her hands as she looked at the area where the Council had disappeared.

"I don't know, Delphine. I really don't know."

Chapter Forty-Four

TIME DRIPPED BY.

There wasn't much we could do while we waited for the Council to deliberate. We weren't allowed to leave the Council building, and if we wanted to go anywhere within the building, we would need to ask for an escort. It hardly seemed worth the effort.

Delphine was so full of nervous energy, I thought she would either faint or break apart from the strain.

Shelda, looking toward the closed chamber door, growled, "What's taking them so long?"

Uncle Baxley put a steadying hand on her arm. "Easy, Shelda. They need time to come to a fair decision."

"They've had days and days to decide what's fair! Anyway, that lecherous lout attacked Kaernan's family in their own home! And he faked his own death! Well, the first time anyway." She smiled smugly at the memory. "Surely that's all the evidence the Council needs to know that Delphine is innocent."

Baxley frowned. "Even though all of Lord Olivera's actions should weigh against him, it is a sad truth that powerful people still hold sway, even in death."

"Spare me all this talking, I think the way the Family metes out justice is much better."

Baxley hushed his niece as the six-member Council of Seekers came back into the courtroom and took their seats. Delphine looked about nervously, unsure if she should move back to her original seat at the front of the room. Fortunately, the Council seemed to ignore this breach of courtroom etiquette. Instead, Pellham Ravenwood folded his hands together and regarded my group.

"Lady Delphine Pahame, please stand and approach the Council."

Shelda leaned over and squeezed Delphine's hand. Delphine gave us all a nervous look as she stood and did as Pellham commanded.

"Lady Delphine Pahame, the Council has discussed the matter of the death of Lord Olivera and what part, if any, you played in his death. We have decided ..."

Delphine began to sway under the collective stares of the Council.

"... that you, Lady Delphine Pahame, daughter of Lord and Lady Pahame ..."

"My goodness, can they drag this out any more?" Shelda muttered to me.

"You should have seen how they were at my trial," I muttered back.

Uncle Baxley stood up, moving toward Delphine in concern.

"... are innocent of any wrongdoing in regards to Lord Olivera's death. Both his faked death, and his true one," Pellham finished.

Delphine swooned. Baxley reached her just in time to catch her before she hit the ground. Alarmed, both Shelda and I stood and hurried toward the two of them.

Baxley was holding Delphine gently, waving a hand in front of her face. "Delphine? Delphine!"

Her eyes fluttered and she sat up gingerly, with Baxley assisting her.

"I'm all right, I'm fine," she said. "I didn't mean to cause a fuss." She looked up at Pellham and the rest of the Council. "Did you just say ... I'm free of all charges?"

Pellham smiled. "Yes, my dear, you are. Are you well enough to hear the rest of our ruling, or would you prefer to go home and rest?"

"No, no, please continue," Delphine insisted. Already the color was coming back to her face. Baxley and I helped her to her feet and walked her to a nearby chair, then Baxley, Shelda, and I took seats of our own and waited to hear the rest of the Council's verdict.

When Pellham was satisfied we were all settled, he continued, "While the evidence from both sides was equally convincing, the Council had reached an impasse until today's testimony from Kaernan Asthore." He leveled his gaze on Delphine. "Young lady, I believe you owe him quite a debt, for without his story, we may have ruled that it was a murder, and not self-defense. Actually, a magical accident."

Delphine nodded, eyes shining.

I couldn't help myself. "Sir ... what do you mean?"

Pellham studied me carefully. "What is one of the main Seeker tenets?"

"Do no harm to those we have been tasked to find," I recited automatically. It was the first, and probably the most important, principle drilled into every potential Seeker from an early age.

"Yes," Pellham affirmed. "If Lady Delphine had truly been a murderer, and harmed Lord Olivera deliberately, you would have been attuned to that. And if she was accompanying you for dishonorable reasons, you would definitely have sensed that, giving you a chance to abandon her mother's commission."

"But there have been cases where Seekers had misgivings about a commission, and undertook them anyway," I said, recalling a story I had heard about the famed dragon Seeker Kye. It had happened many years ago, before I was even born, but it was still whispered about in the Seeker community as a cautionary tale.

"Much to their peril," Pellham said. "And oftentimes when those cases occur, it's because the Seeker is near the end of their career and their gift is beginning to wane. But you are at the beginning of your career. And your gift is rather unusual, as well."

I understood what he was tactfully trying to say. "Unusual" was one of the more polite ways I had heard someone refer to my unwanted ability to find others' lost loves.

"Your particular Seeker ability means you are more in tune with the darker human emotions. The ones that help define us, but that we don't want to examine too closely or experience over and over. Sadness, regret, pain — those are all related to what you are able to do. You would have specifically picked up on any negativity surrounding Lady Delphine, her mother, or your circumstances. If she had deliberately committed murder ... you would have felt that. You would have sensed it as clearly as if she had shouted it in your face.

"You might argue that any Seeker would have picked up on a negative emotion, and that is true to varying degrees. But you and your sister are a special case. Twins who share the Asthore gift of seeking someone's true love, but split into its purest form between the both of you. It's what makes each of you such powerful Seekers.

"Kaernan Asthore, you should feel very proud right now. Your story, and your gift, saved your friend's life."

Chapter Forty-Five

"I HONESTLY THOUGHT the Council was going to condemn me," Delphine said as she, Baxley, Shelda and I left the Council building and walked through the streets of Orchwell.

"It seemed to be going that way," Baxley admitted.

"How did the Council ever doubt that it was a magical accident?" I wondered.

"They believed it, but they also didn't," Delphine said.

Baxley explained, "Lord Olivera was not beloved of the Crown or the Council. But he was a relative of the queen's, and he had a lot of money and power at his disposal. He wasn't someone you'd want to cross. As well, some of the Council didn't want to set a precedent where it might be perceived that it was ... shall we say, 'acceptable' to harm someone connected to the Royal Family. Even if it was in self-defense."

"But even royalty is not immune to consequences, if they break the law," I pointed out. "The King and Queen have always been adamant about that. It's one of the things that endear them to the people."

"That's true," Baxley acknowledged. "But in many ways, by design and by necessity, the royal family and even the

Council of Seekers sometimes have to be outside repercussions."

It was a constant debate, both in the Orchwell government and among its citizens, and not one that we would solve in that moment. But I nodded at the familiar argument.

"I wondered how the Council would view Lord Olivera's actions after the incident with Delphine," I said. "'Faking your own death to then seek revenge is not something a person in their right mind would think of doing, but as such a high-placed noble, it was quite possible the Council would have ... well, not *sanctioned* it, but perhaps looked the other way?"

Baxley nodded. "That was our biggest worry, too. We trust the Council to be fair, and for the most part they are, but there have been times when their rulings were obvious compromises."

"It was your testimony that did it," Delphine said, eyes shining. "As Pellham told you, it was what tipped the trial in my favor. Up until that point, all of the evidence brought before the Council kind of balanced out."

I frowned. "What do you mean? I would think that Shelda and Uncle Baxley's story alone would be enough to condemn Lord Olivera's actions."

Baxley said, "Not entirely. The Hausters are barely respectable in regular society. Many people would consider us, if not outright criminals, then quite close to it. And as a former Seeker of Orchwell — one who left in disgrace and has since used my abilities to aid the aforementioned crime family — my words hardly hold merit in the Council's court.

As my niece and a Hauster, Shelda's even less so. Our stories added an interesting twist to the trial, but Lord Olivera's representatives tried very hard to discredit us."

"But I thought Lord Olivera never married, and had no children? Unless there was some buried indiscretion that no one knew about," I said.

Baxley snorted. "I wouldn't have been surprised if there was some sort of suppressed scandal in that man's life. No, he had no wife or child. The Crown represented him in this case, which in some respects made things even worse. If you're going to say the Crown is in the wrong, you need to have a very strong argument as to why."

We were close to Asthore Manor. To Delphine, I said, "I suppose you're headed home?"

"Oh, yes. Mother wasn't called in to the court today, and I'm sure she'll be anxiously waiting at home, wondering what happened. She'll be thrilled to know the trial is over."

"Well, why don't you go get your mother and bring her over to Asthore Manor? Everyone will be excited to hear about the trial. Not that they wouldn't want me to tell all about it, but I bet they'd rather hear it from you. Plus, if you come by, it will make Jondan stop moping about the house."

Delphine blushed. "It would be nice to see him again. And your family, of course."

"Of course." I winked, causing her to blush deeper.

She cleared her throat and changed the subject. "Shall mother and I see if Rhyss and Farrah are available to join us?"

"No need," I said. "I'll send one of the servants to their homes to extend an invitation."

We said our goodbyes as Delphine turned down the street toward the Pahame residence, and Baxley, Shelda, and I continued on to the Asthore home.

When we arrived, I found I didn't need to send anyone to fetch Rhyss or Farrah; they were already there. Rhyss was working on repairs in the study. Farrah was chatting with Kaela in the parlor while they waited for us to come home.

Farrah stood up when she saw us. "There you all are! Finally!"

"Is something wrong? What are you doing here?" I asked.

"And hello to you too," Farrah said pointedly. "I'm here for several reasons. One, you're all my friends and I wanted to visit. Two, I wanted to see how Shelda's health was doing, make sure she hasn't had any magical issues lately."

"And three, you're incredibly nosy and curious and you want to see if you can glean any information about the trial," Rhyss said, walking into the room.

Farrah looked put out at being exposed so easily. I laughed. "One, it's good to see you. Two, Shelda will have to tell you that herself. And three, if you can wait a little bit longer, the Pahames should be arriving soon, and Delphine can tell you herself."

"Delphine will be here?" Jondan asked as he joined us. "It must be good news, then."

"Yes," I said. "But that's all I'll tell you right now. She can fill in the details herself."

My parents, alerted to the commotion, trickled into the parlor as well. I sent a waiting servant off for refreshments. We all settled in and made small talk while we waited for the servant to return. When the servant came back, bearing a tea tray and a plate filled with small sandwiches, she announced, "Lady Pahame and her daughter have just arrived."

Adallia and Delphine appeared in the doorway, with matching smiles on their faces.

"If you're here, you must have been freed of all charges," Kaela stated.

Delphine nodded. "Yes, completely and absolutely. Thanks in large part to Kaernan. Because of his wonderful Seeker gift, because of *him*, the Council declared me innocent. He saved my life."

Her words settled into the silence that had now fallen over the room. My sister, sitting next to me, reached over and squeezed my hand, her broad smile and bright eyes clearly letting me know her thoughts. Across the room, my mother dabbed at her eyes with a lace handkerchief, smiling mistily through her tears. And as for my father ... I couldn't quite read the expression on his face.

I was so busy trying to decipher the look my father was giving me that I nearly missed what Delphine said next.

"I know some of you — the ones who were at the trial — know the whole story. I told mother everything on the way over. But before I get into the details ... here, look at this ... a messenger brought it to the house just before we left."

She thrust a piece of paper at me. I took it, looking it over curiously. On one side of the thick, creamy paper was the seal of the Council of Seekers, which had been broken.

I opened the letter and read aloud:

LET IT BE KNOWN, AS restitution for the physical peril and emotional harm caused by Lord Olivera to Lady Delphine Pahame, the Crown and the Council of Seekers of the kingdom of Orchwell hereby award the entirety of the late Lord Olivera's estate to Lady Delphine Pahame. This includes all his residential properties located in Orchwell and the surrounding areas; the monetary allowance given him by the Crown; and his business properties located within Orchwell.

IT WAS SIGNED BY PELLHAM Ravenwood, the other Council members, and the King and Queen of Orchwell.

My wide eyes and look of amazement as I gave the letter back to Delphine matched everyone else's in the room.

"Lord Olivera's entire estate is more than enough to keep Mother and me comfortable for the rest of our days. And because it's so much ... we'd like to share part of it with each of you." Delphine looked at me, Rhyss, and Farrah in turn.

My jaw dropped. A side glance told me that Rhyss and Farrah's mouths were wide open too as they gaped at Delphine.

"And I'd like to use some of Olivera's money to repair the study here at Asthore Manor. It's only right, of course."

I shook off my bewilderment. "Delphine, that's incredibly generous of you. But we couldn't —"

Delphine cut me off.

"Think of it as a well-earned bonus to your completed commission," she said. Rhyss and Farrah looked at me hopefully. Seeing that Delphine was determined to gift us from her new bounty, I sighed and nodded.

Rhyss nudged Farrah. In a voice that was meant to be an undertone but clearly carried to where I was sitting nearby, Rhyss said, "Wait until Beyan hears! This never happened on any of *his* commissions."

Farrah nudged Rhyss back, harder, causing him to yelp. Loudly, she said, "What my friend is trying to say is, thank you, Delphine. This is a truly wonderful surprise."

Rhyss nodded in agreement as he rubbed his arm in the spot where Farrah had nudged him.

The look on his face made me burst out laughing. Rhyss looked at me reproachfully.

"Well," I gasped, trying to get myself under control. "Congratulations, Delphine. And to you as well, Lady Pahame. I look forward to visiting both of you in your new home. Assuming you want to move into any of Lord Olivera's properties."

"Why wait?" Delphine asked. "If you're not busy, you should visit now. So you can decide which one you might want as a reward. Mother can tell the others what happened."

My jaw dropped as Delphine grabbed my hand, unresisting, and gently tugged me through the parlor's entryway and out the front door. The sun dipped low in the sky; sunset would soon be here.

As we walked down the flower-lined walkway, we heard several footsteps hurry to join us and turned around, stopping. It seemed we were to have some company: Rhyss and Farrah.

"Can't leave us behind," Rhyss said. "We're a team."

Farrah smirked. "Plus we want to hear the story of the trial straight from Delphine." She tactfully didn't state the other reason they wanted to tag along.

I looked back to see my sister Kaela, my cousin Shelda, my uncle Baxley, and my father and mother, the Lord and Lady Asthore, standing at the front of the manor, waiting to see us off.

My family.

Kaela beamed as she waved at me, her arm linked in Shelda's. Mother was still dabbing at her eyes. Uncle Baxley said something quietly to Father, who nodded. My eyes met my father's. His gaze, normally harsh and unyielding when he looked at me, was different this time. Father looked surprisingly ... proud.

Of me.

My father was proud of me.

As Delphine led the way, and her chatter with Rhyss and Farrah flowed around me, I carried my father's look in my mind ... and in my heart.

Epilogue

"AND SO, YOU MAY NOW seal your marriage with a kiss. May you have a lifetime of love and light. I give you all, Lord and Lady Asthore!"

We all cheered and clapped wildly as the recently reinstated Lord Baxley Asthore kissed his new bride, Lady Adallia Asthore, formerly Adallia Pahame. It was the following spring, and we had all gathered to celebrate the wedding of Baxley and Adallia. I now had a new aunt, and my uncle had been officially recognized as an Asthore again after years of disgrace.

As the bride and groom walked down the aisle to receive the congratulations of the wedding attendees, Rhyss nudged Farrah. "Two weddings in two years. Kind of makes you wonder when it will be your turn, doesn't it?"

Farrah got a strange look on her face. "Maybe. I guess I never really thought about it. Until you brought it up just now."

Kaela, sitting on Farrah's other side, giggled at their conversation but didn't comment. Instead, she turned to me and winked. I just smirked and shook my head. Let Kaela play matchmaker if it pleased her; that definitely wasn't my area of expertise.

Just a few seats ahead of us, the newly married couple was hugging Delphine, Jondan, Juneyen, and Carissa. Shortly after the trial's completion, Juneyen and Carissa had left Rothschan and moved to Orchwell to be with Jondan. Jondan's family adored Delphine, and the feeling was mutual. And from the loving looks Delphine and Jondan gave each other, I knew it was just a matter of time before theirs was the next wedding I attended.

Delphine had been true to her word and had generously gifted Rhyss, Farrah, and me each with a substantial reward. Rhyss and Farrah had opted for a monetary reward.

As for me, I was now the proud owner of one of Lord Olivera's smaller estates. It definitely wasn't as large or fancy as Asthore Manor, and it was in need of some repair, but I was happy to have a place of my own, as well as work to keep me busy in between commissions.

Not that I had a lot of down time.

In a strange and unexpected turn of events, the truth of Delphine's trial and the story of Lord Olivera's treachery had spread throughout the Gifted Lands, making my services now highly sought after. Sometimes people would hire my sister and me together, which added a new dimension to our commissions. I had never worked in tandem with Kaela before, and it strengthened both our bond as siblings as well our magical abilities to work together.

And the oddest thing was, I now didn't mind my work as a Seeker.

Before I had resisted the darker side of emotions, thinking it less valuable or something that shouldn't be touched too often. And while I still didn't enjoy delving too deep into sadness, regret, or despair — who does? — I had now learned to embrace them when needed, and viewed them as just one side of the same coin of the human experience.

Uncle Baxley and my now Aunt Adallia had reached my row. Embraces and handshakes were exchanged as Farrah, Rhyss, and Kaela congratulated the new couple. When they reached me, Uncle Baxley clapped me on the shoulder, pulling me in for a big hug.

"Kaernan, you've given us both so much to celebrate this day," he said. "You brought my family back to me, as well as given me a new one."

"Yes," the new Lady Asthore said as she embraced me in turn. "Without you, this wedding may never have happened. Thank you for giving us our love back. And for giving me hope."

My uncle and aunt smiled at me, then moved to the next group of people waiting to congratulate them. As I watched the joyful couple, I felt my lips tug into a smile.

Perhaps I was capable of helping people find their happy endings after all.

Dear Reader: THANK YOU so much for reading this book.

IT MEANS SO MUCH TO me that you took the time to read *Heir of Memory and Shadow*. I hope you enjoyed this second journey in the Gifted Lands as much I enjoyed creating it.

If you liked this book, please leave a review wherever you like to buy books and learn about new titles.

Want to be the first to know about new adventures? Let's be friends!

Instagram: @rachaneelumayno[1]
Twitter: @rachaneelumayno[2]
TikTok: @rachaneelumayno
Sign up for the newsletter on the Website:
www.rachanee.net[3]
Join the community on Discord: Kingdom Legacy[4]

---

1. http://www.instagram.com/rachaneelumayno

2. http://www.twitter.com/rachaneelumayno

3. http://www.rachanee.net

4. https://discord.gg/Ru6qPxq

Acknowledgements

If it takes a village to raise a child, here's all the people who helped me raise this baby!

Thank you thank you THANK YOU to Tom and Jaime for reading the early drafts, giving amazing notes, and taking a lot of late night (for Tom) phone calls.

Thank you to my husband, for listening to me blather on about my writing issues without giving any context. You are a patient, patient man.

Thank you to my cat Riley, whose constant "must need to sit on mama's lap" meant I was forced to sit at my computer and work on my story when what I really wanted to do was laundry ... grocery shop ... vacuum ... anything but actually write. Couldn't have done it without you, cat. (Well, I could have, and much easier, but I did enjoy having you around constantly getting in my way.)

About the Author

RACHANEE LUMAYNO IS an actress, voiceover artist, screenwriter, avid gamer, and amateur dodgeball player. She grew up in Michigan, where she spent way too much of her free time reading fantasy novels. She still spends too much of her free time reading fantasy novels, although now she writes them too. *Heir of Memory and Shadow* is her second novel, and the second book in the Kingdom Legacy series. You can find her online at www.rachanee.net[1] or on Twitter, TikTok, or Instagram[2] (@rachaneelumayno).

---

1. http://www.rachanee.net

2. http://www.instagram.com/rachaneelumayno

Don't miss out!

Visit the website below and you can sign up to receive emails whenever Rachanee Lumayno publishes a new book. There's no charge and no obligation.

https://books2read.com/r/B-A-JWOM-SEDUB

BOOKS 2 READ

Connecting independent readers to independent writers.